BACK OFF OR YOU'RE NEXT!

I set the appointment book carefully in the far left-hand corner of my desk and turned my attention to the mail. Phone bill . . . electric bill . . . junk mail . . . flyer . . . coupon booklet . . . manila envelope addressed to me with no return address. Curiously, I turned the envelope over and saw nothing unusual. Intrigued, I opened the flap and pulled out the contents, then quickly sucked in a breath of shock and horror. Spilling out onto my desktop were several 8×10 glossies of yours truly, all taken from just a few yards away.

There was one of me at the grocery store, one walking Eggy, another of me out with Dirk, yet another of me talking with Marco at the dealership. My hands shook as I pawed through each one, a feeling of vulnerability like I'd never known creeping down my backbone. Underneath the photos was a folded piece of paper with glued-on letters cut out from a magazine that read:

BACK OFF OR YOU'R ██████

That was all I really ██████████████ ointment book close ██████

"This is a serio██████████████y Cooper is a fresh, exciting add██████████ateur sleuth genre, and *Psychic Eye* is ██████e and humorous page-turner. Laurie has t██████ to spare—she's a writer to watch!"

—J. A. Konrath, author of *Whiskey Sour*

ABBY COOPER, PSYCHIC EYE

A Psychic Eye Mystery

Victoria Laurie

A SIGNET BOOK

SIGNET
Published by New American Library, a division of
Penguin Group (USA) Inc., 375 Hudson Street,
New York, New York 10014, USA
Penguin Group (Canada), 90 Eglinton Avenue East, Suite 700, Toronto,
Ontario M4P 2Y3, Canada (a division of Pearson Penguin Canada Inc.)
Penguin Books Ltd., 80 Strand, London WC2R 0RL, England
Penguin Ireland, 25 St. Stephen's Green, Dublin 2,
Ireland (a division of Penguin Books Ltd.)
Penguin Group (Australia), 250 Camberwell Road, Camberwell, Victoria 3124,
Australia (a division of Pearson Australia Group Pty. Ltd.)
Penguin Books India Pvt. Ltd., 11 Community Centre, Panchsheel Park,
New Delhi - 110 017, India
Penguin Group (NZ), cnr Airborne and Rosedale Roads, Albany,
Auckland 1310, New Zealand (a division of Pearson New Zealand Ltd.)
Penguin Books (South Africa) (Pty.) Ltd., 24 Sturdee Avenue,
Rosebank, Johannesburg 2196, South Africa

Penguin Books Ltd., Registered Offices:
80 Strand, London WC2R 0RL, England

First published by Signet, an imprint of New American Library,
a division of Penguin Group (USA) Inc.

First Printing, December 2004
20 19 18

 REGISTERED TRADEMARK—MARCA REGISTRADA

Printed in the United States of America

PUBLISHER'S NOTE
This is a work of fiction. Names, characters, places, and incidents either are
the product of the author's imagination or are used fictitiously, and any resemblance to actual persons, living or dead, business establishments, events, or
locales is entirely coincidental.

The publisher does not have any control over and does not assume any
responsibility for author or third-party Web sites or their content.

For my sister, Sandy Upham Morrill.
You are my rock, my rainbow, and my sounding board.
I'm so extraordinarily lucky to be related
to you—my very best friend!

ACKNOWLEDGMENTS

I would like to thank the following people for all their help, support and encouragement in the development of this book. My sister, Sandy Upham Morrill, who offered love, support and encouragement along with that now (in)famous conjunction "Or . . ." My amazing agent, Jim McCarthy, who never fails to tell me the truth, but only after wrapping it in a blanket of kindness. My incredible editor, Martha Bushko, who truly "gets" me and allows me so much freedom to roam and explore and experiment. Detective Don Swiatkowski of the Royal Oak Police Department, who generously offered his time, ideas and expertise. And of course that band of gifted intuitives, mediums and psychics who are my dear friends and supporters and who have each "seen" this all along: Thomas Robinson, Kevin Allen, Kimmie Kroll, Joy Austin, Laurie Lipton, Laurie Comnes, Patty Tanner, Debbie Sparling, Silas Hudson and Rebecca Rosen. A heartfelt thanks to you all.

Prologue

On May 28 of this year, at approximately four thirty
P.M., Officer Shawn Bennington was summoned to
1865 Meadowlawn in response to a 911 emergency.
The following is an excerpt from his notes in that file:

> *Victim was a twenty-eight-year-old female Cau-*
> *casian dead at the scene from a single gunshot*
> *wound to the left temple. Victim was discovered*
> *in a quasi-fetal position on the bed in her room. A*
> *neighbor at 1863 Meadowlawn reported hearing a*
> *"loud popping noise" at approximately 3:00 p.m.*
> *Victim was discovered at approximately 4:20 p.m.,*
> *when her fiancé came over to check on the victim*
> *after not being able to reach her by phone. 911*
> *emergency was alerted within minutes of dis-*
> *covery.*
> *The handgun used was a twenty-five-caliber*
> *Smith and Wesson, registered to the victim. Fin-*
> *gerprints found on the gun appear to match those*
> *of the victim. A suicide note was recovered from*
> *the top of the victim's dresser (see enclosure in*

file) and a mutilated wedding dress was also discovered crumpled in a heap near the bed.

Signs of depression were recently noted by the victim's sister, who suggested that the victim seemed tense and edgy in last few days, and had complained of feeling tired. Lately the victim had been known to take long naps in the afternoon. Victim's sister was not present at the time of shooting.

File is tentatively being marked as "Suicide," pending completion of forensic evidence for powder burns, fingerprints and handwriting analysis. S. Bennington

Chapter One

My basic philosophy is simple: People are like ice cream. Take me, for instance. You'd think that by my profession alone—professional psychic—I'd be a ringer for Nutty Coconut, but the reality is that I'm far more like vanilla—consistent, a little bland, missing some hot fudge.

The exception, of course, is my rather unique ability to predict the future. Okay, so maybe with that added in I'm at least a candidate for French vanilla.

Still, overall my life is sadly *that* boring. I'm single with no immediate prospects, I rarely go out (hence the no immediate prospects), I pay all my bills on time, I have very few vices and only two close friends.

See what I mean? Vanilla.

Now, I'm not saying my life is *all* bad. At the very least I'm privy to the richly flavorful lives of my clients. Take the Tooty-Fruity sitting in front of me for example. Sharon is a pretty young woman in her mid-thirties, with short blond hair, too much makeup, a recent boob job and not a clue in sight. On her left hand dangles a rather opulent diamond wedding ring, and over the course of the last twenty minutes all I've been able to do is feel sorry for the poor schmuck who gave it to her.

"Okay, I'm getting the feeling that there's a triangle here . . . like there's someone else moving in on your marriage," I said.

"Yes."

"And it's someone *you're* romantically interested in."

"Yes."

"And they're telling me that you think this is true love . . ."

"Yes, but, uh, Abigail? Who are 'they'?" she asked, looking around nervously.

I get this question all the time, and you would think I would have learned by now to prepare my clients before beginning the session, but change was never my strong suit. "Oh, sorry. 'They' are my crew, or rather, my spirit guides. I believe that they talk to your spirit guides and it all gets communicated back to me."

"Really? Can they tell you their names?" she whispered, still looking around bug-eyed.

We were getting off track here. I pulled us back on course, afraid I would lose the train of thought flittering through my brain. "Uh, no, Sharon, I don't typically get names, I only get pictures and thoughts. So, as I was saying, we were talking about this love triangle, right?"

"Yes," she answered, leaning forward to hang on my every word.

"Okay, I'm just going to give it to you the way they're giving it to me. . . . They're giving me the feeling that this other guy is saying all the right things, that he may say he's interested in you and that he wants to be with you but he's not telling you the whole story." Sharon's bug eyes squinted now as she looked at me critically. "Okay, does this other guy have blond hair?"

"Yes."

"And he works some sort of night job, like, he works at night. . . . Is he a bartender?"

"Oh my God . . . yes, he is!"

"And your husband, he's the guy with dark brown hair and a beard or facial hair, right?"

Sharon sucked in a breath of surprise and replied, "Yes, he's got a goatee."

"And your husband does something with computers, like he has something to do with making computers or something."

"He's a computer engineer . . ."

"Okay, Sharon, they're telling me that the blond is a liar, and that you may not think your husband is Mr. Don Juan but he loves you. They're saying if you leave your husband for this other guy with the blond hair that there won't be any going back. You won't be able to fix it once it's out in the open. And I get the feeling that if you continue to fool around on the side you're going to get caught. If you think you won't, then you're kidding yourself. They're saying there is already a woman, I think she's older than you, with red hair, who's *very* nosy and she already suspects, and she wouldn't think twice about telling your husband. I think this is like a neighbor or something . . ."

"Oh my God! My neighbor, Mrs. O'Connor, has red hair, and she *would* tell my husband!"

"See? She's already very suspicious, and I get the feeling that if you don't rethink this whole thing you could end up divorced and alone. This bartender guy isn't going to marry a divorced woman with two kids. You have two, right? A boy and a girl?"

"Yes, but . . ." she squeaked.

"No," I said firmly. "No buts. You need to do some hard thinking here, 'cuz there will be no going back, and if you continue down this path I'm seeing nothing but heartache in your life. You won't really know what you've lost until it's gone."

At that moment I heard the blissful sound of my chime clock dinging and the tape in the cassette player clicked off. I instantly felt relieved. This woman wasn't picking up what I was laying down and it was pretty frustrating to me. I stood and said gently but firmly, "And that's all the time we have." I flipped open the cassette player and removed the tape, enclosed it in its plastic case and handed it to her along with a tissue. Sharon got up with me and walked with bent head and a forced smile toward the door.

She thanked me for my time and was asking when she could come back when I said, "Actually, Sharon, I'd prefer it if you made an appointment with a friend of mine." I walked back toward my credenza and retrieved a card from a stack piled there. "This is Lori Sellers. She's a psychotherapist with an office over on Eleven Mile. She's very good and I think it would be a good thing for you to talk to her about the choices in front of you." I put the card in her outstretched hand. "If you want to come back and see me, I allow only two visits per year, and that's a good rule of thumb. You shouldn't get hooked on readers; remember that all of the answers are inside you. All you have to do is trust yourself and listen."

Sharon didn't look convinced, so I placed my hand on her arm and walked her gently to the door. "Now I want you to go home and replay the tape and consider everything I've said. You have the gift of free will, and it's a powerful force. You can change your own destiny if you put your mind to it. Just be careful, okay? I mean, you've been married, for . . . what? Ten years?''

Another sucked-in breath of surprise. "Yes. How did you know that?"

I smiled and spread my hands in an "aha" gesture. "I'm psychic."

As I watched Sharon leave I couldn't help but consider for the billionth time how much that word "psychic" still caught in my throat. It's just too close to the word "psycho" for my taste. Typically, when asked what I do for a living I tack on a softer word, like "psychic *intuitive*" to lend a smidgen of legitimacy. I'd even had business cards made up reading, ABIGAIL COOPER, P.I. with teeny-weeny little letters underneath in parentheses spelling out PSYCHIC INTUITIVE. Most people think I'm trying to be clever. The truth is, I'm a chickenshit.

I never wanted to be a psychic, professional or otherwise. It's something that was more or less thrust upon me, and I've never really felt comfortable with it. It isn't that I'm not proud of what I do; it's just that I've always been conscious of the fact that I'm *different*.

For instance, there are plenty of people out there who will engage me in casual conversation and might even find me amusing until they discover what I do for a living . . . and then they recede like a tide from the beach and I'm left in the sand feeling like I've got a big red *X* on my forehead. I've been a professional psychic for four years now, and I'm still waiting for the proverbial tide to come back in.

I was just about to close the door after Sharon when one of my regulars, Candice Fusco, came walking down the corridor, carrying a large manila envelope. "Hey, Candice," I called as she caught sight of me.

"Hi, Abby. I'm on time, right?" She glanced at her watch and hurried her step.

"Yup. I was just seeing my last client out." I stepped sideways, holding the door open and allowing her to enter. Candice was probably only an inch or two taller than me, but the three-inch heels I had never seen her go without made her tower over me. She was an elegant woman, with a fondness for expensive suits. Today she wore cream silk that flowed and rippled with the breeze of her movements and set off the tan of her skin and her light blond hair. Her femininity usually makes me a little self-conscious, but within a minute or two I'm over it, eased, I think, by her genuine nature. You would never guess by her dress and mannerisms that Candice is a private investigator, and a damn good one at that—although her most recent successes were helped a bit by yours truly.

"Would you like to sit here or in my reading room?" I asked, closing the door behind Candice.

"Here would be fine, Abby, this shouldn't take us too long," she replied, pulling the straps from her purse and shoulder bag off her shoulder.

"So how's Kalamazoo these days?" I asked, gesturing toward the two chairs in the office waiting room for us to sit in.

"Still there." she said taking a seat, "I swear this drive takes longer every time."

"The way you drive? I doubt it. How long did it take you today?"

"An hour and forty-five minutes."

"New record?"

"Nah. I've done it in an hour and thirty-five before. Of course, I was doing ninety-five the whole time, but I've slowed it down a notch since you told me to."

"Yeah, not a good idea to ignore a warning like that when it comes up." I'd told Candice the last time we saw each other to watch her lead foot or she could end up with a hefty speeding ticket. "So, is that the stuff?" I asked, pointing to the manila envelope she still held.

"Yes, these are the three employees we've narrowed it down to," Candice said, extending the envelope toward me. I took it and opened the flap, extracting three pictures—two women and one man, all posing for mug shots of the employee-badge variety. I flipped quickly from photo to photo, then back through more slowly, taking my time to open my intuition to each person. Candice had called me the previous evening about a new case she was working on. A large company that handled mutual funds had discovered several thousand dollars missing from its clients' portfolios. The company had not made the discovery public yet and wanted Candice's help in identifying the embezzler.

"Okay—these two?" I said, holding up a photo of a man in his mid-forties, with droopy jowls and yellowed teeth, and another of a woman in her mid- to late twenties, with bangs poufed high above her head and gobby eyes coated with too much mascara. "There's something going on between them. I get the feeling that they two have some sort of romantic connection. This guy"—I pointed to the photo of the man—"He's up to no good. I get the feeling that he's sneaky, and it's not just about fooling around with another employee. There's something more sinister here. Did he just buy a new boat?"

"He's made quite a few purchases lately, which is one of the reasons the company suspects him. And yes, one of his purchases was a boat."

"Okay, this is your guy. There's something about this boat, though. I get the feeling that he's covered his tracks pretty good, but there's evidence hidden on the boat. I'd start by snooping around on it and seeing what you turn up.''

"What about the third photo?" Candice asked.

I looked at the third photo, an older woman roughly in her late fifties to early sixties, with washed-out gray hair, a prominent nose and muddy eyes. I held the photo and felt around using my radar. "I get the feeling this woman has no clue about what's going on, that she's being used as a pawn or something. This guy may be using her in some way to cover his tracks, setting her up to take the blame for the crime."

"That makes a lot of sense," Candice said. "Most of the evidence is pointing to her right now, but she's been an exemplary employee at the company for almost thirty years. She's about to retire, and we couldn't figure out why, after all this time, she would start stealing from the company."

"Yeah, I agree with your instincts. It really feels to me like she's being set up. Look on the boat, Candice. There's something there."

Candice gave me a big smile as I put the photos back in the envelope. "Thanks, Abby. You've probably saved me a ton of legwork on this."

"No sweat, Candice. By the way, what's the deal with Ireland?"

Candice gave a startled laugh. "God! Does anything get by you? I'm going there next month for a six-week vacation."

"Wow," I said enviously. "Well, you're going to have a great time, but you'll need to pack warmer than you think."

"Thanks. I'll make sure I do. I'll be back in September, and I'm sure I'll be calling you for help on the next big case I get."

"Anytime," I said, standing up as she handed me a check and we walked to the door.

"Say, by the way," Candice said as she stooped to gather up her purse and briefcase, "I saw this documentary the other night on the Discovery Channel about a psychic who works with the police to solve some of their toughest cases, and while I was watching I immediately thought of you. You know, I think you'd make a great police psychic."

My eyes widened at the suggestion. She had to be kidding, "No way!" I laughed as if she'd made a particularly funny joke.

"Why not? You've helped me find all sorts of clues to white collar crimes. Why not lend that same talent to your community?"

I looked at Candice for a long moment, struggling to come up with a valid reason she would accept as to why I wouldn't go near the police, when my intuition went suddenly haywire and several very quick flashes bulleted through my mind's eye. The vision was so intense that I stepped back abruptly, nearly losing my balance as Candice reached forward quickly to grab my arm and steady me.

"Abby?" she asked alarmed, "Abby, are you okay?"

Startled out of my trance, I snapped my head up and quickly recovered myself. "Yeah, just a really weird déjà vu moment there," I said, shaking my head to clear it. Trying to reassure her, I said, "Listen, you drive safe back home, okay? And call me next time you get into town and we'll have lunch or something."

Candice still looked worried, but being the talented detective that she is, took the hint that I didn't want to talk about what had just happened. "Sounds great. Take care, Abby," she said, squeezing my shoulder.

I closed the door behind Candice and sighed deeply, rubbing my temples. It had been a long morning. I walked over to my appointment book to check what the rest of my day looked like, scrolling my finger down to the next appointment. My eleven o'clock had canceled, and my next client wasn't until one. I did a small "hurrah" with my hands. With the cancellation I had a two-hour break for lunch and whatever.

Not wanting to waste a minute of it, I blew out all the candles I'd lit earlier, grabbed my purse and bolted out the door. As I entered the hallway of my office building, the coolness of the central air wafted over me, instantly rejuvenating me.

One of the hazards of my job is that air pressure and temperature often change when I'm in session with a client. Cold rooms get warm, warm rooms get hot, and sometimes my ears ring with a high-pitched whine. I'd learned over the past few years to ignore most of it, but in the middle of July it was typically more of a struggle. My office was located in one of the older buildings in town, and the central air, while fabulous in the main hallway, seemed only to leak stingily out of the vent in my suite.

Reaching the stairs, I pitched forward, grabbing the railings and thrusting my hips out in front of me, launching myself down several steps at a time. What can I say? I was always the last kid off the monkey bars when recess ended.

Hitting the ground floor with a loud *thunk*, I stood for just a minute in the marble enclosure, soaking up the cool air before braving the heat and the bustle of people I knew would be waiting for me outside.

I live and work in a suburb of Detroit called Royal Oak, which stands as one of the last great bastions of middle-class neighborhoods buffering Detroit from its much wealthier suburbs slightly to the north, thus saving the area from total plutocracy.

Royal Oak is a city bursting at the seams, sandwiched between Ten Mile and Fourteen Mile Roads. In southeastern Michigan, the mile roads measure roughly how far from Detroit you are—the farther north the location, the bigger the mile number and the farther north the real estate's price tag. A single mile can be the difference of a cool quarter million or more.

In the past several years Royal Oak has transformed from a place to avoid to *the* place to be seen. These days many of its residents spend their time in the city's downtown area, strolling the streets and lounging on benches, doing nothing but ogling. All kinds are welcomed and represented here: Gens X & Y, homos, heteros, winos, midlifers, boomers and dinks. The place is a regular United Nations.

My office is located in the Washington Square Building, which rests on the northern tip of downtown, just before Eleven Mile. I share the four-room suite with my best friend, Theresa, who is a psychic medium. We chose this particular location because not only is the building the biggest in Royal Oak but it's structurally one of the quirkiest.

By all appearances the building is an absolute marvel of architectural indecision. Its layout is a hodge-podge of brick and mortar, chalky brown in color. Boxy sections contrast drastically with sharply angular wings, and windows range from arch shape to retangular depending on what floor you're peering up at. A huge neon sign advertising a local newspaper drapes the cornice like a necklace and can be seen for miles, making it easy for Theresa and me to give directions to new clients.

Inside, small shops, galleries and restaurants make up the street level establishments, while professional suites occupy the upper floors. Theresa and I are sandwiched between an accountant and a computer graphics firm on the building's northern square end. The rent is reasonable, the building is well maintained, and nobody in the other office suites has complained yet about our liberal use of candles and incense. For four years it's been the perfect place to operate.

After sufficiently soaking up the cool lobby air, I stepped courageously out into the furnace of the mid-July day. I turned right toward the center of downtown and pulled my cell phone out of my purse. Flipping the phone open I hit the number for voice mail and listened intently as I walked down Washington heading three blocks south to the Pic-A-Deli Restaurant for a tuna on honey whole wheat with extra-hot peppers. I had one message, from Theresa.

Theresa and I had met four and a half years earlier through very unusual circumstances, and to this day I still marvel at the magnitude of the gift that led her to me.

I was working in a bank at the time, trying my best to fit into a world that never really accepted me. My childhood had been filled with unusual singular events that since they occurred over the spread of several years were fairly easy for me and my family to ignore: my announcement of a fire in our basement a week before smoke alarms woke us from a sound sleep; my premonition of my grandfather's death ten minutes before the phone call from my aunt; and finally, to the chagrin of my social-climbing parents, my proclamation that my father's high-paying executive position was going to fall victim to corporate downsizing a full month before he received his pink slip.

To parents who distrusted anything metaphysical, it was as if my divining such things meant I was forcing them to happen and that if I had just shut my mouth we could have avoided such hardships. I learned pretty quickly that it was better to keep my premonitions to myself.

As I grew older, my "episodes," as I'd come to call them, happened much more frequently and were much stronger. One day when I was in college I was overcome with a feeling that forced me against my better judgment to approach my statistics professor just before class. I hopped from foot to foot behind him, anxious to get his attention, and when he finally turned to look at me I blurted out in a rush that he needed to get to the doctor right away because I saw a problem with his heart.

He looked at me oddly for a long moment before asking me to take my seat so that he could begin his lecture. A week later the class was canceled due to the death of our professor. You guessed it—heart attack.

That single event convinced me far more than my parents' insinuations that I had somehow been the cause of a terrible thing. I felt that by speaking the words aloud I had somehow caused my professor's premature demise. I didn't know anything about intuition back then, how it worked, what it felt like. I just knew the pattern of causation: I saw things in my mind's eye, I said them out loud, they happened— ergo, I made them happen.

For the rest of my years in college and into my early career in banking I refused to speak things that I saw aloud again. If I had a flash of something in my mind's eye I quickly focused on something else and began humming. By the time I was twenty-six I was humming *constantly*.

Then one morning when I was working at my desk in a local bank I got an odd feeling that someone was looking at me. Glancing around I saw a young woman across the lobby with curly chestnut hair and large brown eyes staring at me in an odd, almost blank way.

I smiled at her, wondering if I knew her from somewhere. She smiled back and continued to stare. I shrugged my shoulders slightly in question; she nodded back, then exited the bank. Even as I puzzled over her strange behavior, I couldn't shake the feeling that I would see her again.

The next day I had just come out of the supply room, my arms loaded with flyers and pamphlets for the lobby, when I noticed the same woman sitting at my desk. I set down the pamphlets and hurried over to her, eager to find out how we knew each other.

"Hello," I said as I settled into my chair. "May I help you?"

She looked at me for a moment, and it was as if she was looking through me. "You're Abigail, right?"

"Yes?" I said, nudging the little nameplate at the front of my desk closer to her.

"My name is Theresa, and I know this is going to sound really crazy to you, but I'm a medium and I have a message for you."

I'm sure the look on my face changed in an instant from polite inquisitiveness to caution. I didn't know what a "medium" was, and so I was prepared for some sort of Bible-thumping lecture that I was sure would end with my calling Security.

When I said nothing Theresa continued. "Do you know someone named Carl?" she asked.

My mouth fell open a little. "My grandfather's name was Carl." He and I had been very close, and he'd died when I was twelve.

"And who is Sum— Summer?" she asked, working to get the name right.

"Sumner," I corrected. "He was my other grandfather."

I was conscious at that moment that I had suddenly

stopped breathing, as if the sound of my breath would distract her from talking further.

"And Margaret?"

Unbidden tears sprang to my eyes; no one I socialized with knew the names of all my grandparents, "My grandmother—she was married to Carl and died when I was six."

"Okay, well, your grandparents have been talking to me for two days, and they have a message that I'm supposed to deliver. They want you to know that they know you can see things. They know that you have a gift, and they want me to help you develop it. You're supposed to be using your gift, not *this*"—she waved a hand at my desk—"to make a living."

For a very long moment we just stared at each other. To her credit, Theresa looked as unsure of the message she'd just delivered as I felt. I considered the possibility that this was a joke, that some sick bastard thought this was funny and had put an actress up to it. Or maybe this woman was crazy, and she'd just made three very good guesses. But what I couldn't discount was the fact that she had just voiced aloud what I'd inherently known all my life: that I was, in fact, "gifted."

Up to this point, it hadn't felt much like a gift, but when I understood what kinds of emotions could be stirred by the encounter I was now having, I felt that term was more than appropriate.

I'd love to tell you that I had a *Jerry Maguire* moment, jumping up and announcing to one and all that I was quitting my boring bank job to go be a professional psychic, but the truth is that it took a long time for me to warm to the idea.

Theresa left me her card—she was doing readings out of a little coffee shop back then—and told me to call her when I decided to trust my own intuition and follow the path I was meant to be on.

For three months I mulled it over, unwilling to make a decision either way; then fate intervened and the decision was made for me. A larger conglomerate bought the bank I was working in, and I was downsized. Finding myself unemployed and a bit desperate, I looked up Theresa, who's been my tutor, best friend and partner ever since.

Together we've built a business that combines our talents: She connects people with their deceased loved ones, and I connect them to their futures. It's a great mix, as we really don't compete, and we like to compare notes a lot. Yes, we do that—we intuitives love to talk to each other about what kinds of messages come through. It helps us calibrate our skills and understand the mechanics of what's happening.

People think that we can hear these magic beings in our head, or that we get this full-color film reel of an event and that's how we predict the future. In truth, the reality is much less glamorous.

What happens is that a thought or an image that feels like a memory will pop into my head, and this is coupled with a strong compulsion to blurt out what's swirling around in my mind's eye. It's a little like psychic Tourette's, things seem to tumble out of my mouth that have no forethought, and somehow these are always the most accurate bits of imformation.

The best way to describe it is to compare it to the game of Clue. In my mind's eye I may see a peacock, a pool table and some candles. When I see these images, I will have a strong compulsion to say something like, "Who's the pool player who wears peacock feathers and likes to play by candlelight?" which would be the way my logical mind might translate what I'm seeing. It's then up to the client to put together the clues and figure out that Mrs. Peacock did it in the billiard room with the candlestick. My readings tend to be very interactive that way, and the more cooperative the client the better the results in the end.

Walking to the deli, I smiled as I listened to Theresa's voice sing over the recorded voice mail. She was currently in California, where she'd been for the last three weeks meeting with producers and other Hollywood types negotiating a possible television pilot centered around her ability to connect people with their deceased loved ones. As a psychic medium, Theresa's focus isn't like mine, where I use my talents to predict the future. Her ability rests almost solely on bridging the gap between the living and the dead, and Theresa wasn't just good at what she did, she was amazing. Her sessions were most powerful in large group settings, with lots of tears and jaw dropping drama as she is able to intuit with incredible accuracy names, places and dates relative specifically to people who have crossed over, giving hard proof that life continues beyond the headstone.

Watching her at work is really mesmerizing, which was why Hollywood had come knocking on her door one day and asked her to come out and talk. These days, if you want to become famous for having a sixth sense, you gotta be able to talk to the dead, and as I don't relish a lot of attention, I'm lucky not to have this particular talent. Besides, Theresa's far more suited for all the attention. Of the two of us she's much more poised, and even though she's a few years younger than me, she's typically the grownup between us.

Her message was short and excited. "Hey, girl! I've

got news! Call me!" I immediately hit speed dial to her cell phone and waited for the sound of her voice. She picked up on the fourth ring.

"Hey, what's up?"

"Oh, hi! I was just about to try you again. I don't have a lot of time—they're calling our flight in a minute here—but I had to tell you that we signed this morning!"

"Told you so," I said, smiling. There is no greater feeling to me than being right. I had given Theresa a reading before she left for California, and it was music to my ears to hear that something I'd predicted had come true.

"And you were right about the house too. We found this adorable little three-bedroom for rent in Santa Monica, and we just confirmed with the woman who owns it that we're going to rent it beginning the first of the month!"

Most of me was damned happy; however, the part of me that had grown used to hanging out with Theresa and Brett, her husband, felt sad and abandoned. "So you're really leaving me, huh?"

" 'Fraid so, my friend. But I'm headed back today, and we have the rest of the month, and there are like a billion planes a day flying between Detroit and L.A. You can come out here, I can come there . . . really, it will be okay."

I reached the Pic-A-Deli, but my appetite had disappeared. I walked inside anyway and stood in line, pouting like a three-year-old. I'd always known this day would come, but that didn't help—it still felt cruddy. As I listened to Theresa talk about her exciting new television career I feigned interest and forced my voice to higher octaves of excitement. I don't think I was a very good actress though, because she finally said, "Hey, I'll be home later tonight—I'll call you and we can talk it through then. You could always move out to L.A. too, you know."

Since intuition is a right brain activity, I mentally asked the question on the right side of my head—a technique I used when I needed a yes or no answer: *Should I move to California?* The difference between a "yes" and a "no" is that "yes" feels light and airy on the right side of my body and "no" feels thick and heavy on the left. Now my left side felt thick and heavy.

Putting my acting voice back on, I said, "Sure, give me a call tonight, Theresa. We'll talk more then."

I was next in line, and Theresa's plane was boarding, so we disconnected. Marching up to the counter, I smiled at the heavyset man with receding white hair and forced a smile I didn't feel.

"Abigail! The usual today?"

"Sure, Mike, but extra extra-hot peppers. I'm feeling reckless."

Mike laughed and nodded at me. As he reached for the bread knife, however, a thought flickered into my head. Most people think that psychics are "on" all the time, like we walk through the streets able to detect good people from bad and at a moment's notice know everything there is to know about total strangers. The truth is that we're only "on" when we want to be. In other words, it's very similar to a phone ringing in the distance; it's always ringing, sometimes loudly, sometimes not. If we pick up the phone, we know we'll get some info, but if we don't pick it up, we get nothing. As Mike began cutting the bread, my intuitive "phone" was ringing very loudly. Annoyed, I answered it, and got a flash and a feeling. I looked at Mike. He knew what I did for a living; in fact, he let me hang my card on his bulletin board and didn't seem too unnerved by it, so I decided to blurt out the thought that was now zipping through my head.

"Uh, Mike?"

"Yeah, Abby?"

"You drive a silver car?"

"Yeah! How'd you know?"

I smiled and tapped my temple, winking conspiratorially. "I think your car's leaking fluid—oil or antifreeze or something. You may want to check it later."

Mike stared at me for a long moment without blinking, his mouth hanging slightly open, then a huge grin spread across his face. "Abby, you're good! I noticed a small stain on the floor of my garage this morning and I was thinking I'd take it to the gas station this weekend. Hey, can you tell me the winning lotto numbers?"

If I had a nickel for every person that asked me that question, I wouldn't need to work anymore. I'd be retired and rich, rich, rich!

"Pal, if I knew, I'd be playin' 'em!" I said as he wrapped my lunch and handed it over the counter to me. I paid for my sandwich, throwing in a Coke and some potato chips, and headed back to the office.

As I trundled up the stairs to the hallway leading to my suite, I noticed a woman pacing impatiently just outside the locked door. I felt a moment of panic and looked again at my watch. It was a little after eleven thirty. Had I misread my appointment book and looked at the wrong day? Did I forget to write in an appointment?

Truth be told, I wasn't the best at the administrative side of the business. I usually considered it a pain-in-the-ass part of the job, and sometimes I took a little longer to get back to people than was appropriate, and sometimes I missed an appointment or two altogether.

Red-faced now, I walked briskly up to the woman and smiled my most winning smile. "Hello," I said. "I apologize—I don't remember booking an appointment for this time. Did I goof?"

The woman was tall and thin with shoulder-length

chestnut hair, horn-rimmed glasses and big brown eyes that looked both exhausted and anxious at the same time. "Are you Abigail?" she asked in a voice soft as Minnie Mouse.

"Yes."

"Oh, thank God. My name is Allison Pierce. My friend Connie canceled her eleven o'clock with you, and I thought perhaps if you hadn't filled it you might be willing to see me?"

I checked my watch again and looked at the bagged lunch I now carried. My initial reaction would have been no, I don't do "please-please-please-with-sugar-on-top-just-fit-me-in-this-one-time" readings. Experience has taught me that the moment you make an exception you can count on it becoming the rule.

Something about her anxious face and the wringing of her hands tugged at me, though. I sighed and checked in with "the crew," hoping they'd back me up. Instead I got a very firm "yes!" Crap.

Well, I wasn't that hungry anymore anyway. "Okay," I said, "I've got some time before my next appointment arrives. Come on in."

I unlocked the office, letting us both in, put my lunch in the small refrigerator in the waiting room, locked the front door and ushered Allison into my reading room.

Our office is laid out in a T-shaped floor plan. The front door deposits you in our tiny waiting room, where two chairs sit facing the door and a small table holds several magazines. Directly behind that room is our administrative office, with a small desk in the center of the room to hold the phone, the computer, and two large filing cabinets, which hold client release forms and mailing lists. Two other rooms also open off the waiting room: Theresa's reading room to the right, and mine to the left.

The space that I use to read people is one of my favorite places on earth. The room is rather small, only eleven by nine feet, but to me it's the perfect size. I'd painted the walls an azure blue that always reminded me of one of those travel calendars I'd seen with a photo of the Greek island of Mykonos and the sea surrounding it. The room has an abundance of trim, and this I'd painted a rich buttery cream that complemented the blue. Daylight pours in through two long horizontal windows that run almost the full length of the room. Seven very tall bamboo shoots sprout from a rainbow-colored glass vase, which rests on a credenza butted up against the windows.

Dotting every possible surface are clusters of crystals and lightly scented candles. In the center of the room two overstuffed cream-colored chairs sit facing each other, between them a small table that holds a tape recorder. On the walls I'd hung a favorite photo of Hawaii and a beautiful mosaic glass mirror. Tucked into one far corner, a mammoth linear waterfall gave rhythm to the room.

I pointed to one of the chairs, and as Allison settled herself, I quickly walked around the room with a lighter, igniting several of the candles. Finally, I went to my chair and pulled a blank tape from a stack on the credenza next to me. I stuck the tape in, set the clock and got comfortable.

For most people, intuition is little more than a whisper, a flutter in the white noise they've grown so used to ignoring. For me, it's an actual physical sensation involving flashes of pictures, pressure changes, ringing in my ears and tugs on my body. There are times when I feel so compelled to say something to someone that I can't focus on anything else until I've said it. I've even had instances where I've had a kind of tunnel vision, the world slipping from my peripheral vision as the message I'm supposed to relay plays over and over in my head.

Over the past several years I've discovered ways to control the beast, so to speak, and have found it best that before each session with a client I establish a regular routine. I begin by closing my eyes, and in my mind's eye envisioning white light surrounding me and filling the room. I then invite my crew in.

My "crew" consists of five spirit guides, and one by one I can "feel" their energy enter the room and stand on my right. Think of it like closing your eyes and sensing someone entering the room; there is almost a radiance emanating from them that you can detect without really understanding why you can detect it. This is how it feels to me when I ask my guides to attend.

Once my guides have entered, I then ask the client for their full name and date of birth, which is sort of like painting a bull's-eye on a target for me. Once I have the client's name and birth date I open my intuition, pointing it directly at the client, like an arrow at a target. When I feel a connection to their energy, I know it's time for me to speak.

After a few moments in front of Allison I felt a strong connection to her energy and got several images right away. "Okay, the first thing I'm picking up is pottery. They're showing me a potter's wheel and that scene from *Ghost*, you know, where Demi Moore is making clay pots?"

Allison replied in a surprised breath, "I teach a pottery class at the Art Institute."

"Cool! Okay, they're giving me the feeling that you've been very sad lately. I feel like someone close to you, a woman, has left the picture and that this has made you very depressed; your pottery is suffering or you're neglecting your class as a result."

"Yes," she said as I paused between sentences.

"They are making me feel like you used to be an outdoorsy kind of person, like you enjoyed planting flowers and tending the garden and you've been spending all this time indoors with the shades drawn."

"Yes."

"Your guides are telling me that you need to get on with your life, that this sadness needs to pass and that there is a big giant world of discovery out there if only you'll venture out."

Silence.

I rarely look at my clients when I'm doing a reading as I've found that their facial expressions tend to distract me. I typically point my gaze to an empty corner of the room or just close my eyes. The only time I will look at a client is when they don't confirm something I've said. Allison hadn't responded yet, so thinking that I might have gotten the last statement wrong, I glanced at her to gauge her physical reaction. What I noticed was that her mouth had formed a grim, thin line and her hands were gripping the sides of the chair so fiercely that her knuckles were turning white.

A little confused at her reaction, I checked again with my crew to make sure I was on track. They replayed everything I'd just said again in my head, a sign that I was in fact getting it right. I focused again on Allison, and I suddenly noticed the tiniest shift in her energy. She was closing herself off. Experience had taught me that this meant that either I was way off or I had struck a nerve. I mentally asked the crew for a different topic.

"Okay, now they're showing me a FOR SALE sign. . . . Are you selling your house?"

"Yes."

"Good, they're saying move forward with this. I feel like this is a really good thing you're doing, like they are really happy you're doing this. I get the feeling that there was too much of the past here and that by moving out you're letting go of things that have been weighing you down."

More silence. I refused to look at Allison anymore, deciding to keep my eyes closed. Her reactions were throwing me off, and I just wanted to concentrate on what I was getting. I could feel her energy both accepting what I was saying and holding it at bay. The incongruity of it was making me mentally scratch my head. Feeling slightly frustrated, I again asked my crew for another topic.

"Okay, they're saying there is a dark-haired man around you, and they are attaching a warning to him. They're saying that you need to have nothing to do with him. I get the feeling this guy is connected to you in some obscure way, like he's a family member but not, a brother figure or something, someone you've lost touch with, and you should keep it that way—he's just got bad news written all over him. They're also connecting him to this feeling of loss for you, like he was why this woman you were close to left, and that you want to blame him, and they're saying that it's okay to blame him, but not to his face. Like he really did do what you think he did, but you need to tread carefully here. They keep saying 'Leave well enough alone' and I get the feeling that you're sticking your nose into something that is bigger than you thought it was or that you could be getting yourself into trouble with this dark-haired man. They're saying that there's really nothing you can do and just to leave it alone."

Silence.

Once in a great while I will get a really "icky" feeling connected with a possible future event. The icky feeling with the professor and his heart condition was what compelled me to warn him that day in class.

I was getting the same type of very icky feeling around Allison and this dark-haired man. Hearing no confirmation for what I had just said, I finally opened my eyes and looked at her. She had gone very pale and very still and her eyes were liquid, tears on the verge of spilling over.

The warning continued to play over and over in my head, so I emphasized it by saying, "Allison, I'm telling you, they are making it clear that you need to stay away from this guy, whoever he is. You have the power to change your destiny. It's called free will, and you can choose to ignore this advice and bring one kind of future to yourself, or you can take my advice and stay out of trouble. Do you understand?"

"Yes," she whispered and nodded her head.

In retrospect, I suppose I wanted to believe that I'd gotten through to her; I wanted to believe she'd listened to the warning and taken my advice. Why I didn't probe a little deeper when I had the chance, I'll never know. What I do remember is that my icky feeling refused to subside, but I asked for another topic anyway, and the rest of her reading was actually rather bland. Other than the initial warning nothing jumped out at me. I've gone back over it many times since then, wondering continually if I could have altered fate in some way. Maybe if I'd just pushed a little harder, used my gift to probe a little deeper, perhaps I could have saved Allison's life in the end, and in doing so prevented a serial killer from setting his sights on me.

The tricky thing about fate, however, is that it's all in the timing.

Chapter Two

"Theresa?!" I shouted up the stairs.

"Yeah?" she called back, the sound of paper crumpling emanating from her bedroom.

"I'm finished in the living room. Did you want me to start in on the kitchen, or the study?"

"Um, the kitchen, I think. Brett promised me he'd do the study, so leave that for him. I'll be down to help you in a minute. I'm almost done up here."

"Okay," I said, shuffling into the kitchen and patting her cat, Mystery, on the way.

My face was set in perma frown, and I'd done so much heavy sighing lately that I'd practically hyperventilated twice. The day after Theresa and Brett had arrived home they'd begun packing, making the past week a whirlwind of activity. I'd helped as much as I could in the hours after work, and now, as I stared at the kitchen table where Theresa and I had shared so many late-night talks and so much pizza, I found my eyes becoming blurry, and my throat felt tight—again.

With a sigh, I taped together a moving box, lugged in the wrapping paper from the other room and began unloading the kitchen cabinets. Theresa joined me about ten minutes later, her curly brown hair pulled up in a ponytail and her big brown eyes wide with energy. For a long time we didn't speak. Then, breaking the silence, she looked at me a little askance and asked, "Abby? Have you been holding out on me?"

"I'm sorry, what?" I asked, surprised by the question.

She looked at me more intently now and said, "Honey, you've got the love bug all over your energy! Did you meet someone?"

When Theresa and I first met, she was in the very early stages of dating Brett, the love of her life (and now her husband). I, on the other hand, was in the middle of letting go of mine. I had fallen in love with Ben Newman the moment I'd met him, and we'd been inseparable for three solid years. Then one day we'd talked marriage, and I had taken the bull by the horns and planned the entire wedding in a record-breaking fifteen minutes. I remember him getting a rather pained look on his face, and over the course of the next few weeks he had faded slowly away, like summer into fall, and I'd gotten the message. Okay, so it took him saying, "I don't want to marry you," for it to *really* sink in, but eventually I got there.

It was nearly four years later and I hadn't dated a single soul since. Six months ago I'd been ready to get back in the saddle, finally convinced that Ben just wasn't going to come to his senses and call me begging for forgiveness. I'd started fixing myself up a bit, making goo-goo eyes at attractive men, and wearing lingerie with an underwire and maybe a *little* bit of padding. Then one afternoon I was walking around the mall doing some shopping for more of the underwire push-up stuff when I spotted Ben standing outside a clothing store holding several packages. My heart did a flip-flop, and I looked in a nearby mirror, thanking the powers-that-be that I'd fixed my hair and was wearing makeup. "Play it cool," I muttered to myself, as I began to trot over. "Be breezy."

When I was ten feet from him I saw a woman come out of the clothing store pushing a stroller complete with baby. She stopped in front of Ben. He greeted her with a kiss and loaded some of the packages onto the stroller, the two of them laughing at something the woman said. Just then she caught me staring at them all bug-eyed, and she turned Ben's attention in my direction. He looked at me for a moment, trying to place the face, and just as recognition dawned I bolted away from him, straight out of the mall.

I cried for a week—okay, maybe four, but after that I made up my mind. No more men! Theresa indulged my heartache with open ears, boxes of Kleenex and lots of ice cream. One of the things I loved most about her was her ability to just listen, without judgment or unwanted advice. She let me cry and rage and fall into a well of self-pity. Smart woman that she is, she knew if she just let me heal, I would eventually find my way out of that well and put an end to my self-imposed spinsterhood.

So the day I heard that she and Brett were officially moving to California, I panicked, finding the thought of spending every weekend alone quite daunting. After mulling it over for a little while, I decided to stop living like plain old vanilla and start looking for some topping—or at least some chocolate sprinkles. So I'd joined Heart2heart.com, an Internet dating service, three days ago out of total desperation.

One of the other hazards of my job is that it doesn't invite a stream of eligible bachelors. To a very large degree my clientele is female; the men I do read are typically gay or in the throes of girl trouble themselves. Not exactly the perfect profession for meeting Prince Charming.

I hadn't shared joining the Internet dating service with Theresa, mostly because I just wanted it to happen naturally. For once I didn't want to know the outcome. I wanted it to be a surprise. I also meticulously avoided asking "my crew" about joining the site, for the same reason. The problem with being an intuitive is that you get advice *all* the time. I strictly told them to butt out until I was ready to ask them; so far they had listened and hadn't sent me any feelings one way or another, but that didn't mean they couldn't give Theresa a little hint. I frowned at how sneaky my crew was, but then again, I was a pretty stubborn pupil.

"Well?" she asked, hands now firmly on hips.

Rolling my eyes, I confessed. "Don't get your panties in a bunch. I just listed my profile on an Internet matching service to see what I'd see."

"*And* . . . ?"

I sighed. Clearly I wasn't going to be able to get away with a simple answer. "*And* I have a date tomorrow with a guy who actually took a decent picture."

Theresa squealed and punched me in the arm, which caused me to roll my eyes so far back I had a lovely view of the top of my skull. "Don't make a big deal out of it. It's just a date."

"So what's his name?" she asked, now pumping me for details I was very reluctant to give. I just didn't want the pressure of it all. I was struggling with my own insecurities of being alone, so the fewer people who knew and felt pity for me the better.

I sighed again and gave her a look that pleaded for her to back off. She smiled winningly back at me and batted her eyelashes. There was no way she was letting me off the hook. She could be pretty stubborn too.

"His name is Dutch."

"Dutch?"

"Yep." If Theresa was going to continue fishing for details, she was going to find it a pretty dry lake.

"Hmmm, interesting name. Is it a nickname?"

"I'm not sure. He just signs his e-mails 'Dutch,' so it could be."

"What's he do?"

"I'm not sure. His profile said something about security, or securities. He might be a stockbroker or something."

"Uh-huh—and?"

I sighed again, as audibly as I could, feeling myself on the verge of getting rude and struggling to pull in my horns. "*And* what? He's in his mid-thirties, he's got wavy blond hair and blue eyes, he's over six two, and he's divorced, no kids. He's a nonsmoking, social-drinking, Michigan native, and he currently lives in Royal Oak. He's probably a walking cliché and I'm probably going to have a rotten time and go home convinced that I will never marry and should reconsider my idea of breeding cats."

Theresa laughed and rubbed my arm. "Wow! I gotta say I'm so proud you have such an open mind about the whole thing."

The next day was Saturday, and it promised to be intense. On weekends I book the most readings, six to eight per day, which allows me to take Mondays and Tuesdays off. During the week I schedule no more than four to six per day; any more than that and I'm too tired to do a good job. It's great work if you can get it, and I feel very lucky that I make a pretty good living this way.

My alarm clanged at seven—my first reading was at nine. Sleepy-eyed, I pulled my waist-length light brown hair into a ponytail and slipped on jeans and a tank top. I slapped on a little makeup, thankful that the complexion god had smiled on me and no blemish had cropped up during the night. I had my date with Dutch tonight and was feeling nervous enough already.

At thirty-one I feel pretty lucky. I neither look nor act my age. I'm usually pegged as about three to five years younger than I really am, a myth I encourage.

At five six I'm a comfortable height, and thankfully I'm one of those supremely lucky souls blessed with a fast metabolism, allowing me, with a little effort, to maintain my 123 pounds. Overall I've always been content with my looks. I'm neither bombshell nor plain Jane, but somewhere comfortably in between. My looks allow me the freedom to float unnoticed among the masses when I'm makeup-less and sloppy or to turn a few heads when I need an ego boost and I've spent an hour in the bathroom priming and primping.

Throughout my twenties I'd been a fitness buff, and regular gym workouts were on my daily agenda. These days, however, I'm more into yoga, finding it just as toning and a lot gentler. It just seems to fit better with the whole intuitive image too—I mean, who wants to get a reading from Buffy the Vampire Slayer?

After dressing I went downstairs and greeted my very spoiled, very adorable dog, Eggy. Eggy is a four-year-old chocolate-brown dachshund whom I had purchased shortly after my breakup with Ben. I came to the conclusion rather quickly that I got the better end of the deal; Eggy never hogs the remote, doesn't leave the toilet seat up and has the decency to leave the room when he farts, niceties that Ben had never mastered.

Eggy gets his name from his absolute love of eggs.

To this day his breakfast always includes one fried egg, which he somehow manages to devour first even when I mash it into the rest of his dog food.

As I set out Eggy's breakfast, I heard a familiar truck rumble into my driveway. Climbing over the various tools, stray pieces of wood and cabinets that littered my living room, I opened the front door to greet one of my greatest pieces of good fortune, Dave-the-Handyman.

Dave is a throwback to the sixties and looks like he'd be mighty comfortable riding down the highway looking for adventure. He has very long blond hair, going gray and braided into a ponytail that snakes down his back, ending in a fine point. He's a pretty big guy, around six two, in his early fifties and extremely easy going. Very talented too. And did I mention that he works for a paltry fifteen dollars an hour?

About six months ago I'd looked around the tiny studio apartment I'd been squished into for years and had come to the conclusion that I finally needed to act like a grown-up and dive into the mature world of homeownership. I'd gone right out and signed up with a realtor who gave me the cold hard facts: Based on my income, credit history and the fact that I insisted on living close to my office—a rather expensive neighborhood—the best I could hope for was a handyman's special.

To my naïve mind, that sounded pretty good. I mean, I could be handy. Being the proud owner of both a hammer *and* a screwdriver made me feel brave enough to throw caution to the wind. "Bring it on," I'd said to my agent confidently.

In hindsight I probably should have paid a little more attention to her reaction, which involved some "tisking" noises and a head shake or two, but I was too excited to be reasonable and watched the real estate listings diligently, waiting for my dream home to pop up.

After three months of looking, a house finally came on the market that fit perfectly for me. It had the right location, the right price and, like my agent repeated over and over again, "potential." As I signed the mortgage papers I couldn't wait to put my hammer and screwdriver to work.

I'd come to my senses about two days later, standing in the middle of crumbling walls, a dilapidated kitchen, missing floorboards and smells emanating from the upstairs who's orgin I didn't even want to guess at. The only updates to the house in forty years had been a new roof and central air, otherwise, I was in home-sweet-hell.

Dave had been recommended to me by one of my clients, and his arrival to my front door had been a Godsend. Although he was cheap, I quickly discovered that the repairs weren't, and all the savings I'd tucked away to furnish my new home had quickly vanished once Dave got to work.

I found myself cramming more and more readings into the workweek, trying to keep pace with all the repairs. There was no furniture downstairs save a small computer desk and chair in the second bedroom, off of the living room. My kitchen, which sat in the back of the house behind the living room, had only a card table and a couple of folding chairs, which didn't go very far in making it look homey.

I watched as Dave lugged his toolbox and various drills, saws, buckets and extension cords up the front walk and considered once again how lucky I was to have found him. I made it a point never to rush him, or appear impatient. He tended to be slow and meticulous, and his work was sheer genius. So far he had replaced the hardwood floor upstairs, fixed my stairway, laid a tile floor in the bathroom, installed a new front door and re-screened my back porch. Now he was working on installing new cabinets and recessed lighting in the kitchen. The hardwood floors in the living/dining room were next, along with new windows, but years of working in a bank on a salary just above poverty level had trained me to be cautious with debt.

"Good morning, honey!" Dave said jovially as I held the screen door open for him.

"Hey, Dave. How's it hanging?"

"Low and to the left, if you really want to know," he said chuckling, and bent down to get a face full of wet tongue from Eggy, who, I was beginning to believe, liked Dave better than he liked me. "You going to work?"

"Yeah, got a full list today. There's a check on the counter for all the supplies for this week, and another one for your labor from last week. I should be home by five thirty, but let me know if you need me to stop at the Depot on the way home to pick up anything else."

"Will do. Have a good day!"

As I drove to the office I thought about my date. I ran through my wardrobe choices again and tugged at my lower lip with my teeth, worrying over the two selections I'd resigned myself to. I'd made a firm commitment on dressing my lower half, deciding on a pair of hip-hugging black cotton pants that were painted onto my thighs and flared out with a little bell at the bottom. I had strappy sandals and a new pedicure, so I was fairly confident with these items.

What to wear with the black pants was the dilemma. My date and I were slated to meet at a restaurant not far from my office in downtown Royal Oak, which suited me on two counts. One, I'd been to the restau-

rant before and felt confident about the atmosphere
and acceptable attire, and two, if the date was a total
disaster there would be no uncomfortable walk to my
front door, because I could simply get in my car and
drive home.

The debate I was having with myself this morning
was whether to go slightly sexy or slightly conservative. I had a choice of two tops: The first was a black
halter top with built-in bra that wrapped around my
neck and left my shoulders bare. I have good shoulders, and I hoped they would divert attention from
my barely B-cup cleavage.

The alternate choice was a silky peasant blouse with
a V-neck and long sleeves that fell open a little past
the elbows, making the sleeve hang wide when I
moved my arm upward. Not the sexiest shirt; however
it would allow me to wear the push-up bra and en-
hance the barely B cup to something more like "I
got boobs, and I know how to use 'em!" The debate
continued straight to the office and endured through
breaks between readings.

At exactly five thirty I walked through my front
door again, to see Dave packing his toolbox for the
night. "Hey there," I said.

"How was your day, honey?"

The fact that Dave called me "honey" never bothered me in the slightest. I knew he was deeply devoted
to his "old lady" at home and called every woman he
liked "honey." I actually enjoyed the endearment;
from anyone else it would have bugged the crap out
of me.

"It was good, paid the rent, you know . . . the usual.
I'm ready for a shower and a glass of wine."

"My cue to leave," Dave said, winking at me as he
patted Eggy and scooted out the door.

Alone again, I looked around the corner at what

was slowly but surely becoming a kitchen and smiled again at my good luck in finding Dave. I fed Eggy, and while he was happily munching, headed upstairs for a much-needed shower and pre-date primping.

When I was a little kid, my mother decided that I would look adorable with a Dorothy Hamill—the famous ice-skater's haircut. She said she was tired of keeping up with my long, often tangled hair and that this was what every pretty little girl was wearing. Effectively, what my mother did was turn her eight-year-old daughter into a son. My round face, freckled cheeks and penchant for climbing trees made every stranger think I was a boy, which forced a lifelong hatred of Miss-Goody-Two-Skates. The saga continued for years, my mother always insisting that I keep my hair short, that long hair was too much to keep up with. Throughout my twenties I'd kept it only shoulder length; working at a conservative bank dictated no long hair, open blouses, short skirts or personality. How I lasted so long there remains a mystery.

For the past four years, however, I've only trimmed the very ends of my hair once every couple of months, letting it grow as long as it liked. It hung now all the way to my waist, and I loved it. It framed my angled features in a complimentary way and left me feeling feminine when it swished across my back. Tonight, I blew it dry, then rolled it in hot rollers to add body, a slight curl and some bounce for the evening. Wearing a well-worn flannel robe I walked to my closet and surveyed my choice of outfits. I pulled out the pants and grabbed the black halter top first, holding it up to my full-length mirror. I made several pouty faces and bent my knees in a pose that magazines suggested was alluring. Looking critically in the mirror I thought I just looked silly.

I switched to the peasant blouse, but after checking out the effect I went back to the halter top. I had no idea what this guy preferred, so I just decided to go with what I liked, and I liked bare shoulders better than pushed-up boobs.

While I was getting ready I turned on the TV in my room for background noise and caught the lead story on the local news. A distraught young woman surrounded by microphones stood crying into the face of the camera and pleading for her little boy's safe return.

The camera switched back to the reporter, who explained that four-year-old Nathaniel Davies had been abducted at the Oakland Mall while his mother had her back turned to him and was looking in a store window. The screen switched to a very grainy image of security cameras capturing the shadowy image of a large man in a baseball hat, long sleeves and big jeans grabbing the hand of a little boy and ushering him out the mall's door. The police were unable to make a positive ID and the public was being asked to come forward with any information on little Nathaniel. The broadcast then plastered across the screen a picture of a smiling little boy holding a rubber ball, and my heart did a little thud in my chest.

One of the very odd talents I have is being able to look at a photograph and immediately know if the person pictured is alive or dead. I can't explain how I know, other than that when I look at regular photos of people who are still alive, they look almost three-dimensional to me; people who are dead appear flat and plastic. Little Nathaniel was sadly the latter as he smiled at me from the TV screen, and I mentally said a prayer that he was being well looked after wherever he was now.

The screen flashed back once again to Nathaniel's

mother, and as she sobbed, the phrase *Liar, liar, pants on fire* danced through my head. Focusing on my intuition for a moment I sent out a question: "The mother's lying?"

Yes. My right side felt light and airy.

"But what about the video?"

Liar, liar, pants on fire . . . and then I knew. I knew that the video was fabricated somehow and that whoever was at the mall knew they were being taped and that Nathaniel was already dead. I got the word *brother* in my mind, and then a flash of an old abandoned house and the image of a lily. There was another flash, and I saw a hint of blue fabric poking out from some rubble. Not only was Nathaniel dead, but he was buried under some rubble in an abandoned house and either there were lilies nearby or a lily had something to do with the location.

I walked over to the TV and switched it off, hanging my head for a moment. I hated the news, and in general refused to watch it because often, like tonight, I got more of the story—much more—then I ever wanted. It was so frustrating because I knew without a doubt that people were terrified that what had happened to Nathaniel could happen to their child. It further angered me because I was sure there were other people who cared about Nathaniel that were still hoping he was alive and were worried that he was alone, scared and suffering. Mostly, however, it bothered me because Nathaniel's mother was a child killer and was likely going to get away with it. I struggled with the thought of going to the police with my suspicions, and then I remembered the story of Monica Madden.

Monica Madden was a very gifted, albeit undeveloped, clairvoyant who lived in a small town in Colorado and one day had a nearly debilitating vision of a woman being raped and murdered, then left in the hills surrounding the town. She had gone to the police with her vision, and they only laughed in her face. She was so overwrought by the vision, which continued to plague her, that she and her daughter went looking for the body up in the hills. After two days of searching, led by Monica's intuition they found the body of a woman who'd been missing for several weeks. The pair scrambled away from the scene and called 911.

When the police arrived they were skeptical of Monica's story and kept her for questioning. They were convinced that she must have had something to do with the homicide, as she'd been the only one to locate the body and she had intimate details of how the murder had unfolded. Eventually she was even charged with murder and spent several months in jail pleading her innocence while her seventeen-year-old daughter was left to fend for herself until the real killer was finally caught and brought to justice.

As I remembered this story, I came to the same old conclusion I had in the past—that the world was not ready to take intuitives seriously, and there was no way I wanted to be held under suspicion for something I'd had nothing to do with. I sent up a prayer that the police would find Nathaniel's body quickly and bring his mother to justice. Then with a slightly heavy heart went back to the business of getting ready.

At seven o'clock I took one last long look in the mirror and winked at my reflection. "Oh yeah, you got it goin on, baby!" I said as I made my finger and thumb into an imaginary gun. "Pow!" I said, following that by more winking. The phone rang just then, and if I'd had a real gun I would have shot myself in the foot. Laughing nervously, I picked up the phone and heard my sister's voice on the other end of the line.

Catherine can only be described as a force of nature. She is as different from me as night is from day: Petite, dainty and blond, with a mind that can cut steel, she is a self-made gazillionare, lives in a huge, completely furnished house in an affluent suburb outside Boston, owns her own successful multinational company, is the happily married mother of two kids and has an obedient dog that can do fourteen separate tricks and is surrounded by a slue of people who formally call her, "Yes-ma'am."

She is organized to the point of fanaticism, utilizes every nanosecond of every waking moment and accomplishes more by six a.m. than the entire United States Armed Forces. She is the double-decker banana split to my one plain scoop of vanilla.

Oh, and Catherine always acts her age.

Oddly, with so many differences between us, we never get tired of talking to each other. I couldn't remember a day I'd had in the last ten years that we hadn't spoken at least once. She is my biggest supporter, my closest confidante and my Rock of Gibraltar.

"So which top did you pick?"

"The black halter."

"How's it look?"

"Me liiiiikes it!" I sang, smiling into the phone.

"Wonderful. I just called to wish you good luck and to tell you to be careful. And of course, I will be calling you early tomorrow morning to make sure you didn't sleep with him."

"Cat!" My sister the booty police.

"Oh, and I read in this magazine that you're not supposed to compliment him on his clothes or his looks, but on the restaurant he chooses. So if you like him make a big deal about how much you like the restaurant and the food."

"Yeah, right, got it, Cat. Gotta go!"

"Okay, love you and we'll talk first thing tomorrow."

"Love you too. Good night."

I clicked the phone off, let Eggy out one last time, then headed out the front door, pausing to check my purse for the three essentials: money-keys-ID. I locked the front door, then eased into my Mazda and fastened the seat belt before turning the ignition. I'd had my car for a couple of years, and I loved it like the dickens. The fact that it was paid for made me love it all the more.

I arrived at the restaurant, parked and went around to the front. Dutch and I had agreed to meet at seven fifteen, and I was right on time. I walked into the lobby and was met by the host, a young man with tousled blond hair, an earring and an attitude. I told him that I was there to meet a gentleman named Dutch and that I wasn't sure if he'd arrived yet. The young man looked down at his seating chart and said that my dinner partner had just been seated and that he would have someone take me back to our table in just a moment. He then turned to one of the less important hostesses and asked her to show me to table twenty-nine.

I worked hard not to laugh out loud at that, because my crew was so obviously at work. Twenty-nine is my number. I was born on the twenty-ninth of the month, and ever since I was a little kid I'd had a special affection for the number.

It's more than just my birthday, twenty-nine is also a way for my guides to send me a message that they approve of something I'm doing or thinking. For example, take the day I decided to join the Internet dating service. While I was filling out my profile online my eye drifted to the clock at the bottom of the computer and at the exact moment I looked, it was twenty-nine minutes past the hour. It was their way of giving me the thumbs-up.

The hostess walked me out of the lobby and toward a quartered section of the restaurant. Sitting in the booth that we approached was one of the most attractive men I'd ever seen in my life, and I nearly wet myself with relief. He won extra points for standing up as I approached the table.

The hostess left us to ourselves and as we smiled gamely at each other and shook hands, I'll have to admit that mine had suddenly gone sweaty. I sat with as much grace as I could muster given my heels and the butterflies doing the whoop-de-doo in my stomach.

"Wow!" Dutch exclaimed as he took a gander at me. "You are a beautiful woman, Abby."

"And *you* have excellent taste!" I deadpanned. I'd waited for *years* to say that line.

Dutch threw his head back and laughed, a sound I thought I'd fall in love with. His voice was deep and throaty, smoke through velvet. His features lit up when he smiled, like a house aglow with Christmas lights. I compared him in person to the picture that had caught my interest on the computer and I had to admit that he was *way* better-looking in real life; I could hardly resist the urge to fan myself with the menu.

Thanks to his old-fashioned manners, I had been able to check out his height—the man definitely hadn't lied about being six two. He had broad shoulders that molded nicely under a cream-colored knit shirt and well-defined biceps that bulged slightly when he bent his elbow. His hair was light blond, and his complexion was subtly ruddy, like he'd spent his fair share of time in the sun. The most alluring thing about him, however, was his eyes. They were an electric midnight blue and peeked out at me with a stare that could have melted ice cream. He had a narrow nose and a prominent square jaw. He reminded me a lot of a young Ed Harris, who it just so happens, I have a huge crush on. He had an infectious, brilliantly white smile, full, suggestive lips, and he smelled fabulous. To hell with it—I picked up the menu and began fanning.

"Whoo, it's a hot one this year, huh?" Oh God, did I actually say that?

He smiled and politely played along with the temperature theory. "Yeah, I don't remember it being this hot last year, but I guess we were due. Can I get you a drink?"

Yes! "That would be lovely. I hear they have wonderful margaritas here. And by the way, excellent choice for a restaurant. I love Mexican."

Dutch and I made small talk for the next half hour and finally ordered when the waitress stopped by for the sixth time to see if we were ready. We'd both kept forgetting to look at the menu every time she walked away. I ordered the Sante Fe chicken and Dutch ordered the pepper steak, and we each added another margarita. After our waitress departed we nibbled gingerly on the complimentary chips and salsa and began in earnest the delicate task of getting to know each other.

Dutch had charm that rivaled his good looks, and I wondered why he'd had to join a dating service to find someone to go out with. I asked him as much, and he turned the question back on me.

"Well, I've never been one for the bar scene, and in my profession I don't meet that many eligible men," I said.

Abruptly Dutch grimaced and reached down to his belt buckle, pulling a small cell phone up from a clip fastened there and focusing his attention on the display. "I'm really sorry Abby, I don't mean to interrupt, but I have to answer this page. I'll be right back," he said, reaching across the table and squeezing my hand, which I thought would melt onto the table like candle wax. Then he let go, eased out of the booth, and turned to walk in the direction of the restrooms at the back of the restaurant, giving me a fabulous view of his ass. I wanted to stand up and applaud, but settled for dropping my jaw as I watched his small, firm buns bounce along. Suddenly both buns stopped and swiveled, and I realized he was looking back in my direction. Belatedly I looked up and snapped my mouth shut as he chuckled and pointed directly in front of him. I followed his finger and saw that the wall he was pointing to was one gigantic mirror—he'd watched me watching his ass!!!

I felt a look of horror plaster itself onto my face and quickly lowered my gaze, absolutely humiliated. Several minutes went by and without looking up I felt his presence as he eased back into the seat. "Sorry it took me so long, I used the men's room while I was up. So, what do you think of the décor?" he asked in a serious tone.

Mortified, I looked up and caught him winking with a playful smile. "Dutch, I really have to apologize for my behavior. I'm normally much more of a grown-up than that . . ." *Liar, liar, pants on fire.*

"So does that mean I can't watch you walk to the ladies' room when you have to go?" He was toying with me, and my face turned a darker shade of red. I didn't care if it meant ruining a kidney—there was no way I was going to the ladies' room tonight.

Just then the waitress walked by and I flagged her down to order yet another margarita, as my second one had magically disappeared while Dutch was in the men's room. Dutch smiled and asked for another as well, and a few minutes later the waitress brought the drinks and our food at the same time.

Grateful for something to do other than twist my napkin into a knot, I attempted to cut my chicken, but for some reason I was having trouble holding the knife and fork. In fact, I realized with sudden alarm, I was having a hard time feeling my hands at all. It dawned on me in a moment of panic that the alcohol was hitting me a lot harder than I'd anticipated. I finally managed to cut off a piece of chicken and get it into my mouth—okay, so it fell on my plate a few times, but eventually it got there. We ate in silence for a few minutes, me looking down at my plate, Dutch looking at me with a playful grin. I realized that he was humoring me and that's when I decided I really didn't care anymore that I'd been caught taking a lookey-loo. The view was nice, and it was a free country.

"So, Abigail," he said, breaking the silence, "you said that you haven't met any eligible men in your line of work. I know your profile said you were in counseling, but what specifically do you do?"

Feeling suddenly full of bravado, or perhaps gratitude for the subject change, I said, "You wouldn't believe me if I told you."

"Try me."

"I'm an intuitive."

"A what?" he said, looking confused.

"Psychic."

"Really?"

Either he was very good at masking his true feelings or he actually was open to the idea because judging by the look on his three faces, he seemed genuinely interested. "Yup," I said, nodding to the middle Dutch. "I tell people their futures."

"You make a living doing that?" he asked.

"Yup, and a good one."

"So, what do you do? Look into a crystal ball or something?"

I'm always amazed at the common man's theory on psychics. We're all a carnival act. A sideshow. A bamboozle. "No, I just tune in and go for it."

"How?"

"Well, I sit in front of someone, focus on their energy and ask to see stuff. The stuff comes to me and I just blurt it out."

Putting his fork and knife down and looking directly at me, Dutch said, "Show me."

Normally I don't give away my services. I'm not a circus act, and what I do has value. I've had plenty of people ask me for a free reading as a way of demonstrating my talent. It irks me when people assume that I need to prove my ability to them, but tonight my usual defenses seemed to have melted away with the ice in the second margarita. "Okay," I said, closing my eyes and setting down my silverware. "Tell me your full name and date of birth."

"Roland Dutch Rivers, May eighth—do you need the year?"

I cracked open an eye and said, "Roland?"

"Yeah," he smirked. "My mother was kind of a free spirit."

I shut my eye again and worked very hard not to give in to the guffaw tickling the back of my throat. Dutch told me his birth year and I quickly did the math, figuring him for thirty-three, then concentrated on his energy.

The thing about alcohol, and why I don't indulge in it very often, is that it makes me particularly brave and uninhibited. Bad on a first date with a guy, but very, very good when opening up for a reading. I have absolutely no fear of being wrong when I've had a drink or two, so I say anything and everything that comes to mind; there's none of the filtering that I normally do.

"Okay, first off, I'm picking up a badge all around you, so if you've been speeding lately you need to slow down because you're likely to get a ticket. Your guides keep showing me a cop's badge or something, so I think you need to ease off the gas pedal. Next, I'm picking up that you either just got or are about to get a promotion—congratulations by the way—at work, but that you work all the time, all day and night. They're saying you work too much.

"Next I'm picking up a partnership with a woman—she has brown hair, and it feels like it's everywhere, so she may have messy hair or something. They're telling me that this partnership is good, but that you two struggle to understand each other. Like you're both right, but you come at it from different directions. You two need to learn how to communicate with each other better and accept what the other is saying.

"I'm also picking up a connection to you and New York. And there's something about you and the military—like either you were in the military or maybe you have a family member, like a brother, who is. I'm picking up a cat, too, a big fat gray cat that thinks he owns you, and he's got this problem with peeing all over your house or something. They're making me feel like the reason he's doing this is because the house next door also has a male cat and your cat is just marking his territory. What you need to do is put kitty litter boxes all over the place and just let him pee in those for a while. Then gradually cut back on the number of pans. He'll be back to normal before you know it.

"Now I'm picking up skiing, like snow skiing, and something out in Utah or out West. Like you go there to ski. Also I'm picking up a woman who comes back from your past. She's blond and pretty, and you just don't know what to do with her. But you're going to need to make a decision, and it's not what she's hoping for. You need to follow your gut with her, because I'm picking up that there's some sort of tension between you two, like unresolved business, and you'd prefer it if she would just go away, but unless you say those exact words to her she's not going to get the hint."

Near our table a tray slipped and crashed to the floor, sending broken glass and plates everywhere. I started at the noise and snapped my eyes open and looked at Dutch, who was looking straight at me with a shocked expression on his face.

"How did you do that?" he asked.

"I told you, I'm an intuitive. It's what I do." My buzz was starting to wear off, and it suddenly dawned on me that I might have been a little too over the top for a first date. I looked down at the tabletop, embarrassed now.

"Hey," I heard him say after a moment, "how about we get this stuff wrapped up and go for a walk? I think the fresh air will do us both good."

I smiled back at him and nodded. Dutch flagged down the waitress, who delivered our check and gave us Styrofoam boxes for our leftovers. After we'd packed up our food, he laid down some cash and grabbed my arm, and out the door we went.

We walked around town for a little while, idly talking about where we grew up. Dutch, as it happened, had grown up in New York, and his father, his brother and he had all served in the Marines. Lastly Dutch divulged that along with a house about three streets over he also owned a condo in Utah that he used several times a year to go skiing.

"So tell me more about this stuff. Can you read my mind?" We had stopped at a little bistro on the second floor of an old brick building and found a table outside on the balcony that overlooked the street and pedestrians below. It was close to nine thirty and the sky was finally beginning to darken. My buzz was nearly completely gone now, and I had a glass of wine in front of me that I'd barely touched.

"No, not really. I can't carry on à conversation with you by reading your every thought, but if I concentrate on what emotions or feelings you're having, I'm usually in the ballpark. Mostly what I do is just to focus on the events, opportunities and obstacles going on in your life and discuss the possible outcomes connected with them." I noticed that Dutch had nonchalantly edged his chair a little closer to me and was leaning hard in my direction. Slowly his hand swung over to my arm, and with one finger he began to stroke from the top of my shoulder down my arm to a little circle around my wrist, and then back up the arm. The sensation was fabulous, and I congratulated myself over and over again for wearing the black halter top. After crossing and uncrossing my legs a few times, I continued, "It's more like I just get an image that flashes in my head, and then I know things about that image. For instance, tonight I was watching the news and this woman says she's lost her little boy, Nathaniel, in the mall, but while I'm watching it I know she's lying."

The finger paused almost imperceptibly midway up my arm, then continued as Dutch asked, "How do you know?"

"That's what I mean. I'm not sure. I kept hearing,

'Liar, liar, pants on fire,' ring inside my head, and then when they showed Nathaniel I knew he was dead. And I think he's buried in some abandoned building somewhere near lilies, or near something with lilies painted on it. He's on the bottom floor, buried in rubble. And the mother did it, but she had the help of a relative, and that's who I think is in the video. I think that the image of the little boy isn't even Nathaniel; I think the whole thing is a setup to throw the police off and let the mother get away with murder."

Dutch's finger had stopped at my wrist, and he was staring off into space somewhere around the arm of my chair. "Sorry," I said. "I don't mean to freak you out, but this is what my life is like. Sometimes stuff just comes to me."

In a cautious tone he asked, "Have you considered going to the police with this information?"

My eyes were resting on the finger, light as a feather resting on my pulse. I obviously *had* freaked him out with all the psychic stuff. "No, I haven't. I don't like cops. I mean, it's all well and good that they're out there defending us against anarchy and all, but most of the cops I've met are suspicious of everything and everyone. Every little thing needs to have a motive behind it. As a rule I find them cynical and too analytical, very one-plus-one-equals-two types. There's no way a cop would take me at my word. I mean, I could just see myself walking up to the police counter and saying, 'Hey, I have some information about a murder. I'm a psychic, so please take me seriously.' They'd laugh in my face as they locked me up in the looney bin." I paused, but when Dutch didn't say anything I decided to continue. At this point I figured I might as well put all my cards out on the table.

"And what if I was right? What if the information I had did help them? You can bet that instead of taking my gift seriously they'd think I had something to do with the crime. No, I don't want any part of it. There's no way I can prove how I got my information, and cops are big on proof. They'd want some evidence as to how I knew such and such. Well, in my profession, proof is a hard thing to come by. I live in an intangible world. I don't know why I know things, I just do, and that doesn't translate well in the world of your average lawman. Know what I mean?"

Dutch looked up and met my eyes, regarding me critically, and for a moment his face changed in a way that made me wish I had never told him what I did for a living. Cold, calculating eyes stared at me, and his expression was so blank it was scary. I pulled back just a bit, startled at the sudden change, and then it was gone. He blinked and the man I'd had dinner with returned.

"So, Abby, what kind of music do you like?" he asked, noticeably changing the subject.

An hour later Dutch walked me back to my car. He held my hand and stroked my fingers, and I hoped he was okay with what I'd revealed to him. I was feeling a little vulnerable, and he must have sensed it because it seemed like he was working hard to make me feel reassured. When we reached my car, he turned me toward him and lifted my chin. He lowered his face to mine, held my gaze for a moment and then kissed the bejesus out of me. I felt my toes curl, my stomach go mushy, my limbs go numb—my lips were in serious heaven. This man knew how to kiss! He stroked the side of my cheek with one hand and pulled my waist tight to him with his other. I was so absorbed in the kiss I think all I managed to do was clutch at his shirt in return. For several minutes we lingered there in the parking lot, smooching it up, until he finally pulled his lips away. He continued to hold me close, his forehead resting on mine, rocking me gently back and forth. Then with one last peck he let me go and stepped back. "You're going to be all right getting home?"

"Absolutely. Besides, you're the one with the cop on his tail. You need to be careful, okay?"

Dutch looked at me strangely for a moment, before bursting into a grin and shooting me a wink.

"Can I call you?" he asked.

"Absolutely," I replied, smiling like a little kid with a secret.

"Good night," he whispered and leaned in to kiss me passionately again.

"Mmmmm," I said, as we finally unlocked lips, then I got into my car and waved at him as I backed out of the space. I floated home and upstairs to bed, where I replayed his kisses over and over again.

Chapter Three

Anyone quick enough to label *me* eccentric for being psychic should spend just one day as a fly on my wall hearing perfectly "normal" people walk in, sit down, and lead me down a rabbit hole.

"All right, Penny, I'm picking up on a hospital," I said to a woman in her mid-forties who bore a striking resemblance to June Cleaver. Penny was tall and leggy, with mousy brown hair shaped in a perfectly bouncy bob, subtle makeup applied just so, and pearls circling her neck, with two more tucked demurely in her ears. She sat stiffly in her chair, her feet crossed at the ankles, hands folded adroitly in her lap. She was dressed in a lavender short-sleeved knit sweater with lacy collar, khakis, and, of course, completing the ensemble . . . penny loafers. I was pretty sure Penny thought it was hilarious to parade around in shoes that shared her name, but personally I'd mentally yawned when she first came in.

My attention shifted with the hospital reference. Maybe this wasn't going to be so bad after all, I thought morbidly; maybe she had come to me because she was sick and was looking for a ray of hope. But as I scanned the ether around her I couldn't find a thing wrong with her.

I continued, feeling my way along. "It's weird," I said. "I feel like you spend a lot of time in a hospital, but you're not sick, and I'm picking up that you aren't a doctor or a nurse—do you spend a lot of time in a hospital for some reason?"

She smiled encouragingly. "I work at Beaumont Hospital, in the billing department."

"Ahhh," I said, hiding my disappointment and stifling another yawn. "That makes sense. Okay, now I'm getting that there is some kind of a feud, or a fight, or something, with another woman. She's got blond hair and light eyes, and I think she's considerably younger than you. . . ." Maybe they'd had a fight in one of their Junior League meetings.

"That's Brandy," she confirmed.

For a second I wondered if she was talking about the drink, but then I mentally shook my head and got back to business. "Okay, well, they're saying that this Brandy woman is one big liar. I get the feeling you may have trusted her to tell you the truth about something you confronted her on, but she didn't. And this lie has to do with some sort of an argument involving another woman who's also got blond hair, but short—"

"I knew it!" Penny said, thumping the arm of her chair with her fist, interrupting me. "She said all they did was kiss, but I knew that slut was screwing around on me!"

I jumped slightly in my chair, completely taken aback by Penny's reaction; it was like June had just sworn like a sailor during Sunday dinner.

Also, I hadn't picked up the lesbian thing, and I mentally chastised myself for allowing my first impression to cloud my intuition. I smiled tightly, collecting myself as Penny looked expectantly at me. I turned slightly in my chair and closed my eyes; I couldn't look at this woman and not be thrown off by her appearance. After a moment, I continued, "Okay, the next thing they're saying is that there's this issue about money. I feel like you loaned this woman some money and you two were going to use it to start a business or something? And it has to do with wiring, or copper wire or something like that, but I don't think it's electricity."

"Yes," Penny said. "She makes this really fantastic jewelry out of copper wire, and we thought we could sell it on the Internet, but she needed some start-up money, so I loaned it to her."

"Okay, they're saying 'two,' like two hundred. Did you loan her two hundred dollars?"

There was a pause, so I opened my eyes. Penny's cheeks had rosied to a light pink. "Uh, no," she replied, looking carefully at her feet. "Actually it was two thousand."

My jaw dropped. Who needed two thousand dollars for some copper wire? I recovered again and closed my eyes. "And she hasn't paid you back yet, has she?" I said, more fact than question.

"Well, no . . ."

"I see," I said knowingly. "I'm afraid, Penny, that my feeling is you're not going to see this money again. I also get the feeling that she didn't put it to very good use. In fact, there is a connection to drugs here," I said, sensing the familiar bitter taste that always came into my mouth when I picked up someone using drugs. "Did you know she's a heroine addict?"

"She's been in rehab twice. That's how we met, actually; she was a patient at Beaumont up on the rehab ward."

I wanted to stand up and slap her. In my head I yelled, *You gave two thousand dollars to a recovering drug addict?! What were you thinking?!*

Whaling on my clientele isn't necessarily good for business, so I continued with the reading. "You may not like hearing this, Penny, but she's back using again. This is all the more reason for you to be cautious of this woman, because I'm also picking up the feeling of a jail cell here, and I think Brandy is going to get caught by the law very soon. You don't want to jeopardize your career by getting stuck in the middle of all this. Now your guides are *insisting* that you cut this woman off, that you give her the boot, and the reason you're supposed to give her the heave-ho— uh, sorry, no pun intended—is because there's someone new coming into the picture. I'm feeling like there's another woman on the edge of your energy. She's got brown hair like yours, and I also get the feeling that you two look alike somehow, that you could be mistaken for sisters. I also feel strongly like you know her, or know of her, and I feel like she's a teacher, or she works with small children."

Penny sucked in a breath of surprise. "Oh my God! That's my best friend, Michelle, and I've been in love with her forever!"

"Is she a teacher?"

"Yes, she teaches kindergarten."

"Does she know how you feel?"

"Well, we used to fool around a long time ago, but nothing since college."

"Then, Penny, it's time to throw caution to the winds and tell her about your true feelings. I really believe you two would be great together. Related to this new romance is a move for you. I get the feeling this will happen by the holidays, like around Christmas, and you'll be moving in with this other woman.

Does she have a house that's near a river or a lake? Blue with black shutters?''

A surprised breath in. "Yes, she does, but that's impossible," she said adamantly. "There's no way I'd be moving in with her."

"Why isn't it possible? Do you think Michelle might reject you?"

"No, that's not it. I can't be moving in with her because I'm *married*," she explained, pushing her slender ring finger adorned with a plain wedding band at me.

I blinked in surprise. I hadn't picked that up at all.

"To a man?" I finally asked, looking at the wedding band, rather incredulous.

"Yeah," she answered in a "what else?" voice.

"But, Penny," I said, shaking my head, "you're *gay*."

"What?!" she exclaimed, pulling back in her chair, completely offended. "No, I'm not! I just *told* you, I'm married!"

See what I mean? One minute I'm sitting down to talk with *Leave It to Beaver*'s mother, and the next I'm arguing with a translucent cat sporting a toothy grin. I should just change my name to Alice and be done with it.

After spending ten more minutes with Penny trying to convince her of her sexual orientation I finally gave up and just let her remain in her closet. My feeling was she'd be out by Christmas anyway, so why argue about semantics now?

I closed the door behind her and tidied up the office. It had been a bitch of a week.

What I had thought was a spectacular date with Dutch had obviously been a dud on his end. I hadn't heard from him, which gave him a no-frills membership into my bastard-of-the-month club. For all my psychic prowess, I was as yet unable to divine how the male mind functions. Picking up a book on Mars had made a recent appearance onto my to-do list.

To add insult to injury, tonight was Theresa's last night in town, and I'd barely had a chance to spend any time with her all week. Pouting, I went into my inner office and called her.

"Hey," I said when she picked up.

"Abby! Hi there. We were just talking about you," she said, laughing.

"Yeah, my ears are ringing. You two still on for dinner tonight?"

"Absolutely. Brett and I are heading over to the hotel right now to check in. We'll meet you at Pi's around six."

"Cool. See you there," I said, the light going out of my voice. How was I going to do this? How was I going to let go of my best friend?

I shuffled out from behind the desk and wandered over to Theresa's reading room. The door was open, and I switched on the light. The room was barren and empty, mirroring just how I felt.

Tomorrow an acquaintance of ours, a massage therapist named Maggie, would be moving her things in.

Although I knew Maggie casually and genuinely liked her, I still wasn't sure how I felt about letting anyone but Theresa into my private world. Still, it beat having to pay Theresa's portion of the rent. The other bonus was that Maggie was a night owl who booked most of her clients in the early evening. She would hardly interfere with my daily routine, and I wondered suddenly if that was really how I wanted things to be.

I sighed heavily and shuffled around some more, the weight of calling back clients who wanted to book readings keeping me from leaving just yet. Stubbornly I looked at my appointment book and stuck my tongue out at it. I just didn't feel like putting on a cheerful voice for anyone. Just then the phone rang, and I was considering letting it go to voice mail when the thought that it might be Theresa calling me back moved me to action.

"Hi, this is Abby," I said, taking a seat again at the desk.

"Hi, Abby, this is Allison Pierce. I had a reading with you a couple of weeks ago—do you remember me?"

I smiled into the phone. I rarely remember my clients, and typically remember even less about their readings. The connection I make to their energy never seems to last beyond the forty-five-minute sessions. "I'm sorry, Allison. I have a lot of clients, and after a while they all sort of blend together. What can I do for you?"

"Well, I was wondering if I could sit down with you again—I really need to ask you a few more questions. Do you have any appointments available today or tomorrow?"

I'll regret what I said next for the rest of my life; little did I know that lives were literally at stake and that my answer would have such grave consequences. I know that at the time I was motivated by a sense that the cosmos had rained on my parade in a huge way, and I wasn't in the mood to be charitable or understanding. "No, Allison," I said a bit testily. "I'm afraid that's not possible. I have a hard-and-fast rule that I will do only two sessions per year with my clients, spaced not less than six months apart, and if I make an exception for you then I'll have to make an exception for everyone. I can book you for an appointment in January, but I'm afraid that's the best I can do."

"There's no way you'll consider it? I just have a few questions, and it's really important—"

"Everyone always has just a few questions, Allison," I said, cutting her off, "and then it turns into another full session." I was getting impatient. "Listen, you can answer all of the questions you have by yourself. All you have to do is listen to your own inner voice. You are the most intuitive about yourself. Sit quietly with whatever question remains unanswered, and you'll find the solution. Now, did you want to make that appointment for January right now or call me back in a few months?"

"I'll call you back another time," she said, sounding deflated.

"Fine. Have a good day, Allison," I said briskly.

I hung up the phone with a hint of satisfaction. If I couldn't catch a break why should anyone else? But the satisfaction wore off quickly. The more I thought about it, the more ashamed of myself I became. Why hadn't I been nicer to her? Why hadn't I just asked her what questions she still had and offered an impromptu mini-reading over the phone? I'd done it for other clients. Why was I being such a witch?

The truth was that I was being small and uncharitable, and I was doing it because I was having a crummy day. I felt like I'd just flipped off a little old lady on the highway who'd only been trying to change lanes.

"Crap," I said into the silence. Well, it was too late now. I didn't have Allison's phone number, and unless she called back—highly unlikely at this point—I had no way to get in touch with her. I looked around the office and decided to call it a day before I wreaked any more havoc on my clients. I grabbed my purse and locked up the office.

Lost in moody thoughts, I descended the stairs and stepped out of the building, but suddenly an uncomfortable feeling crept along my spine, and for the hundredth time that week I felt myself looking around anxiously. This had been happening to me since Monday. I felt like someone was watching me, and out of the corner of my eye I kept looking for the bogeyman.

I looked up and down Washington Avenue, but like all the other times, I couldn't see anyone. I trotted across the street to the parking garage and walked quickly up the ramp in the direction of my car, but the moment I neared my assigned parking space the feeling intensified. Someone was following me. I quickened my pace, and instead of going directly to my car I jogged in the opposite direction, to the stairs. Hurrying through the stairwell door, I ran up one flight, letting the door bang loudly behind me, then darted around a pylon and waited. Seconds ticked by, and as I listened I could hear footsteps climbing the stairs. Peeking around the pylon, I saw a tall, good-looking black man dressed in Dockers and a polo shirt step through the door and look around intently. The thing that struck me was that he wasn't just looking; he was listening too, probably for the sound of my footsteps. I watched him move forward a bit, peering this way and that. This was the guy who'd been following me all week.

I'd had this feeling all week that my every move was being scrutinized, and I thought I'd seen a strange car at the end of my block a couple of times, but for the most part I'd just shrugged it off. Now I *knew* I was being watched. But who was this guy and what did he want with me? What had I done to him?

At that moment my purse slipped off my shoulder and hit the pylon with a small *thwack*. The man heard the noise and caught me peeking at him. He seemed startled to see me and regarded me for a brief moment with an odd look before straightening and walking off in the opposite direction, away from me.

I hesitated for only a moment before deciding to beat him at his own game. I started tagging along behind him, crouching low and hiding behind cars. He wandered down to the far end of the garage, then propped himself against one of the back walls and checked his watch. After five minutes he checked his watch again, then pushed himself off the wall and went back to the stairs, moving through the door and disappearing from view.

Cautiously, I hurried forward and followed him on tiptoe down the stairs. I snuck a look through the stairwell opening and saw him several yards in front of me. I darted out the door, closing it behind me without a sound, then duck-walked to a row of cars, intermittently peering up to keep track of the man.

He was walking to a familiar parking slot, and as I watched in near disbelief, he stopped right in front of my car. He regarded it for a moment, checked the hood for warmth with his hand, then came back to the driver's side and cupped his hands around his eyes while he lowered his head to look in my window. After a moment he straightened and glanced around the garage again. When his head turned in my direction, I squatted down low behind a Buick, waiting and listening intently. Finally I heard his footsteps walking away from my car, and after another few minutes I stood up slowly. He was gone.

The ordeal had shaken me, but I attempted to collect myself. My intuition said the man was looking for me, but why? What had I done? Was he a past client? Was he the husband or boyfriend of a client?

A *lot* of my clients cheat on their significant others or vice versa. I've learned not to judge the choices people make, and sometimes the advice that comes through me is to tell the client to get the hell out of their current relationship and run off with the other person.

I wondered if perhaps this was the scenario with my stalker. Maybe he just wanted to talk to me about a reading I'd given to his wife or girlfriend. But if that was it, why didn't he approach me when he saw that I'd spotted him? The whole thing was making me nuts, so as quickly and discreetly as I could I darted to my car and sped out of the garage, checking the rearview mirror all the way home.

At six o'clock I met up with Theresa and Brett at our usual Thai food hangout, Pi's Thai Cuisine, over on Ten Mile. To the average passerby Pi's looks like a run-down shack of a restaurant. The interior isn't much better, with only three tiny, scuffed-up tables and chairs whose last homes were quite possibly someone's Dumpster. The food, however, is absolutely divine. For years it's been the area's best-kept secret, and Theresa, Brett and I were weekly regulars.

When I stepped through the door into Pi's I saw Brett and Theresa already seated, both looking exhausted. They got up and hugged me when I came in, then we all sat down and I made small talk for the minute or two before our waitress came over. She looked at our table and asked, "The usuals?"

We nodded as one and she went off to put our order in. On my way to the restaurant I had planned on telling Theresa and Brett about my stalker, but when I saw their pinched and tired faces I suddenly changed my mind. It occurred to me that my story would no doubt worry both of them, and I knew they had a very long drive ahead. I couldn't afford to have them lose any sleep over worrying about me, so I kept the conversation light.

Within an hour it was apparent that Theresa could barely keep her eyes open, and I knew the time had come to let them go. We paid our bill and headed outside, where we stood hugging each other for long, tearful minutes. I stepped back after hugging Theresa fiercely and held her at arm's length, trying to imprint her image onto my memory. She smiled sadly at me and said, "You take care, Abby. And you'd better come visit us soon, or I'll fly out here and drag you to California myself."

My eyes were watering, and my throat had tightened up. I didn't trust myself to respond, so I just nodded fiercely. We hugged once more, and then she and Brett got into their Jeep, I got into my car, and we pulled out of the little lot in separate directions. I drove home crying softly and wiping my eyes.

Before going to bed I took a long, hot shower, trying to wash away the sad, heavy feeling thumping in my chest. A half-hour later I was stepping out of the steamy room wearing a T-shirt and cotton shorts—my bedtime attire—and I did feel a little better. I was too tired to dry my hair, and tomorrow was my day off, which meant that I didn't need to wake up to a good-hair day. So I settled for draping the long wet strands across my pillow and curling up with Eggy, hugging him in a tight embrace and falling asleep on a tear-stained pillow.

I bolted out of bed the next morning with my heart racing and my senses disoriented. Shaking, I looked around and noticed immediately that Eggy was downstairs barking his head off. Interspersed between his barks was the *"BAM! BAM! BAM!"* of someone pounding on my front door. I scrambled back to the nightstand for my glasses. Shoving them on and walking with unsteady feet and a racing heart, I stumbled down the stairs, gripping the railing tightly. Focusing first on quieting the dog, I momentarily took my eyes off the floor and so I tripped over a stack of plywood that Dave had left in the middle of the room. I went down with a thud and got a splinter in my knee. "Yeeeeeow!" I hollered.

"BAM! BAM! BAM!" My brand-new front door rattled on its hinges.

"Hold your freaking horses!" I yelled, trying my best to settle Eggy, who was wide-eyed with alarm. Limping, I picked him up and put him in the kitchen, behind the baby gate. I paused for a moment to pull out the splinter, then limped back to the front door and pulled it open with the force of an angry tigress, hollering, *"What?!"* for the benefit of neighbors who might think I had somehow invited this loud racket at the crack of dawn. When the door opened, I was suddenly looking straight into familiar eyes, the color of midnight blue. Dutch Rivers was standing tall and magnificent on my front porch.

"Crap!" I blurted as my eyes grew wide.

"Good morning, Abigail," Dutch said crisply, stepping back slightly, no doubt afraid I might bite.

Astonished at seeing him in the flesh, I subconsciously raised my hand to smooth my hair—and felt the uneven lumps of wet head meets bed head. Great.

"How do you know where I live?" I demanded, still angry and more than a little confused. Something was out of place. As I looked closely at Dutch I realized what seemed odd. There was a big shiny gold badge hooked onto his belt, and beside him was the guy I'd seen in the parking garage. "You're a *cop*?!" I gasped, my mouth hanging open in a big O.

"May we come in?" he asked tartly, ignoring my candor.

I looked from him to the other guy and back again,

furiously trying to collect my thoughts. My mind replayed his profile on Heart2heart.com, and I remembered that he said he worked in security. Yeah, just like I worked in counseling. "No!" I said, panicking at the state of my home. It was bad enough that he had to see me looking so disheveled; if he got a peek inside I'd die from embarrassment. "You cannot come in. I just woke up, and *that* guy," I said, pointing to the man behind Dutch, "has been stalking me for a week. What the hell is this all about?" Mornings have never been good for my personality.

"I'd like to explain that, Abigail, if you'll just let us come in for a minute."

I looked at Dutch closely and saw him take an appraisal of me standing there, wearing only a small nightshirt, shorts, no makeup, wet bed head and glasses. I didn't just look bad. I looked scary. I needed to shower, change, apply makeup and eat breakfast. There was no way I was going to readily admit Mr. Gorgeous and his partner to my tousled home to talk to my tousled self. Thinking fast, I asked, "Do you have a warrant?" My mouth had gone dry at the prospect that he'd say yes.

"No," he said calmly, then added, "Not yet," as he looked meaningfully at me.

There was something so smug about his answer and the way he looked down at me that it pissed me off royally. My face flushed and my temper flared. "Fine. Then there's your answer, pal. Why don't you call me later and we'll do lunch?" I said snidely. "I'll hold my breath waiting for your call. Hope I don't turn blue like I did the last time you promised to call me. Now, why don't you two get off my lawn and go terrorize the elderly?" I tried to shut the door in his face, but he stuck out his foot and jammed it in the opening.

"Abigail, listen. We would like to talk to you about

Nathaniel Davies. It's important, and I swear to you that if I go away now I will come back with a warrant and a pair of handcuffs. You get to choose which way you'd rather talk to us. Here, now, in the comfort and *privacy* of your own home or downtown in an interrogation room."

I blinked at him maybe twenty or thirty times with my mouth open, trying to process what he had just said to me. Nathaniel Davies? Who the hell was that? Warrant? Handcuffs? Interrogation room? "Is this some kind of a joke?" I asked, trying somehow to make everything Dutch had said fit into some sort of logical sequence.

"Not in the slightest," he answered in a tone that meant business.

I crossed my arms and looked at him. I was mad, disheveled and in the throes of a really good case of PMS. I clenched my jaw and sighed audibly. "Fine. You may come in, but I am not going to have a discussion with you until I have had a chance to freshen up. You will come in, you will not touch a thing, you will stay away from my dog and you will wait until I come downstairs. Then we talk. *Capiche*?"

"Glad to see you're being cooperative," Dutch said as he edged closer to the open door.

"Listen, buddy," I said, blocking his path again with my body. "Let's get one thing straight here. I waited by the phone for a solid week for you to call me, which of course you said you were going to do but never did. In my mind you rank one notch above the gray gooey stuff growing in the corner of my shower. Do not—and I repeat, *do not*—even *think* of making fun of me this morning."

Dutch smiled his charming smile and saluted. I rolled my eyes and grudgingly let them in.

* * *

Upstairs, I headed first to the bathroom. I took off my glasses and popped in my contacts, avoiding the mirror until the last possible moment. When I had worked up the courage to finally take a peek, I let out a new string of expletives at the sight of my reflection without makeup but with puffy red eyes and wet bed hair. My eyes misted in frustration at the thought of anyone seeing me like this, let alone a man I'd played tongue tag with. I folded my arms across the sink and rested my head on them while I took deep breaths. When the world stopped spinning, I pushed away and turned on the shower, quickly jumping in and dancing around until it got warm as I hurried to wet myself down. I dried off in a rush, ran a comb through my newly wet hair and padded in my flannel robe to the bedroom, where I donned jeans and a tank top, then went back to the bathroom for teeth brushing, mascara and blush.

Ten minutes after ascending the stairs I was back down in my living room, where I caught Dutch's partner standing silently against the far wall and Dutch on one knee poking fingers through the baby gate at Eggy.

Now, Eggy hates strangers, and he particularly hates male strangers. It took him a solid week to get used to Dave, but somehow Dutch had won him over in a matter of ten minutes. I glowered at my traitorous canine and crossed my arms at the two strangers in my house.

"I love what you've done with the place," Dutch said, standing up and waving an arm at the disaster of my living room. I pulled my eyebrows down into a deeper scowl and literally growled at him.

"Is there someplace we can sit?" Dutch's partner asked, looking around at the messy floor and registering the lack of furniture.

"This is going to take that long?" I asked, trying my best to look like I had far more important things to do with my life.

" 'Fraid so," Dutch said.

"Fine. We can go to the back porch. You two head there through the kitchen and around to the left. I'll grab a chair from the study and be right with you."

Neither man moved. Both stood stock-still watching me closely, the unspoken suggestion about my possible flight risk evident in their eyes. I rolled my eyes and stomped off to the study, where I retrieved a folding chair. I walked past them, climbing over the baby gate and leading the way out to the back porch. The two men followed, Dutch's partner a little more wary of Eggy, who was back on duty and doing his best rabid-dog impression.

I opened the sliding glass door and set down my chair on the far side of the card table that was placed haphazardly in the middle of the screened-in porch. Then I sat down and crossed my legs and arms. Yeah, I'd cooperate. When hell froze over.

The whole time I'd been upstairs I kept trying to remember who Nathaniel Davies was. I had come to the conclusion that I must have read for this guy and he must not have been happy with the reading, and instead of calling me for a refund, he must have concocted a phony story and gone to the police. I was desperately trying to recall details of Nathaniel's reading so that I wouldn't be caught off guard, but was having no luck with it at all.

Dutch sat down on the other side of the card table, directly across from me. His partner sat next to him, and both men eyed me skeptically. "Well?" I said, wanting to get this over with.

"Abigail, this is my partner, Milo Johnson. We're detectives with the Royal Oak Police Department working on a homicide investigation, and we're here today to see what you can tell us about Nathaniel Davies."

This was going from weird to scary weird. Why would a pair of detectives working a homicide be assigned to a complaint against my business? "Fellas, you're going to have to clue me in on who Nathaniel Davies is because I'm having a hell of a time remembering him. I read a lot of people, you know."

"So you read for Nathaniel Davies?" Milo asked.

"Didn't I?" I asked.

"Didn't you?" Dutch replied.

"Wait, wait, wait," I said, making a stopping motion with my hand. "I don't know if I read for Nathaniel Davies or not. That's what I'm saying. Did he come to you and say that I read for him?"

"Miss Cooper," Detective Johnson said, "Nathaniel Davies can't come to us and say anything. He was murdered two weeks ago, and his body was dumped in an abandoned house in Pontiac. He was only four years old."

And then it hit me. The night of my big date with Dutch I had seen the news broadcast about the little boy from Pontiac whose mother was sobbing into the camera, telling everyone within earshot that her little boy had been abducted. "Holy crap," I said, "The little boy who was supposedly abducted? *That's* what this is all about?" I asked incredulously.

"We have reason to believe, Miss Cooper, that you may have information about who killed Nathaniel," Johnson said. "We've been able to locate the body of the little boy, and we've brought his mother in for questioning, and she seems to think she knows you."

Liar, liar, pants on fire . . .

I sat back for a moment and turned my head, listening to things only I could hear. My guides were indicating that the police had nothing linking me to the murder other than the information I'd supplied. They were reassuring me that I'd be fine. I could tell it like it was. I turned back to Dutch's partner. "Bullshit, Detective."

Both men looked quickly at each other and then back at me, waiting.

"Nathaniel Davies' mother doesn't even know I exist. There is no link between the two of us except the fact that last week I told you"—I said pointing an accusing finger at Dutch—"some information that came to me intuitively and must have led you to the body of Nathaniel. And the reason you're here is that you can't figure out any other logical explanation about how I knew specific details about the murder other than that I must somehow be involved."

Neither man blinked. They were both poker-faced. "Well, let me tell you something: The truth is stranger than fiction, boys. I'm a clairvoyant intuitive. Knowing things that aren't common knowledge is how I make my living. I don't know Nathaniel's mother, and I never met Nathaniel. You can look into my past, present and future but you'll never find a link. And if you think you're game enough to haul me into court and try and implicate me, you're going to be up against my attorney, who can march in *thousands* of clients to swear I'm the real deal. You're looking for the connection between Nathaniel's mother and the guy who apparently walked off with him, huh? That's really what this is all about, isn't it?"

Again, neither man moved, flinched or blinked. I took that as a "yes" and continued. "I'll tell you the same thing I told you last time, Dutch. You need to look at her family, like to a brother, or someone she thinks of like a brother. There is also a connection to Florida here, and a connection to a blond-haired cop—I think he's close to this guy who's related to Nathaniel's mother. Also there's some sort of a connection to a butcher, or a man who carves up meat, like at the grocery store. That's where you need to spend your energy, gentlemen. Look for the butcher shop and you'll find your guy. But that's all the time we have, folks, so if you'll please excuse me." I stood to indicate that playtime was over.

"We have a few more questions, Abigail," Dutch said sternly.

My head whipped in his direction, and I pinned him to his seat with a look that spoke business, my bad temper getting the best of me. The fact that he continued to refer to me as "Abigail" wasn't lost on me. He was trying to assert his authority by making me feel like a little girl who'd been caught doing something she should be grounded for. I clenched my fists, recalling every night in the past week that I'd sat and waited for the phone to ring, every fantasy that had drifted through my head about what our kids would look like and every insecure thought that had pummeled my ego about why he hadn't called, and I lost my composure. "With all due respect, *Detective*, get the hell out of my house! Go prey on someone else, because I'm no longer interested in *Mr. Charm*. If you come back here again you'd better have a warrant and be prepared to go toe to toe with my attorney because I swear to you I'll be as big a pain in your ass as you've been in mine!" I said this with my hands on my hips and daggers coming out of my eyes. The injustice of this entire interrogation was making my blood boil. Dutch sat in that restaurant the week before looking all gooey-eyed and allowing me to believe he was interested when all he'd really wanted was to pin a murder on me. I had one word for him, and it started with an "ass" and ended in "hole."

For a moment he just looked at me and we had ourselves a little staring contest. Finally, Johnson broke the silence as he cleared his throat and stood up. A moment later Dutch followed. Both men were about to walk out the front door when Johnson turned back, pulled out a card from his back pocket and handed it to me. "Thank you for your time, Miss Cooper. If you think of anything else you'd like to tell us . . ."

I looked at the card and then back at him, my intuition in hyperdrive. "You need to take care of that plumbing problem in your upstairs bathroom pronto. It's your septic tank; it needs to be repaired. Also you've been thinking about buying a new car, but hold off another month. If you wait thirty days you'll get the car you've been dreaming about. And you need to take your dog to the vet. She has a stomach thing going on that she needs medical attention for. The vet can help her out. Oh, and your money worries are going away by early fall. You just need to budget a little better until then. I'd also recommend that you sit your son down and have a heart-to-heart with him about school. He's flunking geography and math. He's really just looking for some attention from you, so the more time you can spare him, the better his grades will be."

I didn't mean to blurt all that out. Sometimes stuff just comes to me and I have to say it.

Milo stared at me with his mouth open and his eyes wide. "How did you . . . ," he began.

I took the card smiling wickedly at both men. "Have a lovely day," I sang and waved good-bye.

Both men turned as one and walked slowly away from the house. I shut the front door and immediately went to the telephone, punching in my sister's number.

"Hello?" I heard Cat say.

"You are not going to believe who just waltzed in through my front door and accused me of murder!" I said as tears formed in my eyes and began dribbling down my cheeks. And then the adrenaline and bravado of the morning gave way to a full-scale meltdown.

An hour later Cat had calmed me down enough that I could listen to reason. She was so damn levelheaded sometimes. Her point was that I had nothing to worry about. I had answered the detectives' questions, I had nothing at all to do with Nathaniel's murder and I had a pretty strong alibi since I had had a long list of clients walk in and out of my office during the time of Nathaniel's disappearance. Cat kept saying, "Abby, you are who you say you are. And I know you're afraid of that whole Monica Madden thing, but there's no reason to worry. You're a professional psychic, and you have about a million people who can testify on your behalf. The police should be working *with* you, not against you. They'll come to the same conclusion. Just give it time."

Sometimes you just had to love my sister. After we'd finished talking, I looked around the house and decided to make it a productive day. I made a couple of eggs for myself and Eggy, then went downstairs and started a load of laundry.

My washer and dryer had been a housewarming gift from my sister and brother-in-law. Cat had originally been intent on furnishing the whole house, but I'd put my foot down and made her promise not to buy one stick of furniture. She'd gotten even with the washer and dryer—after all, technically they fell in the category of "appliances." My sister was great at getting around technicalities.

After doing some other chores around the house

and finishing up the laundry, I decided to take care of some business, so I locked up the house and headed over to the office. On the way I stopped in at the Pic-A-Deli to get my usual tuna sandwich.

"Abby!" Mike said jovially. "I didn't expect to see you here on a Monday. The usual today?"

"Afternoon Mike. The usual would be fine but go easy on the hot peppers today."

"You got clients today?" he asked, reaching for the bread as he began to prepare my sandwich.

"Naw, I'm just trying to keep on top of the paperwork and I thought I'd get it done while I had some quiet time. Besides, I'm in a crunch and I need some lunch," I continued, trying hard to stifle a chuckle.

"You heard our new radio ad?"

"On the way over. Catchy," I said with a twinkle in my eye. The ad consisted of a slightly out-of-tune soprano singing, "If you want some lunch and you're in a crunch, come on down to Pic-A-Deli."

Mike nodded proudly and said, "Well, I'm really glad to see you. I wanted to thank you for letting me know about my car the other day. The mechanic said I had a leak in my oil tank and if I'd tried to drive much farther, my engine would've been toast."

"Cool, Mike. I'm glad I could help."

"Say, Abby, what do you charge, if you don't mind my asking?"

"An even hundred, buddy."

"Do you think I could schedule an appointment with you?"

"Sure. I'm going to the office right now. Why don't you give me a call in about ten minutes and I'll see what I've got available."

"Thanks," he said as he handed me my sandwich. "I'll do that."

I headed to the office and two minutes after I settled into my chair, Mike called. I scanned my appointment book, looking for a spot. "Gee, Mike, looks like I'm pretty well booked until early November, but let me see if I can't find a cancellation."

Whenever I get a cancellation I usually don't fill it. In my mind I see it as the Universe's way of saying that I should have a little down time, but for Mike I'd make an exception. I came across an opening at the end of August, first thing in the morning, a time I'm sure would have been spent sleeping in a little.

"I've got something for August thirtieth, at nine a.m. Does that work for you?"

"I may have to cut it close, but I'll make it work, Abby. Thanks a lot."

I made the notation and gave Mike directions, then returned phone calls and scheduled some new appointments.

An hour later I was finished and headed to the bank, where I deposited the week's earnings and checked the balance. No matter how hard I tried, my bank balance always seemed to hover around the same amount. Attempting to squirrel away any savings always seemed at odds with my house, the money pit. I stopped by the grocery store on the way home. I was in the mood for chocolate to console my bruised ego, so I swung by the candy aisle and grabbed a bag of M&M's with peanuts. I was halfway down the aisle when it occurred to me that I hadn't had M&M's with almonds in a long time either. Backing up, I selected a package of those and then just so I'd have a good variety in my candy jar, I snatched a bag of the plain ones too. As I went through the bakery section, I noticed how many different varieties of chocolate brownies there were and thought I didn't want to go through life not having known what Caramel Double

Fudge Delight was all about, so I threw a box of those into my cart for good measure.

I rounded out the grocery shopping with two kinds of chocolate chip cookie dough, a quart of Ben & Jerry's and enough chocolate covered pretzels to feed an army. About then I decided to head for the checkout line before I dove into a diabetic coma.

When I got home, Mary Lou Galbraith was out in my front yard tending to some newly potted plants.

Mary Lou was my neighbor and a horticultural major at Wayne State University who had an amazing talent for gardening. I'd met her when I first moved into the neighborhood, and she and I had become friendly. She lived in a duplex that she shared with another woman two doors over. One afternoon, after surveying my pitiful and very neglected front yard, Mary Lou had offered some gardening advice. I'd laughed and told her about my brown thumb. She in turn offered, at a very reasonable price, her horticultural skills, and I quickly accepted.

Mary Lou worked for a landscaper by day, and if there were any leftovers from the day's planting, the landscape company threw them away. She often rescued the discarded plants and brought them home, searching for any available space where she could give them a place to thrive. My house had conveniently provided a blank canvas to her creative horticultural genius.

"Hey there," I said, waving as I passed her in the car on the way to the garage.

"Hey, Abby, what do you think?" she asked, standing up and opening her arms wide to my newly acquired mums.

"Gorgeous, sugar. I'll be right there to take a look." I pulled into the garage, extracted the grocery bags and lugged them to my walkway, where Mary Lou was packing up her tools. She reminded me a little of myself when I was her age. She was about my height, with shoulder-length brown hair and a trim athletic body. She had an on-again off-again relationship with a young man I'd met once and instantly disliked named Chad. He tended to refer to himself in third person a lot, and I never really understood what Mary Lou saw in him.

"Wow! You've been busy," I said as I rounded the corner to admire her handiwork.

"Yeah. We were working on this office building today and we ran out of room. We had enough left over in every color, and I thought your walkway looked a little plain."

I thought my walkway looked like everything else not yet updated about the house—shabby. But at least now with the mums lining the cracked cement from sidewalk to front stoop it had a bit of shabby chic. "Yeah, I really like it. Great job, Mary Lou. What do I owe you?"

"How about you let me schedule an appointment with you and we'll call it even?" Mary Lou asked, lowering her eyes.

This was unexpected. Although Mary Lou knew I was a psychic and found stories of my readings rather entertaining, she had never shown a personal interest. Some people don't want to know what's around the corner, and others are just fearful of hearing something they won't be able to handle. I looked at her more closely, my intuitive phone humming in the distance, and my eyes strayed to her upper arm. There was a deep bruise that looked like it had been made when someone grabbed her a little too hard.

"Chad problems?" I asked, careful to keep the malice out of my voice. I hated men who abused women. I found them cowardly and the lowest form of scum.

"No, no, nothing like that . . ." Her voice trailed off as *Liar, liar, pants on fire* rang in my head. "He just, you know . . . we haven't really been getting along lately, and I'm thinking of telling him I want to break up with him."

"Mary Lou," I said in my softest voice, "you don't need a reading to find out that you are definitely worth so much more than someone like Chad."

The moment I said this I regretted it. Mary Lou's defenses shot up, and she squared her shoulders. "No, really, he's a great boyfriend. He buys me stuff and he gives me money and he takes me places. Really, he's got a good heart, he just gets around his friends and he sort of turns into another person. Really, he's a good guy."

Backing off, I said, "Okay, okay, you're probably right. How about you call me tomorrow at the office and I'll check my appointment book and get you in as soon as possible, all right?"

Without looking at me she said, "Yeah, okay," and I knew she had changed her mind. She gathered up her tools and buckets and pinkie-waved a good-bye to me. As I watched her amble across my lawn and head for her house, I fought the urge to run after her and tell her what a wonderful, intelligent, beautiful woman she was. But women like Mary Lou didn't listen to women like me. They only seemed to listen to men like Chad.

I went to bed that night feeling emotionally exhausted. I was thinking about my encounter with the two detectives from that morning and had to laugh at myself for not picking up that Dutch was a cop. I remembered telling him on our date that he had a badge all over his energy, but I'd just assumed it meant he might encounter a traffic ticket or something. Sometimes the obvious just isn't obvious to me.

I curled myself around Eggy, my eyelids feeling heavy, and thought that at least I didn't have to worry about misreading him anymore; chances were, once he figured out I had nothing to do with Nathaniel Davies we'd never see each other again. But as I drifted off to sleep my left side gave that conclusion a thick and heavy "no."

Chapter Four

Three days later I came home to a surprise from Dave. He stood in my foyer as I entered the house, beaming with pride. "You ready to cook in your own kitchen?" he asked.

"What? You've finished? Already?" I asked, setting down my purse and following him with anticipation to the kitchen.

"Ta-da!" he said, spreading his arms wide.

I stood in the doorway and surveyed the scene. It was beautiful. My new wood cabinets had been completely installed, the countertop was in place and the sink with its new nickel-plated faucets sparkled at me, begging to be used. "This is unbelievable, Dave! When I left this morning you weren't even close to being done. What happened?"

"Well, we ran out of decaf this morning, so my old lady put regular in my thermos. I guess I just had a caffeine high all afternoon."

I laughed and gave him an impromptu hug. "You rock! Thank you so much, Dave. I love it!" It was the first time I'd really smiled in what felt like aeons.

I paid Dave for his time and shooed him out of the house, eager to cook in a real kitchen again. Quickly I doled out some food for Eggy, then got busy unloading the boxes under my table that held my kitchen appliances, dishes, and other assorted kitchen items. To keep myself company, I turned on the TV.

As I was putting away the last of my flatware a breaking news story came on during the commercial break of the sitcom I'd been watching. I turned to listen and watched as the anchorwoman gave the camera over to a reporter standing outside the Oakland County prosecutor's office.

The reporter began to speak in quick stop/start sentences, her fluctuations no doubt lending serious journalism to the story. "Yes, Linda. I'm here outside the Oakland County prosecutor's office where we have just learned that an arrest has been made in the Nathaniel Davies murder investigation. You recall that Nathaniel Davies, a four-year-old from Pontiac, was allegedly abducted two weeks ago from the Oakland Mall in Troy. We just learned that his body was recently discovered by police in an abandoned house on Lillian Street in downtown Pontiac. Officials kept the recovery of Nathaniel's body quiet so that their investigation wouldn't be compromised.

"I'm told that investigators from two states and all over metro Detroit helped crack this case. Royal Oak investigators apparently received an anonymous tip that led the police not only to Nathaniel's body but also to an uncle, Chester Davies. Davies had fled the state shortly after Nathaniel was abducted, and was living with extended family in Florida.

"We're told that detectives in Florida worked with

Michigan police to apprehend Davies, who was working at his new job in a grocery store's meat department in Tampa. At this very moment he is being extradited back to Michigan to face murder charges.

"We have also discovered that Mr. Davies at one point worked as a security guard at Oakland Mall and would have had knowledge of the placement of those security cameras. Mr. Davies has a son who is very close to Nathaniel in age and size, and on the day of the abduction Davies had custody of his son. Authorities suspect that Nathaniel was murdered prior to the staged abduction, and that it is actually Chester and his son on video at the Oakland Mall. We have been told that both Chester Davies and Nathaniel's mother, Tameka Davies, will be charged with first-degree murder. We will of course update you throughout the hour as this story develops; however, at this time it does look as if the entire taped abduction was staged and that Nathaniel's mother was in on the plan from the start. Back to you, Linda."

I watched the broadcast with mixed emotions. I was glad that Nathaniel's killers had been brought to justice, but troubled by the brutality of the crime. What had a four-year-old done to deserve such a tragic consequence? I was also rather surprised at the accuracy of my information and couldn't help but smirk a little at the mention of the "anonymous tip" that led police to find Nathaniel and those responsible. I wondered what the press would do if they knew that the tip had come from a psychic. "Probably have a field day," I said aloud to no one in particular. Shrugging my shoulders, I got back to putting things away.

Later that night I was paying bills at the kitchen table when a soft knock on my front door sent Eggy into gales of barking. Wondering who was dropping by my house at nine o'clock at night, I went to the door and peered through the peephole, but I saw only black. I flipped on the porch light and looked again. Still black. Weird.

Curious, I opened the door a crack and saw Dutch, standing on my front step and holding a finger over the peephole.

"Don't you know better than to open the door to someone you can't clearly see?" he asked.

"Don't you know better than to find ways to annoy people?" I responded, opening the door slightly wider. I crossed my arms and raised an eyebrow.

"Got a minute?" he asked, warming up his smile.

"Got a warrant?" I replied, warming up my attitude.

"It's not that kind of a social visit."

The eyebrow held firm and my foot started to tap.

"I'm not here officially."

Eye roll, more foot tapping.

"I just want to talk."

I started to shut the door.

"Please, Abby?" he said, looking at me with puppy-dog eyes.

Damn. Why'd he have to use the eyes? "Fine. Whatever. It's your funeral," I said and walked away from the door. I heard it shut behind me and continued walking into the kitchen. I heard Dutch cooing to Eggy and turned to watch as he lifted him into the air and allowed Eggy to slobber him full on the lips. I told myself that this, of course, meant nothing. After all he'd let me do the very same thing.

Just then the phone rang and I thought about ignoring it but Dutch looked at it, cocked his head and looked at his watch as if to say, "Who could be calling at this hour?" I knew who it was and was faced with the annoying dilemma of not answering my sister's call and having her call every three minutes for the next hour or until she reached me, or answering it and letting Dutch know it wasn't some man who found me utterly irresistible. I gave Dutch a dirty look, snatched up the phone and walked toward the study where I might have some privacy.

"Hey! Where were you? What took you so long to pick up?" Cat asked.

"I was upstairs and the phone was downstairs. It took me a minute to find it. But I'm sort of in the middle of something here and I can't talk long."

"Oh? Like what? Or should I say like whom?" My sister had radar that at times rivaled my own.

"It's nothing. I was in the middle of uh . . . meditating." That was the best I could come up with? I rolled my eyes and hoped she'd go for it.

"Meditating? I thought you only did that at the office. Abby, talk to me. What's going on?"

Ugh. This was going to be tougher than I'd thought. "No, no, really it's nothing big, I just thought I might want to start taking up the practice. I thought it might help me relax. You know, it's been such a tough few weeks and all."

"Ohhhh, honey you poor thing," she said, making little sympathetic mewing sounds. I thought if she didn't quit soon I'd throw up. "Did you want to talk about it?"

"Not really. Cat, listen, can I call you tomorrow? I'm sorry but I just really don't feel like talking tonight"

"Ah, I see," she said. Fabulous. Now I had offended her. I held back a frustrated sigh. "Well, Miss Dietrich, if you want to be *alone*, then I won't keep you. I just thought I'd check up on you, see how you were doing." I checked my watch. She had covered concern,

offense and guilt in just over a minute—had to be a
new record.

"Yes, Cat, and I love you for that. Really. It's nothing personal, I just wanted to center and focus my
energy, that's all."

"Oh all right," she sighed. "I love you and call me
tomorrow, okay?"

'First thing in the morning, I promise. Love you
too."

We hung up and I shrugged my shoulders. Odds
were that I'd hear about this later, but maybe I'd get
lucky and she'd forget about it. Then again, who was
I kidding? My sister had a memory that would put a
herd of elephants to shame.

I put the phone on the desk in the study and padded
back out to the living room. No Dutch. I looked at
the front door to see if maybe he'd gone and saw that
the bolt had been thrown from the inside. I hadn't
locked it, so that meant that Dutch must have and he
must be around here somewhere. Okay, so he was somewhere in my house. I felt a sudden wave of panic that
maybe he'd decided to head upstairs and search through
my panty drawer discovering the horrible pair of whi-
ties I reserved for that time of the month. I was about
to head upstairs when I heard a faint *clink* coming
from the back porch. I went through the kitchen and
out to the sliding glass door and sure enough, there
he was, comfortably seated at my card table spooning
Ben and Jerry's Jubilee ice cream into his mouth.

"What do you think you're doing?" I asked, hands
on my hips and the eyebrow back on duty.

"You didn't have any beer, so I thought this would
be the next best thing. I got you some too, so take
a seat."

Flustered, and not knowing what to say, I sat down in the chair next to him and saw that in fact he had scooped some ice cream out for me—although his portion looked considerably larger. Without touching the ice cream I turned to face him and asked, "What do you want, Detective?"

"First I'd like you to eat your ice cream, Abby, and then I'd like to chitchat for a little bit. How's that for a plan?" He said this with his eyes on his bowl and a small smirk on his face.

I rolled my eyes and took up the spoon, not really knowing what else to do. I swirled it over the two scoops in my bowl, but didn't eat any just yet. What can I say? I'm a rebel. "I saw that you arrested Tameka and Chester Davies today," I said, making small talk.

Dutch smiled but continued to look either at his ice cream or at my backyard. Dusk was falling, bathing my backyard in soft purple and orange hues. "Yeah. We wouldn't have nailed him if you hadn't pointed us in the right direction. Oh, and the cop who tracked him down in Tampa? He had blond hair."

"Told you so."

"Yes. Yes, you did, Abby, and that's what's so . . ." His voice trailed off as he searched for a word.

"Strange? Bizarre? Freakish?" I supplied, suddenly struggling to keep the hurt from my voice.

"Unusual," Dutch said, smiling some more. "I've never believed in fortune-tellers, and truth be told, I'd pretty much made up my mind that you were all a bunch of con artists relieving the gullible of their money."

I sighed, and a sharp little pain stuck me right in the heart. It always hurt to be stereotyped. "Uh-huh," I said dully.

"And then on our date you blew me away. I

thought I'd been set up by one of the guys in the department, that maybe someone had found out I posted my profile and they'd conned you into this crazy story about being a psychic and knowing all this personal stuff about me."

"Mmmm," I said, now eating my ice cream.

"And then you started talking about Nathaniel, which was a case that had just come into the department that afternoon. It wasn't our jurisdiction, of course, but all police departments in Oakland County had been put on alert due to the high visibility of the case. Nathaniel was one cute kid, and a lot of people were out looking for him. So when you started talking about how Nathaniel was dead and the mother was to blame, I thought you were involved somehow. Maybe you'd been able to find out who I was and dug up some stuff on me and snookered me into a date because you wanted to relieve your conscience."

"Well, of course!" I said, my voice dripping with sarcasm. "That makes total sense. I posted my profile on an obscure Web site knowing full well that you would choose me out of the thousands of postings. Then when *you* actually contacted *me*, I went around to all your friends and family asking silly questions about your personal life—which somehow never got back to you—and in the middle of dinner, I decided I couldn't take the guilt anymore so I unloaded my conscience about Nathaniel. Yes, Dutch it was all part of my *giant master plan*!" I was glaring hard at him, my chest heaving because I'd said all that without taking a breath.

"Yeah, well, it made sense at the time," Dutch said, looking sheepishly into his bowl.

"Agh! Men!" I said and went back to eating my ice cream.

"What I needed, Abby, was a little time to think it

through and maybe run a background check and see if there wasn't something else there. I filled Milo in on everything you'd said, and we took it to our captain, who got permission from the Troy police to run with it. While I chased down leads on Nathaniel, Milo kept an eye on you. We started with Tameka's family, and it turned out she had a brother who just so happened to have once worked security at the mall. Oakland Mall hasn't updated its video equipment in about ten years, so the quality of the video was pretty crummy. Chester knew that. Then we discovered that Chester had picked his four-year-old son up on the afternoon of the abduction, and Chester's son looks a lot like Nathaniel. When we analyzed the video a couple of times we noticed that the little boy on the tape went over to the man in the footage a little too quickly. We also looked closely at Tameka, and the more we watched her on video, the more convinced we were that she's one hell of a bad actress.

"We figured if Tameka had killed her son she probably hadn't stashed his body too far away from her home in Pontiac. On your advice we started looking at abandoned houses. You had mentioned lilies, and one of the worst streets for abandoned homes in Pontiac is Lillian Street. It didn't take long to find Nathaniel; it's summer and the smell pointed the way."

I dropped my spoon into my bowl, leaving my ice cream only half eaten. I shoved it to the center of the table and grimaced. Dutch eyed my leftovers and asked, "If you're not going to eat that, would you mind if I polish it off for you?"

"Help yourself," I said flatly.

Grabbing my dish, Dutch continued. "So the coroner approximated Nathaniel's death to have occurred at least a couple of days before the alleged abduction.

Cause of death was severe brain hemorrhaging, most likely from violent shaking. Tameka has a long history of owning a bad temper. We think she accidentally killed Nathaniel, then called her brother to help her hide the fact. They came up with this whole abduction scheme to divert attention from them and also to solicit sympathy money. They had a hot line for tips and donations set up almost immediately."

My stomach was turning over. I didn't want to hear any more. I put my hand up and said, "Stop," my voice barely more than a whisper.

Dutch looked at me and set the ice cream aside. "Oh, hey, I'm sorry," he said. "I didn't mean to upset you. I guess I'm just used to this kind of stuff. It doesn't even phase me anymore." As he said this he took my hand and squeezed it, and when he touched me I felt a different kind of flutter in my stomach.

"Well, I'm not used to it. I'm really glad I could help you out and all, but stuff like this is too heartbreaking, you know? How do you guys do it? How do you see the worst of people and still find the energy to get out of bed every morning?"

Dutch was quiet for a long moment before he answered. "There are days, Abby, when it's really tough. I've seen things that I wish I'd never seen, but it's the choice I made when I joined the force and I made that choice because I thought I could make a difference. That's all, plain and simple—I just wanted to make a difference. Still do."

I looked up into his magical blue eyes and saw a side of him that was sweet, vulnerable and so totally accessible that I impulsively leaned forward and kissed him. I took him by surprise with that, but he went with it and I swooned a little as our kiss deepened. Just then a loud chirping noise sounded. Pulling abruptly away, Dutch reached to his belt and un-hooked his cell phone. Pressing a button, he raised the phone to his ear and barked, "Rivers."

He listened for only a moment before saying, "On Maplelawn. Got it. I'll be right there."

Turning to me he smiled and said, "Duty calls."

"I understand," I said shyly.

Dutch grabbed me by the chin and kissed me long and deep again, and I thought I was going to melt into one giant puddle right there on the porch.

Breaking off the kiss, he said, "Listen, I'm sorry about the other day. That's really what I came here to tell you. We weren't sure where you were getting your information, and to be honest, we're still not. I mean, it's pretty hard to believe this stuff is for real . . ." His voice trailed off, and in an instant, I suddenly felt embarrassed for kissing him and assuming he had come over because he believed in me.

"Well," I said tartly, "you're right, Dutch, you really do have to go. Oh, and thanks *so* much for the apology. It was swell." I said this with a sneer, and Dutch looked at me, confused.

"Did I miss something?" he asked.

"You've missed a lot of things. But mostly I think you've missed several opportunities to leave. Let me assist you to the door so that you won't miss this next one." With that I began to push him out of the porch, through the kitchen and toward the front door. Of course, Dutch allowed himself to be pushed. I had a feeling given how much muscle my hands were con-necting with, that if Dutch didn't want to go some-where all he had to do was plant himself and I certainly wouldn't be able to make him budge. As we neared the door, I rounded him and stepped quickly to the lock, unfastening the bolt and throwing the door open. I stood in the doorway and made a gesture with my hand that said, "Right this way." Dutch walked out onto my front step and turned to look at me, opening his mouth to say something, but he ended up saying it to the door because I slammed it in his face. Just in case he was slow on the uptake, I clicked the bolt into place and turned out the front light. I waited twenty seconds, then peeked through the peephole. I could just make out his departing figure as he headed for his car. Oddly, as I watched him drive away, I felt deflated.

I walked back to the porch, collected the ice cream bowls from the card table and stared down at Eggy-the-traitor. He wagged his tail at me and gave me a look back that said, "Who, me?" when the phone rang. Cat, I thought. Sighing, I set the bowls in the sink, then went to the study to retrieve the cordless. Punching the TALK button, I said, "Cat, I'm really tired tonight. Can we please do this tomorrow?"

A silky deep chuckle wafted through the line. "Who's Cat?" Dutch asked, obviously calling from his cell phone.

"My sister. What do you want?"

"I just want to say one last thing. I wanted to tell you that I have a cat of my own, only he's the furry four-legged kind. His name is Virgil and he came with the house I bought eight years ago. Anyway, the day before yesterday I came home and discovered that Virgil had decided to make my entire house his litter box. He peed on my floor, he peed on my rugs, he even peed on my bedspread. Normally this would have made Virgil prime pound material, but then it hit me that you told me two weeks ago this was going to happen. I checked around the neighborhood, and sure enough one of my neighbor's kids just moved back home from college and brought her tomcat with her."

There was a long moment of silence while I struggled to recall the details of Dutch's reading and come to an understanding about why he was now sharing all this with me. Finally I said, "Okaaaaaay . . . ?"

"See, this is why I'm calling, Abby, why I came over tonight. I wanted to apologize for suspecting you were involved in Nathaniel's murder but I also wanted to clear the air and let you know that this psychic stuff is really throwing me for a loop. I'm not sure what to do with it. The problem is, I'm attracted to you."

He had my full attention.

"But I think it would be better for both of us if we just gave ourselves some time to get used to the idea of what we each do for a living, and maybe pick this up at a later date."

"I'm sorry?" I asked, at first not following what he meant by that and then feeling a pang as the realization that I was being brushed off hit home.

"Look, I have a feeling that my being a cop didn't exactly thrill you. After all, you were the one who told me over dinner that you didn't like cops."

I chewed my lip and pondered that for a while. He was right. My view of cops was perhaps just as stereotyped as Dutch's view of psychics.

"Gee, Abby, don't rush to contradict me," Dutch said with a chuckle.

"It's not that simple, Dutch," I said, trying to explain.

"Then let's keep it simple and step back for now," he answered. "Listen, I'm at the scene—gotta go," and with that there was an abrupt click and I was left listening to dead air.

I set the phone back on the charger and sighed heavily. In my next lifetime I wanted to come back as a guy. They seemed to always get the upper hand.

*   *   *

The next morning as I was getting ready for work my phone rang again. Cat, I thought. I forced myself to answer it using my Top-o-the-morning! voice. "Good morning, Sugar, how are you?"

There was a throaty chuckle on the other end, and a baritone voice that was definitely not Cat's answered, "Very well, Muffin. How are you?"

"Don't the local police have anything better to do other than harassing the city's tax-paying citizens?" I demanded. I was still angry that he'd hung up on me the night before.

"Sorry about that," he said, clearly understanding the source of my irritation. "Listen, we need to talk. Soon. It's important."

"What about?" I asked, curious at the instant change in his voice from playful to dead serious.

"Not over the phone. When are you free?"

"Uh," I said, as I rubbed my forehead and mentally reviewed the clients I had for the day. "My last client leaves a little before four. Will that work?"

"I'll meet you at your office at four sharp."

"Okay, I guess," I said, but I suddenly realized Dutch had already hung up. The guy was definitely abrupt. Running back upstairs, I rethought my ponytail and wound my hair into a slightly more elegant twist. I told myself I wasn't doing it because I was going to see Dutch later . . . *Liar, liar* danced in my head.

At four o'clock I was seeing my last client out of my reading room when we both came up short. Dutch was sitting in my waiting room reading a magazine when we came out of the door, and as he stood up I heard my client's breath catch. He was wearing a light tweed jacket, a white dress shirt and navy blue cotton Dockers. *Yeah*, I thought, *he is hot*.

"Hello," my client, Judith, said in a wispy voice, her eyes doing the Wile E. Coyote *Barroooga!*

"Hello," Dutch answered, giving her a dazzling toothy grin and the full force of his midnight blues. I thought she was going to swoon.

"Okay-thank-you-Judith-really-it-was-great-seeing-you-now-you-take-care-and-we'll-see-you-later-okay?—Buh-Bye-now!" I said, as I practically shoved her out the door and closed it quickly behind her. Sometimes, I have no tact.

"So," I said, spinning around. "What's this all about?"

"Is there someplace we can sit?"

Uh-oh. Sounded serious. "Sure. Come on in," I said, waving him into my reading room.

We sat facing each other, and Dutch reached into his jacket pocket, extracted a photograph and handed it to me. I looked at it closely. Two young women, both with shoulder-length chestnut hair and beautiful brown eyes, beamed back at me. I sighed, my eyes pinching a little in sadness. "These women are both dead," I said and handed the picture back to Dutch.

I could tell by his startled expression that he hadn't expected that, so I said by way of explanation, "It's a talent."

"Weird talent to have, Abby," he said, looking at me with appraising eyes.

I smiled uncomfortably and shifted in my chair. Directing attention back to the photo, I asked, "Who are they anyway?"

"You don't recognize one of them?" he asked, the photo still held loosely in his hand.

I took the photo back and looked more closely. One of the women looked vaguely familiar, but I couldn't place her. She could have been a client, but I didn't want to suggest this after the Nathaniel Davies fiasco. I decided to play it non-committal. "I'm not sure . . ."

Dutch was watching my expression closely. I had to

concentrate on not giving in to the temptation to squirm. Finally he said, "They are Allison and Alyssa Pierce."

Okay, so he wasn't going to give me anything to go on. Suddenly something popped into my head. "Allison Pierce," I said softly and turned my memory banks up to high. "Oh! Now I remember. I read Allison a couple of weeks ago. In fact, she called me a few days ago because she wanted to come in for another reading."

"She called you last week?"

"Yeah," I said, thinking back. "It was Sunday afternoon. I remember because I went out to dinner with my best friend that night. I don't think I was very nice to Allison when she called." *Guilt, guilt, guilt . . .*

"Do you remember what you talked about with her?"

"She wanted to schedule another reading with me. She said she had unanswered questions and wanted to come in for another session."

"And what did you say?" Dutch asked.

I was growing more and more uncomfortable. "I have this hard-and-fast rule, that. I won't read someone more than twice a year because people can base their whole lives on what a psychic tells them and it's just not a good idea, you know?"

Dutch said nothing, waiting out my confession. Nervously I continued. "So I told her I couldn't fit her in this early but that I could schedule her for January if she wanted to come back then."

"Did she tell you what her questions were?" Dutch asked.

"No . . . I guess I didn't ask. The truth is I feel terrible that I was so abrupt with her. I guess I was in a pissy mood and wasn't feeling very open. She just caught me at a bad time."

"I see."

"How did she die?" I asked, wanting to move on with the conversation.

"She was murdered, Abby."

"Oh my God!"

"That was the 911 page I got while I was at your house last night. A neighbor claims that she heard screaming coming from Allison's house, but she waited an hour to call the police."

"What? Why did she wait so long?" I asked, incredulous.

"No one wants to get involved anymore. Anyway, when we got there we found Allison, beaten to a bloody pulp, with her throat slashed. The house looked like a tornado'd hit it. Early this morning the coroner found this hidden in her underwear," Dutch said, as he reached into his pocket and pulled out a clear plastic bag. Inside it was a cassette tape that was all too familiar to me—it was identical to the ones I gave to my clients after each session. A few years ago I'd gotten savvy and had a printing company emblazon both the tapes and the cassette cases with my professional information. My name and my business address were typed neatly across the top of the cassette, including a blank space for the date of the reading.

"Whoa," I said, my mind reeling.

Dutch looked at my credenza, which held dozens of similar blank copies, all neatly stacked in their plastic cassette cases. "Abby, I have to ask you if this tape also came with a cassette case."

I nodded and explained, "Yes, of course. I always put the cassette back in its case and give it to the client. Why?"

"We found only the tape, Abby. The case is missing."

I felt a rush of adrenaline spike through my bloodstream. "What are you saying, Dutch? This makes no sense. Why would someone take the case and not the cassette? Do you think Allison's killer has some sort of connection to me?"

"We don't know. It's just very strange that an ex-client of yours turns up with her throat slashed and hidden in her underwear is a cassette tape of a reading she had with you. Her house gets ransacked and we can't find the cassette case. The brutality of the crime suggests that this wasn't a robbery gone bad; it tells us that the killer knew Allison and hated her. It also suggests he was looking for something. From listening to the tape we know that you warned her about staying away from a dark-haired man. Now I was with you last night, and I know that you couldn't have committed the crime, but what is it about you that connects Allison to her killer? What I'm saying is, why would Allison take the precaution of hiding the tape of her reading in her underwear?"

I looked at Dutch closely; if his eyes weren't accusing then they were damn close. I was still reeling from the shock that Allison was dead, and I didn't really know how to respond. "What do you want from me, Dutch?" I asked wearily.

"You say you're good at knowing things that most people don't. What can you tell me about who killed Allison?"

I blinked several times at him. What did he think I knew? Did he think I had something to do with her murder? I shook my head and said, "I still don't know what you're asking me. I barely knew this woman. I don't even remember her reading. Really, I wish I could but so many of my readings blend together that I can't recall what I said to her."

Dutch refused to offer me an out. He simply continued to stare at me, and the uncomfortable silence stretched out between us.

Finally he tucked the Baggie with the tape back into his jacket pocket and reached around to another pocket, extracting another cassette tape. This he handed to me and said, "Okay, Abby. Here's a dubbed copy of the reading you gave Allison. I hope you'll listen to it and call me if you can think of anything that jogs your memory. Oh, and because we're not sure if her killer has the cassette case or not, I want you to be very careful around here. Always lock your door, never open your front door without knowing who's on the other side and call me if anything even remotely strange happens." With that he stood up, handed me his card and strode out.

I locked the door behind him and walked back to my inner office. There I paced the floor for a while, tapping my finger against my lips in a sort of daze. I couldn't shake my feelings of guilt. What had Allison wanted to ask me? What was it I could have answered for her? Would I have seen this coming? Would she have listened to me?

My attention fell to my desktop and the tape Dutch had left with me resting on the corner. I had two choices: I could let the police figure out who murdered Allison Pierce and keep my nose out of it, thus avoiding any further entanglement and possible finger-pointing in my direction. Or I could quietly resign myself to assisting in whatever way my instincts allowed. After all, I had an invaluable, highly refined tool at my disposal: my intuition. Hadn't it been instrumental in leading the police directly to little Nathaniel's murderer?

I had to admit that assisting with that investigation had given my ego a definite lift. It felt damn good to use my gift in a way that was . . . well, important and meaningful. It certainly beat telling some housewife that she needed to be more careful when she was sneaking out of the house to cheat on her husband.

I picked up the cassette tape and turned it over a few times. I came clean with myself: I needed this. I needed to help solve this case to absolve my feelings of guilt over not being there for Allison when she'd called, and also to send a message to skeptics like Dutch that I wasn't some smoke-and-mirrors performer, but a legitimate, albeit quirky, professional. I paced my argument back and forth in front of my desk, and after wearing a tread in the carpet and cementing my decision to help in any way I could, I headed home.

Dave had already gone by the time I got there, but I could see that he had been busy ripping up the cracked and rotted wood floor of my dining room. Stepping carefully around the plywood, I moved into the kitchen and made Eggy some dinner. While he was happily munching, I threw a quick salad together and took it out to the porch, then came back in and grabbed the old battery-operated cassette recorder I kept in the study. I popped in the tape of Allison's reading and began listening as I ate my dinner.

As my voice emanated from the speaker of the recorder, I was surprised by how flat I sounded. In my head, my voice always sounded clearer, with more range, than it did on a recording. But I pushed those thoughts aside so I could concentrate. I waded through the reading several times, turning up my intuition.

During my session with Allison I mentioned early on something about a loss, a woman who had been very close to her. I remembered that in the photo Dutch had shown me, another woman who had very similar facial features was pictured with Allison. I wondered if she'd been a sister. Either way, I knew she was also dead, her flat plastic-like pose in the photo confirming it for me. Dutch hadn't mentioned two women being murdered, so most likely this other woman had died previously.

I wondered if she also had died violently. My right side lifted in a light, airy feeling. Two women, possibly sisters, dying separate violent deaths: What were the odds? I went into the kitchen and got a piece of paper and a pen. Back on the porch I sat down and made a list of things that came to my intuitive mind. First I had to find out who this other woman was, then I had to know when and how she died. I kept feeling there was a connection, that the two deaths were linked in some way. There was also something about Ohio.

Geography is another one of my talents. Early on in my career as a psychic it became important for me to grasp geography. People today are transient, and many of my clients have all sorts of connections to other states. After a while I had taught myself to picture a map of the United States and in my mind's eye, one state would stand out for me when I was talking about a location. The state of Ohio kept jumping out of my intuitive map now, and I knew there was a strong link there.

I made a few more notes and wondered how I could get started. My intuition flashed a picture of my appointment book. "Hmmm," I said, wondering what my appointment book had to do with this. I kept my book at the office, so I decided to go in a little early the next morning and see if I could look up Allison's reading. Maybe the date had something to do with it.

I went to sleep that night with thoughts that were heavy and still filled with guilt. My conscience wouldn't let go of the idea that maybe I could have prevented this. Maybe if I'd just asked Allison what questions needed answering—maybe I could have told her that she was in danger, that she needed to be careful.

In my sleep I had one recurring dream that seemed to take up the entire night. I dreamed that Allison and I were sitting in my reading room together, but our roles were reversed. She was the psychic and I was the client. As she sat in what was usually my chair she said only two phrases, and these she repeated over and over. "Abigail, you're in danger. You need to be careful. . . . Abigail, you're in danger. You need to be careful . . ."

Chapter Five

The next morning, before my first client arrived, I sat down at my desk and thumbed through my appointment book, looking for Allison Pierce's name, but it was nowhere to be found. This was weird. I couldn't remember the date she'd come in, but I did remember that when she'd called a week ago she said she'd had a reading a few weeks earlier. I went back one week, then two, then three, then four and so on, scanning all the names. When I got to week twelve I gave up and came forward again. No Allison Pierce. Frustrated, I sat for a moment and wondered why I couldn't find her name. Had I forgotten to write her in? Or maybe she'd given me a false name?

I once had a client who would tell me only that her name was Jane Doe. Some people are just weird about wanting the information in a reading to be truly authentic. I guess they think I have some sort of a detective agency that works for pennies on the dollar and can look up all sorts of good personal stuff on a person so I can memorize it and recite it without skipping a beat during a reading. For some people this is easier to believe than accepting that I'm psychic.

I sighed heavily and thrummed my fingers on the desk. I was missing something obvious, but I wasn't sure what. I started again at Sunday and went back page by page, looking closely at the names. On July 21 something caught my attention. I'd had a cancellation that day and there was something familiar about it. The woman's name was Connie Franklin, and I'd listed her phone number right there next to her name. I closed my eyes, concentrating. Hadn't Allison been a substitute for a cancellation? I seemed to have that as a fragment of a memory. Without waiting to think it through, I boldly picked up the phone and dialed Connie's number. She picked up on the second ring.

"Hello?"

"Hi, is this Connie?" I asked.

"Yes?" she said hesitantly.

"Hi Connie, this is Abigail Cooper calling. . . ."

"Oh, Abigail, I'm so glad you called. I've been meaning to reschedule with you, but I couldn't find your number. As a matter of fact, I've been trying to call the woman I gave your card to, to see if she had it, but I haven't been able to get hold of her."

My mouth went suddenly dry. It was clear that Connie was the one who had given an appointment to Allison but clearly she hadn't yet heard the terrible news about her friend.

"Hello? Abigail? Are you there?" she asked when I failed to respond.

"Yes . . . yes, I'm here, Connie. Uh, listen, would it be possible for us to get together? I mean, I'd like to reschedule your appointment, but there's also something I need to talk to you about."

"What?" she asked, wary again. Getting a phone call from a psychic out of the blue was, I'm sure, a rather atypical event for her.

"Are you by any chance free today at noon?" I asked evasively. I'd be giving up my lunch hour, but I figured I owed Allison and Connie at least that.

"Uh, yes, I guess so. Did you want to meet at your office?"

I thought about the comfort of my reading room. With its soft, engulfing chairs, cool color and abundance of tissue boxes, it was probably a more than appropriate setting to hear that your friend has passed away. "Yes, that would be perfect." I gave her the address and said good-bye. I had no idea how I was going to break the news to her, but I'd doled out tough news before; unfortunately it was part of the job.

Connie arrived promptly at noon, looking anxious as she twisted the golden cross dangling from her neck. She was pretty, around thirty-one or thirty-two, with curly carrot-colored hair that framed her heart-shaped face and emphasized her light green eyes. I waited until she got settled, then I took a deep breath and asked her, "Connie, did you by any chance give your appointment with me last month to a woman named Allison Pierce?"

Connie blinked in surprise. Whatever she had anticipated I would ask her, it evidently wasn't that. "Why, yes. Yes, I did. Is that a problem? Because I never told Allison she could definitely have the appointment," she said defensively. "I just gave her your card and told her to call you, to see if you would be able to fit her in. I swear I never misrepresented things."

I held up a hand to let her know that I wasn't angry

and nodded as I searched for the right words. "Connie, I'm not upset with you. That isn't why I've asked you here. I've got some tough news to share with you, and it's about Allison."

More blinking, more twisting of the cross.

"I'm so sorry to have to tell you this, Connie, but I'm afraid Allison passed away two nights ago."

Connie's delicate mouth opened in a round O of surprise, and her almond-shaped eyes grew large. She stared at me as if I'd said that Martians had just landed at the capitol, trying to absorb the news but finding my statement impossible to register. "What?" she said in a voice filled with confusion and denial.

"I'm sorry, but Allison's gone."

"But . . . but . . . how?" she stammered.

I sighed and looked at my feet again. Damn, this was hard. "She was murdered in her home on Wednesday evening."

"No," Connie said, shaking her head. "That's not possible. I just talked to her last weekend. We were going to go shopping. There was a sale . . ." Connie's lip began to tremble, and a single tear slid down her cheek. I got up and walked over to my credenza to retrieve a box of tissues there and brought them back to her then bent down and held her hand. "Connie, I'm just so sorry . . ." Connie began to wail and then the dam burst. I hugged her tightly as she rocked and cried, trying to soothe her as best I could.

After a while her sobs lessened and she sat back in her chair, dabbing at her eyes with a tissue. "How is it that you know about this?" she asked me, her voice full of moisture.

"I record all my readings and give the tapes to my clients for them to take home. The police found the tape from Allison's reading at the scene and traced it back to me. They're looking for any details about her murderer, and they've asked me to assist them if I can."

"The dark-haired man," Connie said, a faraway look on her face.

"I'm sorry?" I asked, surprised.

"Allison played the tape for me, and I remember you warned her about a dark-haired man. We both thought it was really creepy, and that's one of the reasons I hadn't rescheduled my appointment with you yet. I wasn't sure I wanted to know what you were going to say to me."

I nodded my head in understanding. "Yeah, I get that a lot. But stuff like that is such a rarity. It's happened to me only one other time and I've read hundreds and hundreds of clients. But I'm glad Allison let you listen to the tape because you might be able clarify some things that came up in her reading."

"Like what?" she asked.

"Well, there is the mention of the loss of a woman, like a sister. Do you know what that's about?"

"Alyssa."

"Who?" I asked, blanking on the name.

"That was her sister. She committed suicide in May."

Left side, heavy feeling. "She committed suicide?" I asked, following my intuition. Something didn't fit.

"Yes. Two weeks before her wedding, her fiancé came home and found her lying in bed, a bullet through her head and her wedding gown torn to shreds."

I went back to my seat and sat down, thinking about what she was telling me. Why would a woman kill herself two weeks before her own wedding? Something clicked in my head, and I asked, "Did her fiancé have dark hair?"

Connie nodded. "Yes. His name is Marco Ammarretti, and he does have dark hair."

"And he was the one who found her?"

"Yes. He came home from work early, found her in the bedroom and called the police. There was a note at the scene. Allison told me about it. She said that Alyssa had killed herself because she didn't think her marriage to Marco would work.

"Marco seemed crushed. I saw him at the funeral, and he looked devastated. Allison immediately blamed him. She read the note and assumed they'd had some fight or something. She told me she'd confronted Marco about it, but he denied all of it. He said they'd been happy and that they never fought." She paused. "It struck me as very odd that he'd say that. I mean, what couple doesn't fight? I don't know why he'd lie about it."

Connie and I fell silent then, as thoughts of lives taken too young filled the air with heaviness. Connie started crying again and my heart went out to her. "Abby, I think I need to go home. This is all such a shock, and I'm sure the police will eventually catch up with me."

"Do you know of any family they can contact?" I asked.

"No. The girls were orphaned a few years ago," she said. "Their parents were killed in a car crash and they inherited quite a bit of money. They moved up here from Ohio about six years ago, and I met Allison at an art class soon after they'd settled in. Allison only worked part-time, and I don't think Alyssa worked at all. They lived together in a house over on Meadowlawn. I just can't believe she's gone," she said as she stood up and took several tissues from the box.

I got up to walk Connie out of my office, my brain whirling with details. Suddenly, as we neared the door, something flashed in my head. "Uh, Connie, by the way, are you considering a surgical procedure for something?"

Connie stopped, a surprised expression on her face. "Yes," she said.

"I'm getting the feeling that you need to go through with it. It's to remove a blockage of some kind, correct?" I said, my hand going to my abdomen and making circular motions.

"Yes. I have gallstones and the doctor wants to remove my gallbladder."

"I'm feeling like you should stop putting this off and get it taken care of. They're saying you'll be fine. Also, they want you to go back to school. You've been considering that too, haven't you?"

Connie gave a small gasp. "Yes! I was thinking of going back for my master's in art. My goodness, Abigail, you're amazing."

"Sometimes I'm not amazing enough," I said glumly, still feeling the guilt over Allison.

Connie must have read my thoughts because she squeezed my arm and moved past me into the hallway. "I'll call the police this afternoon. Maybe I can be of some help. Would you like me to call you when I know what the funeral arrangements will be?"

"I'd like that very much. Thank you."

I watched her walk down the hall, then closed the door and leaned against it. I had really hoped that talking to Connie would give me some answers, but I'd found only more questions. Why would Alyssa kill herself two weeks before her own wedding? Was it true that she'd had a fight with her fiancé and it depressed her so much that it led her to take her own life? My radar wasn't buying it. I'd read for a lot of frazzled brides-to-be and yes, they sometimes bordered on just this side of crazy, but for the most part the prize of that wedding day loomed large enough in their minds to prevent them from doing harm to themselves or others. Why wouldn't Alyssa's marriage have worked? What was it that drove her over the edge?

I sat down in my chair again and closed my eyes. Answering that question seemed to be the key. Something kept telling me there was a strong connection between the sisters' deaths. Was this Marco character the dark-haired man I'd mentioned to Allison? Was he the man she was supposed to stay away from?

At least my Ohio connection had been confirmed. The girls were from there—but something felt slightly off about that. Why did I believe it was an important link in solving Allison's murder? Sighing heavily, I opened my eyes and looked at the clock on my credenza. I had ten minutes before my next client and I was starving. Bolting out the door, I ran down the stairs and across the street to the little café that served prepackaged yogurt and fruit. I dashed back to my office and up the stairs and down the hallway, and as I quickly jogged to my door, the hair on the back of my neck stood up sharply on end. I stopped just in front of the door and looked around anxiously.

I'm very sensitive to energy, especially energy of a malicious intent. What I mean is, if you blindfolded me and told me to walk into a roomful of people I could tell you what specific emotions were emanating from each individual.

Happiness and rage are the easiest, while sadness and contentment give off a softer energy.

There is one emotion, however, that slices me like a sword when I'm close to it: malicious intent. Once when I was in college working as a waitress in a little dive of a restaurant, a man walked past me on a busy afternoon in the middle of the lunch rush. He was an average man, of average height and build and probably of average means, but as he passed me I felt something akin to a slap on the face and I blurted out in a shocked voice, "Oh my God, he's going to kill her . . . !"

People within earshot looked up at me in surprise, including the man my intuition had hit on. He regarded me with eyes that were flat but wary, then bolted out of the restaurant. I had no idea who he was, nor whom he intended to kill, but my memory of him haunts me to this day.

As I stood in front of my office door I felt surrounded by a lingering cloud of that same kind of energy, clinging thickly to the air. I looked up and down the hallway, but no one was there and yet the small hairs along my arms and the back of my neck were raised in a state of alarm I couldn't shake. I quickly unlocked the door and scooted inside, fastening the bolt behind me. I moved away from the door and regarded it warily. Suddenly a shadow appeared in front of the door. I stepped back, my hand reflexively moving to cover my heart. My door has one of those thirties-style frames, with a frosted-glass pane in the top half of the doorway.

I watched in horror as a large shadow moved to stand in front of the door, my breath catching as the doorknob twisted. Not waiting to see what would happen next I turned to dash into my office and dial 911, but a knock sounded softly on the door's glass pane. A woman's voice called out, "Hello?"

I stopped short and turned back to the door as I warily called back, "Hello?"

"Hi, Abigail. It's Jenny Smart? I have a one o'clock with you?"

I shook my head to clear it and quickly unlocked the door to let Jenny in. She took one look at my rather pale complexion and asked, "Are you all right?"

"I'm fine, Jenny, just a little winded. I had to run out during lunch and didn't think I'd make it back in time. Please come in," I said, being sure to lock the door behind her.

Later that day, as I finished up with my last reading, I decided to forgo hanging around the office making phone calls. Instead, I walked out with my last client. We parted at the street, and I made my way to the parking garage and my car, looking around anxiously.

My intuition was on high and I felt like someone was watching me. However, I wasn't absolutely sure this wasn't a product of my earlier scare, much like walking through cobwebs can make you feel like an invisible spider is crawling all over you.

After practically running to my car, I got in, quickly started the engine, and pulled out of the garage. Just to be safe, I decided to take the side streets to my house.

I was a block away from my home when I noticed a car making its way through the side streets with me. Tired of feeling fearful, I pulled over and waited to see if the car would pass me. Instead it pulled up right alongside and Milo and Dutch looked out from the front seat.

"Afternoon, Abby," Dutch said jovially.

"Why the tail, boys?" I asked, not necessarily annoyed.

"We got a call from Connie Franklin today, and she says you guided her in our direction. She's coming in tomorrow to see if she can offer any information, and as a thank-you we thought we'd just make sure our favorite little clairvoyant got home safe and sound."

So now I'd graduated to "Clairvoyant," huh? Dutch

must have been doing some reading. "Thanks. I appreciate it. This going to happen a lot? You know—just want to be prepared to stop at every stop sign and obey all traffic signals."

"It might," Dutch said noncommittally.

"Okay, good to know. Thanks guys." I waved at them and then pulled away from the curb, fellas in tow. When I got home I had to laugh as they watched me from the street to make sure I got inside safely. As I reached for the front door, it suddenly opened on its own and I jumped back as Dave, coming out at the same time, startled me. I lost my balance on the step and Dave reached over to grab me and prevent my fall. Just then there was a blur of movement and urgent shouts from behind me. Lost in the confusion I was shoved violently aside as two shadows barreled past me into the house as they tackled my handyman.

As I watched in horror, Milo and Dutch tackled Dave, wrestled him to the living room floor, flipped him onto his stomach and had him handcuffed faster than you could say, "Yippee-ki-ay."

"Stop!" I shouted as I jumped into the fray, pounding Dutch on the back with my fists and trying to pull him off of Dave. Eggy, secure behind the babygate in the kitchen was barking like a rabid dog, throwing himself against the gate trying to help both me and Dave.

"Ow!" Dutch yelled as I slapped the back of his head. "Abby, what the hell?!" he shouted at me, still bent down with his knee planted squarely in Dave's back.

"Get off him you IDIOT!" I screamed, and Eggy took his barking to new heights, jumping up and down trying to come over the top of the babygate.

Dave, whose face was beet red and shoved firmly into the wood floor, squeaked out, "I can't breathe . . ."

"This is my handyman, you moron!" I shouted as I

continued to try and pull Dutch off of Dave. Finally I got Dutch to stand up, but he kept a wary eye on the man on the floor.

"Your handyman?" Dutch repeated a moment later when the synapse finally connected.

"Yes! He *works* for me!" I said, helping Dave get to his feet. "Uncuff him right now!"

Out of the corner of my eye I saw Milo reholster his gun, and a chill went down my spine. I'd had no idea he'd even drawn it, and I wondered how close we'd come to real tragedy. Dutch looked around the living room at all the saws, tools, extension cords and plywood, and a sheepish look came over his features. He quickly stepped forward and unfastened the handcuffs.

The moment the cuffs were off, Dave turned to Eggy, who was still barking and held up a hand in a "stop" motion. My dog became instantly silent. In the back of my brain I registered this as something just short of a miracle, but I was more concerned with the state of my handyman as I began to brush off the sawdust and dust clinging to his shirt. Dave gently moved me aside, then wheeled on Dutch with a menacing look. "You're damn lucky there's a lady present, pal, cuz I've got half a mind to take you outside and introduce your face to some concrete."

Dutch stared at him with hard, flat features. He wasn't the least bit intimidated.

Completely flustered and embarrassed, I figured it was time to throw my two cents' worth in as well. "Detectives, I believe you two have worn out your welcome yet *again*. It would be best if you left immediately," I said as I pointed to the open door.

Nonchalantly, Dutch turned to the door and with Milo close behind, left the house. The moment the front door closed, Dave rounded on me. "You want to tell me what the hell *that* was all about?"

I jumped a little, surprised by Dave's tone—I'd never heard him raise his voice before. "Dave, I am *so* sorry! I had no idea they were going to jump you like that! Really!"

"Who are they, Abby?" he demanded.

"They're Royal Oak police detectives."

"What the hell were they doing here?"

"Well, one of my clients was murdered on Thursday, and at the crime scene they found the cassette tape of the reading I'd given her. They think there may be a connection between what I told her on the tape and her killer so they followed me home to make sure I got here safely."

Dave's eyes had grown wide as my words tumbled out of my mouth. After a moment he asked, "Are you in danger, Abby?"

I smiled bravely up at him and brushed some of the sawdust from his beard. "I don't know, Dave, but I'm trying to be careful. We don't know who killed my client, and until we catch her killer I'm not sure who's safe in this town."

Dave's mouth set in a firm line as the wheels in his head churned. "Abby, I know tomorrow is Saturday, but I need to install something for you. Is it okay for me to come over tomorrow?"

I was startled by the question and took a moment to answer. In the silence Dave quickly added, "There won't be a charge for the labor, Abby, but I need to get in here tomorrow."

I found my tongue again and answered, "No, Dave, of course I'll pay for your labor. What is it that you need to install?"

"A burglar alarm."

An hour later I finally locked the door behind Dave. He had put in the overtime measuring and cutting thin pieces of plywood, then inserting them into the frame of every window, locking them into place so that no one could jimmy the windows open from the outside. I felt safer already.

I took my dinner out on the porch that night making sure the back gate was securely locked and the door to the porch was fastened as well. While I ate I thought about what to do next.

The incident at my office had scared me, and although I knew that the smart thing was to leave the detective work to Dutch and Milo, I still felt a heavy responsibility to Allison that I wasn't sure I could let go of. I had let her down in her moment of need, and I wondered what that meant for me from a karmic standpoint. I needed to set things right. I couldn't bring her back, but I could work to bring her killer to justice. No, I wouldn't walk away. Not yet, anyway.

Chapter Six

Sunday evening I had just finished with my last client when my business line rang. Hurrying into my office, I picked it up with a crisp "This is Abigail."

"I need an appointment," demanded a gruff male voice.

"Okay, just a moment while I get my calendar," I said, reaching across the desk and pulling my blue appointment book toward me. "All right, sir, my first available appointment is Wednesday, November nineteenth. You can have your choice of times . . ."

"No. I need one right away," the voice interrupted.

I became aware in that moment of the hair sticking up all along my arms and a chill creeping along my backbone. "I'm sorry, what did you say your name is?" I asked.

"Bob Smith." *Liar, liar, pants on fire . . .*

"Well, Mr. Smith, I don't seem to have anything earlier than November available. I'm sure there are other psychics out there who might be able to fit you in sooner . . ."

Click. The phone went dead. Replacing the receiver quickly, I hit *69 and was told that the number I was calling did not have that feature available. I hung up the phone and stared at it for a moment, then it rang again, startling me. I snatched up the receiver and snapped, "Listen, pal, I am not interested in giving you a reading. Take your business someplace else, okay?"

"Abigail?" a woman's voice asked.

I blinked twice and said, "Uh, hello? Uh, yes, this is she. I'm sorry, I thought you were someone else. Who's this?"

The voice gave a nervous chuckle. "It's me, Connie Franklin. I'm sorry, is this a bad time?"

"No, no, Connie. I apologize. Some weirdo just called me and gave me the willies, and I thought it might be him calling back. What can I do for you?"

"You said you wanted to know when the services for Allison were, so I was calling to let you know. I didn't think I'd get you in person. I didn't know you worked on Sundays."

"Yeah, I'm typically here all weekend, for my clients who can't get away during the week. So when are the services?" I asked, reaching for a pen and paper.

"The coroner won't release her until Wednesday or Thursday, so to be safe her attorney has scheduled the services for Saturday morning. The casket is closed, so there won't be a viewing and, truth be told, Allison had very few friends. She kept to herself quite a bit, you know."

"I know. I told her in her reading she needed to get out more, and enjoy life. It's just too bad she didn't take my advice."

"Oh, but Abby, she tried, you know? When she came back from seeing you, all she could talk about was how what you said had affected her. She vowed to start socializing, and she even went as far as to join one of those Web site dating services."

I blinked in surprise. This was a freaky coincidence. "You're kidding. Do you remember which one?" I asked.

"It's that one that's always on TV. Heart2heart.com, I think it is. She went out on one date, and then that was it. She didn't want anything more to do with it."

"She went on a date?" I asked, amazed at Allison's gumption.

"Yeah, but she didn't really talk about it to me. It was weird. She told me all about this guy before her date, and seemed really excited. Then I called her the day after and she sounded so depressed. She wouldn't tell me what happened though. She said she just didn't want to talk about it. To my knowledge she never went out on another date again."

"Do you remember the guy's screen name?" I wanted to look him up on the Web site. A thought occurred to me that perhaps he had dark hair and maybe this was the man I had warned Allison about.

"Yeah, I thought it was goofy when she told me. He called himself 'Mr. Hardbody.' Sounded pretty arrogant to me, but they exchanged a couple of e-mails and Allison thought he was sweet."

I jotted the name down and thanked Connie after she had given me directions to the funeral home. I promised her I'd be there.

I left the building checking over my shoulder and bumped into Stuart, the weekend and evening security guard.

"Hey, Stu, how's it going?"

"Evening, Abby. Just fine. You calling it a night?"

"Yeah—hey, would you do me a favor? Would you mind walking me to my car?"

"There's still plenty of daylight, Abby. You nervous about someone?"

"I had a client who wasn't really happy with his

reading and has been giving me a little trouble," I lied. "Would it be an inconvenience?"

"Not at all. You parked in the garage?"

"No, I'm out back." I had given up my parking space even though it meant I was now dashing downstairs every two hours to feed the meter. The garage was just too scarey for me.

Stuart walked me to my car, and I took side streets home again. Something about the man who'd called looking for an appointment earlier had given me the creeps.

After dinner I went to my study and got online, calling up Heart2heart's Web site and entering my password. I typed "Mr. Hardbody" into the search field, and within seconds a picture and a profile appeared.

The picture showed a fairly good-looking man beaming out from the computer screen as he reclined on a seat on a boat. I took in his hair color—not quite brunette, not quite blond but a murky in-between light brown. He looked like he was a swell guy. I read the profile, and no alarm bells went off. I drummed my fingers on the desk as I stared at the picture, and in a moment of bravado I sent him an e-mail suggesting that I thought he was cute and inviting a response. Not even a minute later my little mailbox informed me that I had mail.

I read the opening line and fought the urge to roll my eyes. "Dear Mystic Lady, your subtle beauty and dazzling smile suggest a heart I'd love to dance with. Shall we meet?"

Whoa, this guy didn't waste time. Now I was stuck. Did I meet him? What if he was Allison's killer? What if she had gone out on a date with this guy, and things had gone wrong, and he was really some kind of a stalker, or serial killer? I stared at his profile and picture. My intuition gave no bells or whistles of alarm. "What the heck," I said and sent my reply, asking where and when.

Mr. Hardbody's real name turned out to be Dirk, and I arranged to meet him at a coffee shop just two blocks from my house. I figured I'd get a feel for him there, and if I felt even the smallest prickle of alarm I could end it right away.

Ten minutes later, I signed off and put in a call to my sister. "Hey there," I said when she answered.

"Hi, Abby. How was your day?"

"The usual." *Liar, liar, pants on fire* . . .

"Did you have any standout readings?" My sister loved to hear about the people I read. Tales of my clients were a bit of a soap opera for her, and typically I would rattle off a list of the highlights, but I just didn't have it tonight.

"No, not really, Cat. They were all kind'a same-ol', same-ol'."

"Oh," she said, sounding disappointed. "So what are you doing tomorrow?"

"I thought I'd paint the bedroom." My entire house was colored the same mottled gray in every room, and I'd finally gotten sick of it. My thought was to start in the bedroom and work my way down.

"What happened to your handyman?"

"Nothing. He's working on the floors this week. I thought I'd save a little money and do the painting myself." The moment the words were out of my mouth I realized my mistake and wished I could reel them back in.

Cat wasted no time pouncing on the opportunity. "Save money? Abby, I'll get my checkbook, how much do you need? I can wire it to you if you need it. Have you gotten some furniture in that house yet? Why don't I just send you an even ten thousand so you can cover Dave's labor and get some decent furniture . . ."

I groaned as I heard her shuffling papers, no doubt searching for her checkbook. Into the phone I pleaded, "Cat. Cat, stop! Listen, I don't need any money. Please put your checkbook away. We've been over this, I'm *fine!* Plus, you know I won't cash a check from you." We'd had this identical conversation at least a hundred times before. My sister was ridiculously wealthy, and where I was concerned she had an overzealous generosity that knew no boundaries.

"Abby, this is silly. Why don't you just let me take care of this? You wouldn't have to worry about saving up until you got money, you could just get done what needs to get done and be finished with it already."

"Cat," I began, taking a long breath of patience, "like I told you the last time we had this discussion, I want to do this on my own. It's important to me that I do this myself. As always, I'm very grateful that I have such a generous sister, but this is my house, my responsibility, and my choice. Can you understand that?"

There was a long pause and finally Cat relented. "Fine, Abby, be stubborn, but I still say it's ridiculous to be in a home without a stick of furniture. But if you don't want my help then you don't want it."

Ah, guilt, my sister's favorite dish du jour. "Cat, you know I appreciate the offer. You're the most incredibly generous sister a person could have."

"Mmmm-hmmm . . ." Great. I'd wounded her.

Okay, I'd have to toss her a bone. "You know what you could help me with?"

"What?" she asked cautiously.

"Well, I have another date from that Web site set up for tomorrow, and I was hoping you could give me some advice about what to wear."

An hour later my ear was sore from pressing the receiver to it. Cat had given her advice, and given it, and given it, to the point where I was exhausted. I finally managed to end the conversation and crawl up the stairs to bed. I thought about the man I would meet the next day. Wouldn't it be ironic if the last man to date Allison Pierce ended up being someone I fell for? Left side heavy feeling. Yeah, I had to agree. Nothing about this guy struck me the way Dutch's profile and personality first had. But we all knew how that one ended.

Since finding Allison's body, Dutch hadn't given me anything more than a wave. Not that I could exactly blame him for being wary, of course. After all, in the short time we'd known each other, I'd been embroiled in not one but two murder cases.

Still, it was a shame that someone so promising had been scared off. I was starting to feel like I would never meet Mr. Right. Maybe I just needed to lower my standards a little. I fell asleep that night with a scowl on my face.

The next day I woke up early and got to work painting the bedroom. Dave wouldn't be back until Tuesday, so I spent the whole day in quiet solitude with nothing but the sound of a roller squishing up and down the wall.

I finished just in time to get ready for my date and hopped into the shower, taking the time afterward to blow-dry my long hair and pick out a dressy outfit of linen slacks and silk shirt. I applied my makeup with care, then at six-thirty I walked out the door and down the street two blocks to the coffee shop. I arrived right on time, but when I went in and looked around no one jumped up from a chair to greet me and I didn't see anyone matching Dirk's description. I got an iced tea and took a seat in a nearby booth to wait for my date.

Dirk's profile said that he always arrived right on time. We had agreed to meet at six forty-five, and when he breezed through the door at seven o'clock minus an apology for being late, I realized punctuality wasn't all Dirk had lied about. He'd listed his height at five ten, and by my estimation he was off by two to three inches. When I stood to shake his hand in greeting I met him eye-to-eye. Now maybe he'd gotten confused when measuring himself or perhaps he thought that by puffing his hair way up like Elvis he could put one over on us womenfolk. My thought was that we womenfolk just weren't that dumb.

Dirk smiled and winked as he flashed me a grin. I noticed that he also had a pretty severe overbite, and I forced a polite smile when he introduced himself with a slight lateral lisp.

"You must be Abby," he said, thrusting his hand out.

"Yes," I said, extending my hand in greeting. "Hello, Dirk, it's nice to meet you." *Liar, liar, pants on fire.*

"Yes," he said as he took my hand and pumped it exactly once. Looking around, he turned away from me, already in motion toward the door. "You ready?"

Oh my, I thought. No manners, a lateral lisp, Elvis hair and a cocky attitude. How ever did Allison resist the temptation to fall madly in love?

"Where are we going?" I asked, thrown a little by how quickly we seemed to be moving.

"We can't have dinner here," Dirk said, turning back to me and looking around as if the coffee shop were distasteful. "I know a place that's much better."

I hesitated a moment considering. I hadn't brought

my Mazda so I would have no choice but to let him drive, and even though I was hungry, I wasn't sure it was safe to get in a car with him. I asked my crew if it was okay to go with this man, and I got a light and airy feeling right away so I nodded to him, making a small detour to throw away my iced tea.

I walked out of the shop and saw him heading for the parking lot. I wondered what he drove, hoping it wasn't one of those monster trucks; he seemed the type. I caught up with him as he stopped in front of a small red, rather innocuous two-door. I didn't recognize it, so I looked at the painted decal on the back hood. The car was a Ford Aspire. My, how appropriate.

The automobile was tiny, faded red in color with torn seats and tires that looked like they were all spares. I noticed also that it listed slightly to one side, rather like someone very heavy had been riding in the passenger seat.

At least Dirk had the decency to unlock my side first and open the car door, but just as I was moving to get in he stepped in front of me to clear off the seat. Most people would have taken care of that *before* they picked up their date, but Dirk didn't seem like the plan-ahead type. "Sorry," he said as he tossed various papers, bags and junk into the backseat.

He finally finished and moved out of the way. I was about to sit down when I saw that he had left a huge banana comb on the front seat. Ah, now I knew how he got his hair so high.

"Just toss that in the back," he said as he unlocked his door.

I looked at the comb and wished I had a pair of gloves so I wouldn't have to touch it. With the tips of my fingernails, I picked it up and tossed it gingerly into the backseat. I sat down and inconspicuously wiped my hands on my pants as Dirk climbed in. As I watched him get situated I noticed two things immediately. First was that the scent of cheap hair spray that smelled alarmingly like Aqua Net hung cloyingly in the air; and two, that in the time that Dirk had parked and come inside to get me in the coffee shop, he had locked his steering wheel with *the Club*.

He sorted through the keys on his key ring and located a small key, which he inserted into the keyhole of *the Club*. "Let me just unlock this baby and we'll be on our way."

I began to imagine all sorts of scenarios that would save me from this disaster of a date. I imagined a fifty-car pileup with such whimsy that I had to shake my head to clear the image. To distract myself, I tried to make casual conversation. "Have you had your car stolen before?" I asked, pointing to *the Club,* which Dirk was now setting on the backseat.

"No, that's why I carry *the Club*," he replied, in a tone that suggested I might be slow on the uptake.

I looked around the parking lot of the coffee shop. I spied a BMW to my left and a Mercedes to my right, but why would a car thief bother with those when he had the crème de la crème of all cars, the Aspire, to choose from? I mean, who could resist a faded, four-cylinder, two-door, listing-to-one-side *classic* like this baby? More imaginary visions of slapping Dirk with *the Club*.

Dirk started the engine and we pulled out of the lot and headed toward the highway. "Where are we having dinner?" I asked.

"There's this place called the Copper Kettle in Southfield. You'll love it."

"Oh? What kind of food do they have?"

"All kinds."

"Ah." It was going to be a long night.

We arrived at the restaurant ten minutes and only two sentences later. Dirk got lucky with a parking spot right in front. Before we could go in I had to wait while he put *the Club* back on his steering wheel, and I stood wishing very hard that no one I knew would see me. Finally we walked into the restaurant and were lucky enough to get a seat right away.

The Copper Kettle was a microbrewery with a sports bar ambience: waitstaff in jeans and T-shirts and polished copper trim on everything from the beer taps to the picture frames. It was extremely casual, and having taken a shower, I suddenly felt over-dressed. We were seated in a booth on the far side of the restaurant and were immediately approached by our waitress, wearing a name tag that read KELLY.

"Can I get you something to drink?"

Dirk turned to me and asked, "You like red wine?"

"Yes, . . ." I said and was about to follow with "anything but Merlot" when he cut me off.

"We'll have two house Merlots." He turned back to me and said, "I already know what I'm having, so I'll let you look at the menu."

"You come here a lot?" I asked, opening the menu.

"Yeah," he answered and started picking at his fingernail.

I stifled a yawn and kept my eyes glued to the menu.

The waitress came back with wine while I was still looking, and Dirk turned to me and asked impatiently, "You ready yet?" Apparently he thought my name was "You." I was beginning to believe that this man possessed all the charm of a malaria-ridden mosquito.

"You go first," I said, stalling for a little more time.

"I'll have the whitefish, but I don't want it baked, I'd like it steamed. I want the sauce on the side, and no capers or artichokes. And I don't like the carrots or yellow wax beans in the vegetable medley, so can I just have the green beans?"

If I had been Kelly I'd have bonked him on the head with my tray, but she apparently had more patience than I, and only nodded as she scribbled on her pad. After she'd written a paragraph she turned to me, and I quickly chose the angel hair pasta, just as it came.

Trying to be a good sport, I tried the wine. Just like I suspected, it was awful. "Isn't it great?" Dirk asked.

I nodded and sent him a fake smile. Obviously encouraged by my smile, he proceeded to have an "I/me" conversation, where he started lots of sentences with the word "I" and inserted several "me's" along the way, and I was left simply to nod my head and feign interest.

Apparently Dirk was an outdoorsman. *He* enjoyed boating, waterskiing, wakeboarding, camping, fishing, hunting, golf, tennis and racquetball, just to name a *few*.

He worked at a printing company where *he* did "something" with computers. *He* hadn't had much luck with the women *he'd* met on Heart2heart because *they* had been too dishonest, unattractive, conniving, materialistic, shallow and fat. My guess was that they had reached the same conclusion I had and bolted at the first opportunity.

While Dirk chatted *at* me, I thought about asking him about Allison Pierce. I wondered if he would remember her. My instincts said that this man was harmless, and that the two had met, had dinner and she'd gone home discouraged by the encounter. My heart went out to her as I thought about how hard it must have been for her to have made the bold move to venture out on a blind date, only to get stuck with this idiot.

Our food arrived about the time I was considering heading to the ladies' room to find an open window. Just my luck.

The food was horrible, but I figured the faster I ate, the faster the date would be over. Dirk never bothered to ask me a single question, and I wondered how it was possible for a grown man to make it into his early thirties with the social grace of a blowfish.

All that talking about himself must have made him thirsty, because he switched from wine to gin when our food arrived, and all that talking about himself obviously encouraged more rounds. By the time I'd finished my meal, Dirk was three sheets to the wind and was now spitting at me when he talked. Gee, and I could have saved myself that shower.

The waitress came to cart away the last of our dishes and asked if we would like dessert or coffee. I could have really gone for some chocolate, but of course Dirk dismissed her without asking me if I'd like anything. He turned back to me and said, "Well, thish ish going all right, don't you think?"

I looked at him then, into his fourth gin and tonic, with his bleary eyes and slurred speech, and I held up a finger. "Hold that thought, would ya? I'm going to go powder my nose."

I excused myself and took off to the back of the restaurant. I found Kelly, our waitress, and asked if she had a phone book, as I needed to call a cab. She looked at me and smiled kindly. "He's a bit of a jerk, huh?"

"Oh, you're really too kind," I said.

"Yeah, I see him come in week after week always with a new chick he's met on that Web site. He used to meet them here, but most of them left within about fifteen minutes. Now he insists on driving so they get trapped, but they usually end up doing exactly what you're doing. I've never actually seen him leave with a date—in fact, the last girl he came in with slapped him silly!"

"No!"

"Yeah, they were having dinner, and I guess he got rude and she hauled off and whacked him," Kelly said, laughing.

Something tickled in my mind and I asked, "What did this woman look like?"

"Let's see," she said, thinking. "She was tall, with shoulder-length brown hair and glasses. Pretty, and she was nice to me. I remember they were having this really deep conversation, something about suicide. I think she mentioned a sister who'd killed herself. I overheard because I had just set down their plates at the time. He made some kind of a wisecrack about it, and she just hauled off and slapped him."

My mouth dropped open and Kelly gave me a sympathetic look. "Yeah, he's about as sensitive as sandpaper. Hang on just a sec and I'll get you the name of the cab company."

While she was in the back I hid in the narrow space between the back wall and the waitstaff station, which luckily afforded me a view of the booth where Dirk sat now, turning in his seat looking for me. I scrunched down into the tight space as his head swiveled in my direction, praying he hadn't seen me. I stayed ducked like that until I became aware of a pair of Italian loafers standing mere inches from mine. Tentatively I looked up, right into midnight blues.

"Dutch!" I said, never so relieved in my life to see a familiar face. "What are you doing here?"

"Evening Abby," he said, looking at me curiously. "Milo and I are here catching up with some guys from the Southfield station."

"Uh huh," I said, squishing down again as I saw Dirk swivel in the booth again, looking for me.

"Don't tell me you pissed off the host and this is where he seated you?"

"Ha, ha, you're *funny*! No, actually I'm in a bit of a jam."

"I can see that."

"No, not this! I'm on the date from hell and I need a ride home."

Something almost imperceptible changed on Dutch's face. For a moment I could have sworn this announcement upset him, but as quickly as something flickered in his eyes, it disappeared. "Do you have anyone you can call?" he asked.

Oh, so we're going to play it that way, are we? I thought. "Not really. The waitress is bringing me back the number for a cab."

"Do you have enough money for the ride?"

Jerk, jerk, jerk!

I looked in my purse and found a twenty. I held it up and sneered at him, "Yeah, I'm great."

"Okay, then, have a good night." And with that he turned on his heel to walk away.

Irritated I stood up from my hiding space as I watched him walk back toward a group of men at the bar which was on the other side of the hostess stand where I was hiding. Just then I caught sight of Milo sitting on a barstool watching me with a smug smile on his face and I scowled at him. Good naturedly he waved back and mouthed, "Hi Abby," and I couldn't help but smile back as I turned away embarrassed now.

In the next moment the waitress came back and handed me a number on a slip of paper. I pulled out my cell phone and punched in the number. Just as it picked up I saw another pair of shoes in front of me and looked up to see Dirk standing there wobbly-legged. "Where'd you go?!" he slurred.

"Uh, hi, Dirk. . . . Hold on a sec," I said as the cab company picked up.

"Main Street Cab, can I help you?"

"You're leaving, aren't you?!" Dirk demanded.

I held up one finger at Dirk and spoke quietly into the phone. "Hello, I need a cab, as *soon* as possible please . . ."

"You know you're all the schame!" Dirk shouted at me.

I covered the phone with my palm and glared at Prince Charming. "Dirk, listen, it was lovely, but I just didn't feel we had a connection . . ."

"I bought you dinner!" Dirk shouted again.

"Hello? Hello? Lady, you there?" coming through the phone.

I put the earpiece back to my head and said, "Yes, I'm at the Copper Kettle in Southfield."

"You know what you are? You're a bitsch! You schat there through dinner and pretended to like me juscht for a free meal, and now you're juscht going to leave like all the rescht of them! You're juscht a lying leasch who doeschn't even like . . ."

Dirk never finished his sentence because at that moment he was yanked backward by his shirt collar and spun around so quickly that the movement startled me and I dropped my cell phone, effectively cutting off the call to the cab company.

I watched spellbound as Dutch angrily grabbed Dirk by the front of his shirt lifting him to his tiptoes, and in a slow and even tone he said, "That's no way to speak to the lady, buddy. Maybe you need a few lessons in manners?"

Dirk's eyes were enormous and frightened; he looked at Dutch, then down at the ground, and promptly burst into tears. "Oh jeez!" Dutch said and set him down. Dirk buried his face in his hands and continued to sob. As he let out a particularly large sob he also farted, making both Dutch and me back away from him a few feet. At that moment the manager arrived. He was a short fat man with black hair and beady little eyes. "Detective, is there a problem here?"

"Yeah, Sal, this guy's had a few too many. I think you need to call him a cab. He's in no shape to drive."

"This guy again? Christ, every weekend with this one. I'll take care of it—thanks, Detective."

I had watched the scene unfold in front of me with my mouth agape, and it suddenly occurred to me to pick up my cell phone. Dutch had the same thought at the same time, and we bent over together, reaching for the phone. He got there first and retrieved it for me. He handed it to me and said, "Come on, Abby, I'll take you home." I noticed that he avoided my eyes when he handed me the phone.

"Thanks" was all I could muster. I walked behind him as he sauntered back over to his seat, withdrew his wallet and placed a twenty on the bar. He said good night to his friends, who were all looking around him at me, and we walked out the door.

We got to the parking lot, and I had my head bent, feeling really bad and concentrating on just following behind him. We had walked only a few feet when I noticed Dutch's legs had stopped moving and he was standing still in front of a motorcycle. I looked up at him with eyebrows raised in question.

"You ever ride a motorcycle before?"

"You're kidding, right?" I asked, convinced he was pulling my leg.

"Would you rather share a cab with Dirk?"

I stifled a sigh. "No, not really. I've never ridden one of these before, though," I warned him.

"Well, first things first," he replied as he opened a

compartment under the seat, pulled out a spare helmet and handed it to me.

I took the helmet, surprised by how heavy it was, and slipped it on. I felt stupid in my dress slacks and silk top wearing a motorcycle helmet. "But it clashes with my other accessories," I said, holding up my little beaded purse.

Dutch ignored me, fastened his own helmet and mounted the bike. Looking at him decked out in jeans and a T-shirt that revealed well-sculpted muscles and bronzed skin, I felt parts of me go all wet and sticky. He turned his head toward me and motioned for me to get on. I did so tentatively and wondered for a minute what I was supposed to hold on to. It seemed a little presumptuous to wrap my arms around him. I settled for just placing my hands gently on his back. He looked back at me and said, "Abby, you're not trying to give me a back massage. This is a Harley, and they have a lot of power. You're going to have to hug me when we get moving."

Well, if you insist! "Okay," I said.

"Now, when we're moving all you have to do is lean your weight into me. Don't try and lean into the curve, or you could throw our balance off. Just hold on tight and enjoy the ride."

Before I could nod Dutch jumped up and brought his full weight down on the starter. The engine burst to life, and he revved the clutch several times before easing the bike out of the parking lot. I left my stomach at the restaurant as we cruised out onto the service drive and then onto the open highway headed east. I had my arms wrapped tightly around him trying not to strangle him and at the same time holding on tight enough that I wouldn't be dislodged. I could hear nothing but the wind as it whipped my loose hair dangling from beneath the helmet. It was a warm evening, but the wind made goose bumps appear all along my arms, and I hugged Dutch just a little tighter. We reached the exit for my house, but I noticed Dutch cruised right on by. Fine by me. I was having a ball.

We drove the open road, weaving in and out of traffic for another fifteen minutes, and then I became so cold I started to shiver. Dutch turned and glanced at me, noticing my shivers, then pulled off at the next exit. He navigated a U-turn and got back on the highway, heading west again, this time taking the exit for my house.

When we reached my neighborhood he braked slightly and cruised slowly down my street. We stopped in my driveway and he turned off the engine. I stepped off the bike and removed the helmet quickly, patting my hair self-consciously.

"What'd you think?" Dutch asked.

"That's a fun toy you got there, pal," I said, giving in to a huge grin.

"Yeah, she's pretty sweet."

We stood there for a few awkward moments not really knowing what else to say. "Thanks for helping me out there, Dutch. That guy was a nightmare."

Dutch had removed his helmet and he held it in his lap as he sat sidesaddle on the Harley. He eyed me for a minute, thinking thoughts that I wasn't privy to. "What's the deal with him, anyway?"

"Well, it's funny you should ask that," I said shuffling my feet. "I found out from Connie Franklin that Allison Pierce was also a member of Heart2heart, and a few weeks ago she went out on a date with that guy."

"Tell me you're pulling my leg, Abby," Dutch said, his voice suddenly flinty.

"I, uh, that is . . ." I stammered, not really sure why he looked like he was about to explode.

"Tell me you did not go out on a date with a man connected to Allison Pierce to see if maybe he had something to do with her murder." Dutch's eyes now pinned me to the spot, and I found myself looking longingly at my front door.

"It seemed like a good idea at the time. I checked in with my intuition and I knew I'd be fine. Plus the moment I met him I knew he didn't kill Allison," I said, rushing it all out at once.

"You checked your *intuition*, and you knew you'd be *fine*?"

"Yes?" I squeaked.

"Are you insane Abby? Do you know what a stupid thing that was for you to do? Did you ever think of calling us with this information? Hasn't your intuition ever been *wrong*?!" he bellowed, and I felt the wind of his breath across my face, blowing strands of loose hair along my temple.

I don't like being yelled at. It tends to get my dander up. "Well, Detective, as a matter of fact my intuition *has* in fact been off exactly once that I know of and that was when it suggested that going out with you was a good idea!" Point to Abby.

Dutch's jaw bunched at my insult, and he audibly grumbled. After a moment, he reached into his back pocket, whipped out his cell phone and snapping it open, hit a number on speed dial. In a moment the line was picked up and Dutch barked, "Milo, Dutch. Listen, I need you to do a background check on that guy Abby was with at the restaurant. According to her he recently had a date with Allison Pierce." There was a pause and then Dutch said, "I don't know. Hold on." He turned to me and asked, "What's his name?"

"I only know his first name, Dirk, but he's listed on Heart2heart as 'Mr. Hardbody.' "

Dutch's lips formed a mocking smile, and he said,

chuckling, "You went out with a guy named 'Mr. Hardbody'?"

"Yeah, and I also went out with a guy who calls himself 'Cool-Hand Luke.' How's *that* for cheesy?" Point two to Abby . . .

Dutch's smile disappeared and I watched his jaw bunch a few more times. "That happens to be my favorite movie," he answered with a sneer.

"Of course it is, Paul—or do you prefer 'Mr. Newman'?" I said, batting my eyes. Abby three, Dutch zero.

Dutch's lip curled a bit, but he clearly thought better of whatever retort he had on his mind and turned back to the phone. "Milo, the guy's first name is Dirk. Check to see if he left a credit card receipt at the restaurant. If not, he's listed on a Web site Heart2heart. We can find him from there." Dutch paused, listening, then continued, "Okay, I'll see you in ten." Flipping the phone closed, he regarded me with the same flinty expression and cool temperature in his eyes. "Abby, you need to do me one small favor—that's all I want and I don't think it's too much to ask."

I rolled my eyes and crossed my arms. Yeah, I'd do him a favor—right after he taught a pig to fly. "What?" I asked testily.

"You need to butt out of this investigation. The only exception is if your *intuition* tells you from the comfort and safety of your own home exactly where we can find the guy who killed Allison Pierce. Until you're able to perform that little magic trick, you will not have anything more to do with this case. Is that clear?"

"Crystal," I said, my voice at sub zero.

"Then you'll stay away from this?"

"Of course, Dutch," I said. *Liar, liar, pants on fire* . . .

"Abby, I'm warning you. If I catch you anywhere near this I'm going to arrest you for obstruction of justice." *Liar, liar, pants on fire . . .*

Man, was I glad to have an inboard lie detector. I might have been scared off by the being arrested thing. "Like I said, Dutch, I'll back off. Now go on and do your little detective stuff. I'm going inside." With that I stepped around him, opened my front door and closed it without looking back. Game, set, match, Abby.

Eggy greeted me and I picked him up, cuddling him as I sighed into his fur. "Men!" I muttered. He must have understood completely, because he gave my cheek an extra-big slobbery kiss.

Chapter Seven

The next morning I woke up early with one thought I couldn't shake. What made Alyssa Pierce commit suicide two weeks before her wedding? Was she unstable to begin with? My intuitive phone kept ringing on this one, and I couldn't let it go. I just wasn't sure how to find out what really happened.

I got up and went downstairs, where I fixed breakfast for Eggy and me. I talked to him while I cooked his egg—he's a great listener—and consulted him on the topic. Unfortunately he's not such a great talker, and couldn't tell me much.

I sighed heavily as I sat down with my own egg and toast and drummed my fingers on the table. The only person who I could think of who might know what had happened to Alyssa was her fiancé, Marco Ammarretti.

I went to the phone book and looked in the A's but couldn't find him. His number was probably unlisted. I went back and sat in front of my untouched and now cold breakfast. Suddenly, an idea came to me and I decided to skip breakfast altogether and get right to work on it. Quickly, I put my dish in the sink and rushed into my study to get the essential items I would need, which included several pieces of paper and some mailing envelopes. Bringing these items back to the kitchen table, I sat down and closed my eyes, intent on getting into the right frame of mind.

When I first came under Theresa's tutelage, she taught me a game that I discovered I was naturally very adept at and that has helped me develop my intuitive skills more than anything else. What she did was secretly cut out various pictures of people, places and colorful things from *National Geographic*, then place them in sealed security envelopes that you couldn't see through. Then she would give me a sheet of paper and have me focus on one envelope at a time and, when I was ready, she'd instruct me to describe from top to bottom on my sheet what colors, tastes, sounds, textures, smells and emotions I picked up from the envelope. Once I was finished with the written description, I would move to the bottom of the page and draw a very quick abstract sketch. When I was finished with the process—it took no longer than three minutes—I was allowed to open the envelope and see what I had described.

The results of this game always astounded me, as with almost eighty percent accuracy I was able to sketch a rough picture of whatever was in the envelope. I was even more adept at picking up emotions and colors—these I did with near one hundred percent accuracy. The trick, I'd learned, was to keep my logical mind out of it. If I just let the thoughts come, I was far more accurate than if I tried to interpret what I was getting. In other words, round, red and sweet is not always an apple.

My idea for getting a handle on Marco was to try

a version of the game. I still wasn't sure I wanted to encounter Marco on my own. If he had killed Allison, then maybe he was also after me. By this time I wasn't trying to kid myself. Someone was definitely watching me, and it was giving me the willies.

When I felt centered and focused I opened my eyes again and pulled out five sheets of blank paper, setting them side-by-side across the tabletop. In the middle of the first four pages I wrote down the name of someone I knew well and on the fifth page I wrote down "Marco Ammarretti."

My intention was to leave as little to my imagination as possible, and having four other individuals to act as a control group would help keep my intuition on track. I had selected Theresa, Brett, Dave and Cat as my control group, thinking that I would know enough about them to be able to distinguish them from Marco once I had completed giving my intuitive impressions.

After writing down all four names, I carefully folded each piece of paper into thirds and stuffed each envelope with one of the five sheets of paper. I sealed the envelopes then closed my eyes, and began swirling them round and round the tabletop until I was positive I didn't know whose name was in which envelope. I then opened my eyes again and selected each envelope at random, numbering them one through five. I then set them off in a small pile to my right.

Next, I pulled out five more sheets of blank paper and I stacked these neatly in front of me. I then took a deep breath, grabbed the first envelope, picked up a pencil and closed my eyes, focusing my intuition on the name inside the envelope in my hand. When I felt the connection I opened my eyes and began to write.

Blue, salt, cool, slippery, rolling, sand, warm, wind, calling birds, thirsty, freedom, happiness, anticipation.

I picked up the next envelope and focused on it.

Black, darkness, peace . . . Nothing else came. That was all I got, which was strange, but I set that piece of paper aside and selected the next envelope.

Hurry, rushing, searching, anxious, wood, carpet, phone ringing, people talking, car exhaust, horns honking.

I set that aside and reached for the next envelope.

Sadness, overwhelming heavy, heavy sadness. Guilt, metal, pollution, acrid taste, tired, weary, lifting, straining, hurts to breathe, sadness, guilt.

For a moment I paused and regarded what I had written there; the sadness was so deep it was all-consuming. What if that envelope was Cat? Or Theresa? I almost opened it, but I only had one more to go, so I set aside my worry and continued.

Metal, car exhaust, movement, asphalt, stop motion, shoulder aching, metal clanging, walking, wood, barrier . . .

At that moment I heard my front door open and Dave called out from my foyer. I got up to greet him and noticed he was rubbing his shoulder.

"Good morning. What's up?" I asked, pointing to his shoulder.

"Ah, nothing, I think I slept on my shoulder wrong last night and it's a little sore. You got any aspirin?"

I smiled as I thought about what I'd just written. He obviously was the last envelope, and that was good because it meant I was getting accurate information. I rushed upstairs, got him the bottle of aspirin from the medicine cabinet, then hurried back to the kitchen to open the envelopes.

The first one had Theresa's name on it and I checked my watch to see the time difference. Six a.m. Pacific Coast time and she was already at the beach, lucky girl. The second envelope was her husband, Brett, and keeping with tradition, he was most likely still asleep, which was why I couldn't get much out of him.

The third envelope was my sister, still trying to pack sixteen hours into eight, I saw. The fourth envelope was Marco Ammarretti. I considered what I'd written about him for a long time. The sadness I picked up was so intense it left me nearly breathless. I noticed there were also feelings of guilt intermixed, but guilt caused by what? Murder?

Did he and Allison argue over her sister's death? I knew from Kelly the waitress that Allison's emotions were close to the surface; she'd slapped Dirk with little provocation. Had she incited Marco's temper by acting out violently against him and he'd overreacted?

I paced in the kitchen for a little while, considering all of it. Finally my curiosity got the best of me and I called Connie.

"Hello?"

"Hi, Connie, it's Abby. How are you?"

"Oh! Hi, Abby. I'm doing better. Is something wrong?"

"No, no—I just wanted to ask you about Marco, Alyssa's fiancé. You said you'd met him, right?"

"Yes, I'd see him practically every time I went to visit Allison. He all but lived with the girls."

"Do you happen to know how I can get in touch with him?"

"I don't have his home phone number, but I know he works at that Mazda dealership on Woodward and Twelve Mile. He's a mechanic there."

"Thanks, Connie, that's great. I'll see you at the services on Saturday."

"Good luck, Abby," she said and we disconnected.

I stood in the kitchen for a moment, indecision tugging at me. I'd be taking a huge chance going over there. However, if I took my car in for an oil change,

I could see if he was there and if my radar picked up anything about him. That seemed like a viable plan so I zoomed upstairs, threw on jeans and a cotton shirt, then raced downstairs for my purse.

"Heading out?" Dave asked me.

"Yeah, I'm going to get my oil changed," I answered, waving good-bye to him as I left.

Ten minutes later I was pulling into the Mazda dealership and trying to locate the service garage. The dealership wasn't an attractive building, at least not to me. Large and boxy, it was constructed of big concrete blocks painted a brilliant shade of white. With its boxy construction and gleaming facade it looked a bit like a giant igloo in summer suburbia.

I wheeled around to the back and found the service garage. I pulled into the parking area beside it, got out and entered the office. The cashier, a pretty brunette who appeared to be no older than fifteen, looked up when I walked in, setting aside the magazine she'd been reading.

"Hi," I said with a friendly smile. "I'd like to get my oil changed and tires rotated, please." Truth be told, the car was due anyway.

The cashier said, "Keys" by way of reply and pushed a customer information form in front of me. I filled out the paperwork and handed back the form with my car key. I was told to wait in the lobby one door down. I wasn't sure who was watching me, so I followed orders and went next door, where freshly brewed coffee filled the air with a nutty aroma. A large woman sat in one of the chairs set in a U formation sipping noisily from her Styrofoam cup. She gave me an appraising look when I walked in, then went back to watching the game show that was blaring out from the television mounted on the front wall.

After a minute or two I nonchalantly moseyed out

of the lobby, back out into the bright sunny day and walked around the building to a spot near one of the far walls where I had a pretty good look at the mechanics working on the cars inside the garage. The huge garage doors were all open, letting in as much air as possible, and I spotted six mechanics in total working on five cars which were hoisted up on mechanical lifts. The men all wore the same dark blue jumpsuits with their first names embroidered on a patch over their left breast. I spotted Marco immediately.

He was tall, with thick, wavy hair, slicked back with some kind of hair gel. His face sported a narrow nose that was slightly pointed at the end, high cheekbones, a square jaw and thin ruby lips. I could see a large Adam's apple and tufts of hair poking out from the V in his jumpsuit. He was a striking man with elegant fingers that deftly maneuvered nuts, bolts and wrenches with the talent of an artist. I watched him as he worked mostly with head bent, the weight of his sadness slumping his shoulders and causing him to pause at intervals and take a deep breath.

The other mechanics seemed to give him a wide berth, as they joked with each other under the bodies of the cars they worked on. Within a short time, Marco must have felt he was being watched because he looked in my direction, exposing brilliant green eyes, and in that moment I fired my radar at him. Several things flashed into my mind at once, but one in particular caused me to catch my breath in alarm.

Just as I was processing the information, I felt someone tap me on the shoulder and I jumped slightly. I turned to see the garage manager staring quizzically at me. "Ms. Cooper?"

"Yes?" I said, feeling a little foolish.

"Sorry. Didn't mean to startle you. Your car's

ready. You can pay the cashier and pick it up out front."

"Thank you," I said. I was still bothered by what I'd picked up from Marco, so I quickly added, "Listen, would it be possible for me to have a word with one of your mechanics? I swear I went to high school with that guy." I pointed to Marco, who was eyeing me suspiciously. "We're planning our high school reunion this year and I wanted to give him the details." *Liar, liar, pants on fire . . .*

"You remember his name?" the manager asked, testing me.

"If it's the same guy who was in my homeroom then his first name is Marco, and I believe his last name is Ammarretti?"

"Yeah, that's him. Wait here and I'll get him."

The manager trundled over to Marco and began speaking to him. I saw Marco look at me, trying to place the face and I gave him an encouraging "really-I'm-harmless" smile. After a moment I saw him nod reluctantly and setting his wrench down, he walked over to me.

"Hello Marco," I said.

"Hi. Listen, I don't mean to be rude, but I'm really not interested in going to the reunion. I never really liked high school and I've got a lot on my plate right now."

"I know, Marco. I'm so sorry to have misled you, but I'm not from your high school. My name is Abigail Cooper and I'm a psychic."

"Shit. You're the one that Allison went to," Marco said, his eyes looking mean.

"Yes, and that's why I'm here. I need to talk to you."

"Listen, lady, I'm not interested in your hocus-pocus. I think all you people are fakes, and you're not going to get a dime out of me so you might as well go on home now," he said as he turned away.

"Marco!" I called out desperately. "Please don't run your car into that tree!"

He stopped abruptly and turned to stare at me with wide eyes. "What did you say?" he asked.

"Listen, I am the real thing, and when I was standing here, I picked up on your plan to drive your car into a tree. It's near your home, isn't it? There's some sort of really big oak tree near your home, by a park of some kind—I think it's near a children's playground, am I right? And you've recently been thinking of ramming your car smack-dab into the middle of that tree, correct? But you'll wait until nighttime, won't you? You'll wait until there are no children around who could get hurt, right?"

He took a step back, reeling a little. "How could you know that? How could you possibly *know* that?"

"Because I *am* psychic, Marco. And I can tell you that killing yourself will absolutely not end your suffering. I know you're devastated by Alyssa's death, but you cannot escape that pain by ending your own life. The cosmos just doesn't work that way."

Marco walked over to a picnic bench under a nearby tree and sat down. I followed and sat beside him. A tear slid down his cheek and he wiped it with the back of his hand, leaving a black grease mark that looked like war paint.

"It wasn't your fault, was it?" I asked, referring to Alyssa.

"I don't know. I just don't know anymore."

"You and Alyssa were happy together. There was no argument, there was no fight. You just walked in one day and found her dead."

Marco squeezed his eyes shut and nodded his head. "She never let on that she was going to do it, you know? I mean, she kept talking about the wedding, how excited she was. It wasn't going to be a big deal, just a small group of friends and family—actually they were mostly my friends and family. Alyssa and her sister pretty much kept to themselves. They were all that was left of their family, you know. Their parents died six years ago in a car crash and there weren't any aunts, uncles or cousins. I just don't understand why she thought it wouldn't work out between us. We had all these plans for kids and building a house. I'd been saving up money; it was going to be perfect." Marco lowered his face into his hands and wept. "What did I do to drive her to that? Why? Why did she do it? If she didn't want to marry me, all she had to do was tell me—she didn't have to kill herself. I still don't understand why she thought that was the only way out."

I rubbed his back in sympathy as he rambled on, and felt tears sting my own eyes. The saddest part about suicide, I thought, was the wreckage of lives it left behind. I was considering this when an image flashed in my head and I sucked in a breath. Something struck me with brutal force and I jumped up as my intuition jarred my mind like a lightning strike. Marco looked up at me, clearly confused by my sudden movement. "What?" he asked.

"Marco, did Alyssa have any other male friends? Someone with dark brown hair? Maybe someone from her past? Someone who lived in Ohio?"

"No. Not that I know of. She and her sister moved up from there right after their parents died, and Alyssa didn't like to talk about her past. She said the past was the past and she didn't want to revisit it. Why?"

"I'm so sorry to have to ask you this, but why were the police so sure her death was a suicide?"

He swallowed. "There was the gun with her finger-

prints and she left a note. Her sister said it was definitely her handwriting. I never read it, but according
to Allison, Alyssa wrote that our marriage could never
work and that she thought this was her only way out.
She said she just wanted to be free. Allison blamed
me for Alyssa's death."

"When was the last time you saw Allison?" I asked,
something else tugging at my mind.

"Uh," Marco said, looking at the ground, "I guess
it was in early June, at Alyssa's funeral." *Liar, liar,
pants on fire . . .*

I was surprised. It was the first time I'd felt him lie
to me. "How did you feel about Allison?" I asked
carefully.

"Well, she was Alyssa's sister. I loved her like a
sister. But after Alyssa died, she went all crazy. She
said it was my fault, and she wouldn't even let me
come into the house for the wake. I was just blown
away, you know? So I guess I was pretty mad at her
too, and I said some things I shouldn't have. Now
she's dead and I feel terrible about that too."

At least that part was true. "Marco, please promise
me that you will not do to everyone else who loves
you what Alyssa did to you when she took her own
life." That hit home and Marco flinched. Now that I
had his attention I added, "I mean it. It may not seem
like it now, but day by day it will get a little bit easier.
I promise you that. You will never forget Alyssa, but
at least you can honor her memory by living your
life."

Marco nodded noncommittally and stood up. "I
gotta get back," he said, and moved past me at a
shuffle. My heart ached for him, and I knew without
a doubt that he wasn't Allison's killer.

I got up myself and began to walk back to the cashier's office. As I rounded the corner, I bumped right into a broad chest. "Oh! Excuse me!" I said, backing up.

"I'm not sure I can do that, Abby," Dutch said, his eyes pinning me to the spot.

Uh-oh. "Dutch! What a surprise! Small world, huh? Funny running into you here . . ." I was rambling, my cover blown.

"What are you doing here, Abby?" Dutch asked me, his jaw clenched in anger.

"Getting my oil changed." I answered, hoping that would be my get-out-of-jail-free card.

"By Alyssa's ex-fiancé?"

"Oh? Was that him?" I asked, giving Dutch a Little Bo Peep smile and eye flutter. Maybe my dazzling display of femininity would throw him off track.

"Wait for me out front, Abigail, and don't even *think* about not being there when I come looking for you."

Gulp. I moved around him and headed to the cashier's office to pay my bill and retrieve my car keys, the thought of fleeing temporarily crossing my mind. When I came out of the office I could see Dutch and Milo escorting a handcuffed Marco to their patrol car and helping him into the backseat. My jaw dropped. Why was Marco being arrested?

Dutch approached me with a second pair of handcuffs, and I wondered if he really intended to arrest me. The look in his eyes was murderous, and in spite of myself I trembled a little.

"Why are you arresting Marco?" I asked sternly. Maybe I could throw him off by copping an attitude.

"Because we know he killed Allison Pierce," Dutch said, standing in front of me and jangling the cuffs.

"Based on what?" I asked.

"Based on the fact that he was the last person to see her alive. They had dinner together at a restaurant the night she was murdered."

Ah, now I knew why my lie detector had gone off when I'd asked Marco when he'd last seen Allison. "Seems pretty circumstantial," I said, showing off the legalese I'd learned from television.

"He has no alibi, Abby. We have a neighbor of his who witnessed Marco pulling into his driveway looking shaken and upset at midnight the night Allison was murdered. Marco claims he was just out driving around after leaving the restaurant."

"Hardly sounds like solid evidence," I insisted, a little rattled by the restaurant story.

"We also have his prints on her purse, which was found at the murder scene."

My thoughts whirred, and in my mind's eye I saw Allison and Marco sitting at the restaurant, her purse falling to the floor and Marco picking it up for her. "He didn't do it, Dutch."

"We think he did, Abby."

"My intuition says he didn't."

"I see," Dutch said, rolling his eyes.

"Oh, so that's the way it's going to be, is it, Detective?" I sneered, angry and insulted. "May I remind you it was my intuition that led you *directly* to Nathaniel Davies and his killers, but now all of a sudden I couldn't possibly be right about this? So instead of trusting me, you're going to lock up the wrong guy and let a killer walk around loose, possibly preying on other women. How many people have to end up dead before you listen to me?!" I yelled, causing people walking close by to turn and stare at us.

"What do you want me to do, Abby?!" Dutch yelled back. "Set Marco free and wait for your little crystal ball to lead me to the killer? Is that what I'm supposed to do?"

I looked over at Marco, sitting resignedly in the backseat of the patrol car, and thought that, for now, he might be safer in jail with people to watch over him.

I turned back to Dutch and put my hands on my hips. "Take me to the murder scene," I said boldly. "I know there's something there I can pick up on. I just need to connect with the energy of the place and I may be able to get some specific clues."

"What?!" he asked, shaking his head emphatically. "You are out of your friggin' mind, Abby. Go home." With that, he turned away from me and walked toward his car.

"If you don't take me to the murder scene, Dutch," I shouted to his retreating back, "I will call the news station right now and tell them how I helped you solve the Nathaniel Davies case, and that without my assistance, you guys would've been dead in the water! I'll bet the journalist I talk to will, of course, be totally unbiased and paint the entire story with the seriousness it deserves. I'm sure they won't *slant* it in any obscure, tabloidish way or anything. You, I'm positive, will come off sounding like the open-minded, forward-thinking, serious detective we all know and *love*. In fact I'm sure all your friends and colleagues will congratulate you on your ingenuity. Using a psychic to solve a crime—pure genius!"

That stopped him. He pivoted and came stomping back to me, his breath fuming from him like a great manly smokestack. "You wouldn't *dare*."

"Coffee? Tea? Or *try me*, Dutch?" More Bo Peep smiles and eye batting.

Dutch wiped his face with his hand, smearing the

grim expression plastered there, and took several deep breaths. Finally he said, "You are a real pain in the ass, you know that, Abby?"

"I try," I said smugly.

"Fine," he said through gritted teeth. "Meet me at the Royal Oak Police Station in one hour. If you're late, I'm leaving without you."

I saluted and trotted over to my car, which had been nicely cleaned and vacuumed. I drove with a small smirk all the way home.

Exactly one hour later I stood tapping my toe impatiently on the sidewalk waiting for Dutch and looking at my watch every thirty seconds. Minutes crept by and I began to suspect I'd been set up. If Dutch wanted to call my bluff on the news story, he'd be mighty sorry in about two hours. I don't make idle threats.

At quarter past the hour I had my cell phone out and was already getting the number for Fox 2 News from Information when a silver unmarked police sedan pulled up curbside. Reluctantly I clicked the phone closed. I was so mad at being made to wait I seriously considered placing the call anyway, but decided I should quit while I was ahead. I got into the car and fastened the seat belt, not looking at Dutch. "You're late," I said in greeting.

"I know," he replied, then pulled away from the curb while I smoldered.

We traveled through downtown and turned into a small subdivision on the southeast side of Royal Oak. The area, which bordered the dramatically more expensive township of Pleasant Ridge, was immaculately kept, with huge maple trees shading the streets, and well-watered front yards glowing Chem Lawn green.

We made several turns down streets with names like

Hickory Wood Lane and Smokey Oak Drive until we finally came to a small cul-de-sac on a street called Meadowlawn and parked in front of a one-story, rather rustic ranch with a FOR SALE sign on the front lawn.

We walked to the front door, and Dutch removed the only visible crime scene tape still barring the doorway. He pulled out his notebook and flipped several pages, then bent over and turned the combination on a lockbox secured to the railing on the front porch. He extracted a key, but before entering he turned to me and put a hand on my shoulder. "Abby, this place hasn't been cleaned since the night of Allison's murder. There was a lot of blood, and I want you to prepare yourself."

My eyes widened a little, and I took a deep breath, tucking in my emotions, preparing myself. After a moment I said, "I'm ready" and nodded at the house.

Dutch opened the door and we both stepped into a small foyer, where he fumbled with the light switch. The shades had all been drawn to keep out the eyes of the curious, and the room was fairly dark. When the interior was illuminated we walked forward quietly, oddly respectful of what had transpired here.

As I moved into the living room I looked around at the chaotic scene. Several rubber gloves and empty paper bags competed with overturned furniture, pottery knickknacks and various odds and ends littering the floor. The house had been destroyed.

There was garbage everywhere, and a fetid stagnant odor clouded the interior like heavy smoke. I waved a hand in front of my face and stepped in a little farther. I found my chest was moving a little too fast to take air in and out, so I closed my eyes, trying to calm myself. I opened them a moment later and looked more closely at the room. My eye caught the image of a handprint left in what looked like brown rust-colored paint on the wall, and I realized suddenly that the paint was in fact dried blood. I looked questioningly at Dutch.

"Hers. We think she struggled with him before he finally killed her. From the defensive wounds it looks like she put up one hell of a fight."

Dutch's face was set grimly and his mouth was a firm thin line. I nodded and continued to walk carefully among the litter. I hadn't completely opened up my intuition. I could feel messages coming in, but I wasn't picking them up just yet. My rational side wanted to survey the scene first and come up with a logical explanation somehow.

I wandered into the kitchen, and it too resembled the aftermath of a tornado. I retraced my steps and headed for the master bedroom. There, in the doorway, was the chalk outline of the final resting place of Allison Pierce. I stepped around the drawing, subconsciously avoiding a body that was no longer there. My intuitive phone was going haywire, and I was finally ready to pick it up. "Okay, Dutch, this will work better if you can take notes because I don't always remember what intuitively comes to me."

Dutch reached into his pocket and pulled out his notebook, nodding at me when he was ready.

"The first thing I'm getting is that there is this really strong connection to Ohio here. I get the feeling that Allison figured out something that no one else knew, and she thought it had something to do with Ohio. Wait, no, that's wrong. It had something to do with *someone* in Ohio, and there is some sort of reference to Robin Hood here. I keep hearing 'Robin Hood and his band of merry men' in my head. I don't know if that describes the guy we're looking for or not, but

personally I think this has to do with a man who has
dark hair and is a little on the short side. He walks
with a weird kind of walk, like he hops when he walks
or something. I get the feeling he wears big clothing,
oversized clothing, because that makes him feel taller
than he really is. This guy is definitely bad news. And
I feel like he was here. Like he came up from Ohio
because Allison found out about him. Also there is a
connection to sports, baseball or softball, something
about a bat. They keep saying 'bat, bat, bat' in my
head—" I looked at Dutch then, and he was staring
at me with the same wide-eyed expression he'd given
me when I'd touched on something I wasn't supposed
to know.

"We recovered a bat in the front yard. He used it
on her like batting practice," he explained.

I sucked in a breath and was suddenly aware that
my vision was closing in on me. I couldn't seem to
focus and I felt my knees grow weak. Dutch caught
me and helped me outside, where I sat perched on
the front stoop with my head between my legs and
Dutch rubbing my back in slow circular motions. Finally I could see clearly again and smiled a little at
him. "Thanks. I guess it was just the smell and the
scene in there—it caught me off guard a little."

"That's why I didn't want to bring you," Dutch said
in an "I-told-you-so" tone.

"Yeah, well, thanks for trying to shield me from the
ugly, but I need to help you guys figure this out."

"Why, Abby? Why do you have to?" he asked,
looking intently at me.

My lip trembled unexpectedly at the question, and
a wave of guilt washed over me. "I guess I feel like I
let Allison down. She came to me looking for answers
and I only gave her bits and pieces. Then when she

needed a little clarity, I blew her off. Maybe I could have prevented this. Maybe there was something I missed."

"Abby," Dutch said, but I ignored him.

"Maybe if I'd just given a damn I could have . . ."

"Abby, this isn't your fault," he said, gripping my shoulders and looking deeply into my eyes.

I swallowed and fought back the tears pooling in my lower lids. "But what if it is? What if part of my karma was to prevent this from happening and because I didn't listen, because I blew her off, she ended up dead?"

Dutch smiled kindly at me and said, "Abby, I don't know much about karma, but I do know a little about life. Look, you can cause-and-effect yourself into insanity, or you can just accept that you do the best that you can, whenever you can. You're human. There is nothing to feel guilty about."

I took a deep breath and struggled to accept what he'd just said. After a minute, I'd composed myself again. "Okay, I'm ready to go back inside," I said as I stood.

Dutch looked at me for a moment, his eyes summing me up. Finally he sighed heavily and followed me inside.

I walked into the foyer and entered the living room. I closed my eyes and focused again, listening intently to my intuitive phone. Something was tugging me down the short hallway at the back of the house. I followed the trail and came to two doors, one straight in front of me, the other to my left. The first led to a bathroom, the second to a door that had been padlocked, but now hung crookedly on its hinges and was splintered from top to bottom. A large footprint was visible just to the side of where the door's padlock still clung to the metal clip that had once been attached to

the doorjamb. I looked back at Dutch for an explanation.

"Alyssa's door was padlocked. The killer didn't
know the combo and he wanted in there real bad."

I turned back to the entryway, pushing in the
crooked door carefully and stepped inside the small
bedroom. The room was fairly bare. There was a bed
frame but no mattress or linens, two empty
nightstands were toppled over, and a small dresser
rested against one wall, its empty drawers strewn
across the room. The room had been painted recently,
the smell of paint still clinging lightly to the air, and
I noticed small round shadows of color seeping
through the white over the bed frame. The closet door
had been opened but only empty hangers hung inside.
There was nothing else in the room, but my intuition
was telling me something was out of place. I looked
around, staring at everything until I finally got to the
window next to the bed. Something about the window
was off. I moved forward and checked it, but discovered it was locked tight. I stepped back and surveyed
the scene again. The window kept calling to me.
Maybe I needed to view it from a different angle. I
turned and walked out of the bedroom, back down
the hallway and through the kitchen to the back door.
"I need to go out to the backyard," I said over my
shoulder to Dutch, who'd been following me.

"Help yourself," he said, gesturing.

I undid the lock and stepped out onto the lawn
then headed over to the exterior of Alyssa's bedroom
window. There were no bushes or flowers along this
edge of the house, nothing under the window but
overgrown grass. I put my hand on the glass pane,
something still tugging at me. Dutch stood off a few
feet watching me intently as I shut my eyes and listened to my intuition. I had a feeling I needed to

move to my right, so I did and walked around the edge of the house, and there I saw it. A rusty screen lay hidden behind a bush at the side of the house. Dutch followed me and watched as I carefully picked the screen up and moved it to Alyssa's window. It fit perfectly.

"What are you getting, Abby?" he asked me as I stepped away from the now screened window.

"The murderer removed the screen and got in through this window."

Dutch gave me a humoring smile and said, "Abby, this window was locked from the inside. Plus the door was padlocked and the killer kicked it in from the hallway. He couldn't have gotten inside to murder Allison from here."

"No, *you're* missing it. He didn't get in to murder Allison from here, he got in to murder *Alyssa* from here."

Dutch regarded me for a long moment, the muscles in his jaw bunching and unbunching, before he moved to the window and surveyed the screen. Next he moved around to the side of the house and poked at the area where I'd found the screen next to the bush. Finally he finished and walked past me toward the house. "Come on," he said.

"Where are we going?" I asked, trotting behind him.

"Back to the station. We're going to look through Alyssa's file."

Forty-five minutes later we were sitting at Dutch's desk on the second floor of the Royal Oak Police Station, facing Officer Shawn Bennington, a barrel-chested cop with sloping shoulders, fat belly, sloppy food-stained uniform and murky attitude. He seemed to have little respect for the detective in front of him, and I suspected that, given his attitude, he probably treated everyone with authority the same way.

"Thanks for meeting us, Shawn. Sorry to have to pull you off patrol."

"Uh-huh. Well, here's her folder. I had to dig through all sorts of shit to find it. Misfiled as usual," he said, rolling his eyes as he pushed a dark brown legal file in front of us.

Dutch accepted it, seemingly oblivious to the scowl shooting out from the officer's beady eyes. Bennington continued, "We don't normally keep evidence from suicides, but we wrote this one up as an S.P.F.I."

"What does that mean?" I asked.

"Suicide Pending Further Investigation," he explained.

I thought it was curious that he hadn't even asked who I was and why I wanted to know such things. "In other words," he continued, "it means that all the evidence of a suicide is there except the powder burns on the vic's hands. Tough to shoot yourself with a gun if there aren't any powder burns on your trigger finger."

Dutch raised his eyebrows. "Do you know why this information was never turned over to our department for follow-up?" he asked.

"Like I said, *Detective,* it got misfiled and probably never made it up here. Either that or you guys got it and sent it back downstairs to get lost."

Dutch's jaw tightened. Even I could see the delicate dance Bennington was tiptoeing, just to the right of insubordination. "Thanks, Shawn, we'll take it from here," Dutch said firmly, dismissing the officer.

"What's his problem?" I asked.

"Passed over for detective half a dozen times, but he's been here long enough that no one has the balls to get rid of him. His work is so sloppy it's no wonder the file never made it up to us. My guess is that it wasn't misfiled at all, but probably sat at the bottom of a pile on his desk for the past couple of months."

"You're kidding!" I said.

"I wish I was," Dutch answered. "Unfortunately, it's happened before."

I looked again at the retreating back of Officer Bennington and felt anger sweep over me. What if Dutch was right and Bennington had mishandled the file? What if Dutch had been able to look into Alyssa's death? Would he have found her killer in time to save Allison? As my mind wandered to such dark thoughts, Dutch squeezed my hand, pulling me back. "Hey," he said gently, and I turned to look at him. "We need to focus on this, okay? We can't waste our time pointing fingers right now. I'll take care of Bennington later."

I nodded at Dutch and he opened the file. He spread it on the table in front of us, and my eyes darted over the pages of notes and pictures. There were several fairly graphic crime scene photos, and my stomach rolled over when I looked at them. I steeled myself, though, and forced myself to keep going. Alyssa had been shot under her chin at point-blank range but I noticed in one of the photos that her head was turned oddly in relation to the position of her body. It looked as if she'd been leaning slightly to one side, but after she was shot, her head had turned all the way to the other.

The gun had been left on the floor, and Allysa's hand dangled over the side of the bed, hovering in midair over the weapon. There were other photos of the room: a single shot of what was clearly a wedding dress that lay torn and crumpled in the corner; a close-up of the suicide note left on the dresser; and a long view taken just inside the doorway of the bedroom. Something struck me about that particular photo and

I gripped Dutch's arm. I pointed to the window that had had the missing screen. The window was wide open, and curtains that were no longer hanging in Alyssa's bedroom had been sucked through the opening by the wind. The other window on the wall was also open, but the screen was clearly in place, preventing the other set of curtains from being pulled through.

Dutch looked for a long moment at the crime scene photos, his features unreadable. Finally he turned to me and said, "Abby, I think you might be on to something. This whole scene looks contrived."

We focused again on the file. Dutch turned to the back and retrieved a small Baggie containing two pieces of paper. One was the suicide note; the other was a shopping list. I looked curiously at the Baggie and asked, "Why is a shopping list in here?"

"Handwriting analysis. We would have wanted to compare the letter left at the scene with something we were sure was Alyssa's handwriting."

I did a quick comparison through the Baggie and could tell immediately that the handwriting was identical. Alyssa had written both notes. I was waiting for Dutch to pull out the suicide note so we could study it more closely, but before he did, he got up and walked over to a nearby desk, where he opened a drawer and took out a large pair of tweezers. Coming back to his desk, he carefully opened the Baggie and with the tweezers took out both notes. He laid them gently on his desk blotter. The script was big and loopy, and on the suicide note it began at the top of the page. I leaned in to read over Dutch's shoulder.

this marriage can't work. I've tried to be faithful to you, I've tried to be honest, but I don't think we're meant to be together. This has to end

now, and I need to go away, I just want my free-
dom. Please just let me go. I'm so sorry about all
of it. Please forgive me.
   Love always,
   Alyssa.

Dutch used the tweezers to turn the short letter
over, but nothing was written on the back. It started
simply and ended simply, and that simply didn't make
sense. Why had a woman who had apparently ripped
her wedding gown to shreds written a suicide note
only five sentences long? The fact that she tore up her
gown indicated rage, and yet the note spoke only of
regret. As I scanned the suicide note, my eye kept
wandering to the top of the page and I focused on
that for a minute. Then something dawned on me and
I sucked in a breath of surprise.

"What?" Dutch asked.

Excitedly, I pointed to the top of the page at the
first word, "*this*," and said, "Dutch, look at this word.
It's lowercase. Alyssa starts every other sentence with
a capital, but she begins the letter in the lowercase.
And it is a lowercase *t*, because this sentence here"—
I pointed to the fourth sentence down—"this one
starts with a capital *T*. I don't think that's a mistake,
Dutch. I think this beginning sentence is actually the
end of a sentence from another page and this is the
last page of a longer letter!"

Dutch looked closely at where I was pointing; then,
with the tweezers, he held the note up to the light and
studied it, and there were indeed some indentations
there, but whether they were from a longer letter or
something else wasn't clear. Next he checked the file
and the photos and found no evidence of any other
pages. He flipped to the initial interview with Marco
right after he had come upon the body. According to

the report, Marco had been so overcome with grief at finding Alyssa that he hadn't been aware that she'd even left a note.

"See? I told you so!" I said triumphantly. "Someone else murdered Alyssa, someone she knew intimately. Allison must have suspected it and told the killer that she was going to the police, then he killed her to shut her up!" I was full of adrenaline and had gotten up from the table so I could pace back and forth, doing my best Perry Mason.

"Abby, you're drawing a pretty big conclusion there," Dutch said patiently. "At the moment all we have is a suspicious crime scene. I'll agree with you that it looks contrived, but I'm not ready to call this a murder scene just yet."

His statement popped my balloon. "Oh, for Pete's sake, what the hell do you need?" I asked testily.

"Short of a confession?" he asked. "Overwhelming evidence. I'm going to get this file over to the lab and have them run some tests on the note to see if we can make out any of these indentations. You could be right and this could be the last page of a longer letter, or you could be wrong and it's something unrelated like a grocery list. I'll let the crime techs do their job and then we'll see what turns up, okay?" With that he closed the file and stood up, then motioned for me to follow him.

"How long will that take?" I asked, grabbing my purse.

"Couple weeks . . ." he answered, walking down the staircase with rapid movements.

"What? What do you mean, weeks? We don't have weeks!" I yelled as Dutch reached the bottom.

Moving to the door, he finally turned to me and asked, "Abby, what do you want me to do? The lab is backed up to the time of Moses; everything has to wait its turn. We'll be lucky to get an analysis by Christmas."

My mouth fell open. He *had* to be kidding. "Five months?! "But I can't wait that long! I have to catch this bastard!"

Dutch looked at me with empathy. I'm sure he had faced the same sort of impatience from the families and friends of the victims whose deaths he investigated. "Abby, listen to me," he said. "There is an order and a protocol to detective work that I can't ignore. I have to follow the rule book; otherwise, the bad guys would all get off on a technicality. Now, I will admit that you've opened up some things here, but I'm still going to follow the evidence where it leads me. If it leads me in a different direction and I discover someone else is to blame for Allison's murder then I'll have all my investigative efforts to back me up."

"But, Dutch, we're running out of time," I said without really knowing why I said it.

Dutch sighed and wiped his face again in the same frustrated gesture I'd seen earlier at the dealership. "Listen, I'm starved. How about we go to lunch and talk about it there? What do you say?"

My stomach gave a Pavlovian growl at the word "lunch," and I let my shoulders slump a little. "Fine," I said and walked out with him to get into his car.

"Good girl," he said, patting my head as I clicked the seat belt. As we pulled out of the lot I wondered if I should stick my nose out the window and pant like an obedient little terrier.

Dutch drove to a local Royal Oak favorite called Pronto's! He parked and we got out, opting to eat inside instead of in the baking sun. Pronto's! is the place where those who like to ogle congregate when the weather won't cooperate. Formerly an almost exclusively gay hangout, it now welcomes everyone in the loving embrace of delicious comfort food. The menu is gourmet deli, and I had never had a bad meal in my life from the place. As we walked in, the flamboyant male host gave Dutch an appraising look that began at his feet and worked its way slowly up, stopping at his roguishly handsome face. The final conclusion must have been good because he flashed Dutch a beaming smile and sang, "Right this way!" I might as well have been invisible.

As the host led us to our table, I couldn't help but notice all of the heads that turned as Dutch walked by. He had that effect on people; he was someone who quite literally exuded virility, and like a scent in the air it tickled the noses of everyone interested. A flutter of insecurity tickled my tummy, and I wished for not the first time that day that I had put more effort into my appearance before leaving the house.

We settled at a table and picked up our menus. After the waitress took our order, Dutch turned to me and said, "Your boy 'Mr. Hardbody' checked out okay." I looked at him with a question on my face, not following his train of thought, so he continued. "During the time Allison was being murdered Dirk was filling his hard drive up with porn."

"Ewww," I said, making a face. That was a visual I didn't really want to entertain.

"You're lucky the guy turned out to be harmless, Abby. What if he was the killer? You could have put yourself in real danger."

I rolled my eyes and replied, "I told you, my radar never lies, Dutch, and if it says someone's harmless, then they're harmless. I guess it was just morbid curiosity on my part. I wanted to see what kind of guy Allison would go out with, you know, maybe it could tell me something about who killed her."

"You think whoever killed her was involved with her at some point?"

I thought about that for a minute, and played it across my radar. It didn't quite fit but it was close. "I'm not sure. Maybe not involved per se, but I think someone from her past came back and wanted to shut her up. I mean, you saw that crime scene. He didn't just eliminate her quickly and quietly. He *hated* her. Why? What had she done that caused such rage?"

"Marco's someone from her past," Dutch offered.

I gave him an exasperated look. "Oh, please. Why would Marco kill her? What was his motive?"

"According to several people we've talked to, Allison caused quite a scene at Alyssa's funeral, blaming Marco for her sister's death. She humiliated him publicly. Maybe she taunted him. Maybe she was so upset over the death of her sister that she harassed him, even invited him to dinner, taunting him to the point that he snapped."

Our food arrived and I stared at it for a long moment before picking up my fork. It looked and smelled delicious, but my thoughts were far away. Finally I said, "Dutch, I just know he didn't do it. He blames himself for Alyssa's death, and he thinks that somehow he provoked her into it."

"All right, then, let's follow that line of thinking for a minute, Abby. Maybe Marco was responsible for Alyssa's death. Maybe he popped her while she was sleeping and arranged the whole scene to look like a suicide and Allison found out about it."

"But why, Dutch? What was his motive for killing Alyssa? Everyone thought they were happy together."

"Actually he had a very good motive. For starters, Alyssa named Marco as the beneficiary in her will. The girls inherited a couple of million from their parents, and upon her death Marco was entitled to half her parents' estate. The kicker is that Allison named Alyssa her beneficiary, so now that she's dead her half also falls to Marco. I think that sets the table quite nicely for murder, don't you?"

For the first time a ripple of fear traveled down my back. I could see it clearly through a jury's eyes. It made sense in a brutal, barbaric sort of way, and I knew that Marco, riddled with guilt over his fiancée's death, wouldn't fight back very hard. In fact, he would probably embrace a guilty verdict. He felt responsible for Alyssa's death and would probably see a murder conviction as penance. I couldn't let that happen.

"Okay, Detective," I said, cocking my head, "Riddle me this, then: Why would Marco go through all the trouble of climbing in through a window to murder Alyssa? He had a key. Why wouldn't he just use the front door, let himself in, shoot her, and go off and dial 911 saying he'd been in the living room when he heard a gun go off?"

Dutch sighed heavily and shook his head. "You're still assuming the screen was removed the day Alyssa died. What if one of the girls removed it earlier and forgot about it? Why did it have to be removed on the day of Alyssa's death? Also, I think you're right about the suicide note being a longer letter. What if Marco has the rest of the pages? It's possible it wasn't a suicide note at all, but a Dear John letter. He reads it, gets pissed and offs her. Everything keeps turning back to Marco."

Okay, he had me there. I scratched my head and grimaced. I hated knowing that I was right but not knowing the why or the how of it. I sat moodily in thought until Dutch paid our bill and we got up to leave. We drove back to the station in silence, and as Dutch dropped me off at my car he offered, "Listen, Abby, because I think you may have something about

Alyssa, I'll keep looking into it, but I want your solemn vow that you will butt out from now on. *Capiche*?"

"*Capiche*," I said flatly and turned to my car. I hadn't exactly taken a vow now, had I? I just said I understood, and in a foreign language at that.

I drove home and greeted Dave, who was packing it in for the day. He was making some good headway on my floors, and I asked him about his shoulder.

"It's still sore, but hey, I'm not twenty-one anymore. I'll muddle through."

I wrote him a check and sent him off with instructions about moist heat and anti-inflammatories. I then made Eggy's dinner and paid some bills, but my mind was still on Marco. I needed to talk to someone who would understand my point of view, so I called my sister.

"Hey, Abby, how are you?"

"Good. Cat, you got a minute?"

"Always sweetie, what's up?"

And so I started from the beginning not leaving out a thing. I finished with the visit to the crime scene and all that I detected there, and how I was still convinced that Allison's killer was out there, lurking

All the way through my long speech, Cat remained oddly silent, but when I'd finished, an ear-piercing string of words formed themselves into a rapid, machine-gun sentence. I suddenly knew that I'd inadvertently awakened my sister's alter ego—Howler Monkey.

"*YOU WHAT?! You went on a date with someone who could have murdered your client?! Are you insane?!!*"

Oops. Maybe I should try some damage control. I started with the calm down, it's really no big deal approach. "Cat—"

"And then you decide taking chances with one possible crazed psycho isn't enough so you go looking for another?!!!"

Switching to authoritative. "Cat—"

"And you're going to crime scenes?! What are *you thinking Abby?"*

Trying reasonable. "Cat—"

"And the police are just letting *you go pell-mell all over town just asking for trouble?! What the hell kind of a town are you living in?!"*

Moving to exasperated. "Cat—"

"Well I have heard ENOUGH Abby! You get your butt on a plane to Boston IMMEDIATELY or I will fly to Michigan and bring you back here myself!"

Last resort, pissy. "Cat—"

"Don't you, 'Cat' me, missy! You will see reason if I have anything to do with it!"

Sometimes, especially with my sister, all you can do is stand back, cover your ears, and wait for the hurricane to blow itself out. I sighed and sat down, propping my feet up on the kitchen counter. After another ten minutes, Cat still wasn't willing to let me get a word in edgewise, but her voice was starting to go hoarse so she put my brother-in-law on the phone. "Hey, Abby, what's going on?" he asked, his voice somewhere between reason and alarm.

"Hi, Tommy. Nothing, just Cat being Cat. How's the golf game?" I asked, hoping for a little distraction.

"Good, got a big tournament in two weeks." My brother-in-law was a professional golfer.

"In Texas?"

"Dallas," he said, laughing at my hit.

"Are you thinking of switching caddies?" I asked.

"Yeah, actually I was. Any thoughts?"

"Is it to a guy with red hair and lots of freckles?"

"He's one of the selections."

"He's your man, Tommy. Good luck."

In the background I could hear a struggle for the phone before my brother-in-law had a chance to say anything further. I heard my sister say, *"Why are you talking about your damn golf game when your sister-in-law is trying to get herself killed! Am I the only sane person left in this family?!"* Recovering the phone, Cat said in a voice that had calmed just a teeny bit, "Abby, please, be reasonable. This is insane! You could be in mortal peril!"

I loved my sister's flair for the dramatic. "Cat," I said, "listen to me. I'm fine, really. Dave installed a burglar alarm and I've got Eggy here to protect me—"

"You have a guinea pig that barks. A psychopath intent on killing you is not going to be intimidated by a pygmy of a dog."

I bit back the smarty-pants reply I had for her assessment of my pooch. "Cat, I'm fine. My radar is up and running, sweetie, and the moment I sense I'm in real danger I'll be on that plane. I promise," I said through somewhat gritted teeth.

"But what if it doesn't warn you in time? What if you don't know until it's too late?"

She had me there, and for the first time, I actually did feel nervous. I shook the feeling off and said, "I won't take any more chances, okay?"

"Promise me."

"I promise." *Liar, liar, pants on fire . . .*

"Okay, but I don't see how I'll be able to sleep at night knowing someone could be after you."

Ah, what was a conversation with my sister without a heaping plateful of good old guilt? "I'm sure you'll be fine, Cat. I'll call you tomorrow, all right?"

"Fine. But Abby, please, please be careful."

"I will, Cat. Love you."

I went to bed that night with thoughts of Marco,

Allison, and Alyssa swimming in my head. I didn't know why the puzzle wouldn't come together, but I couldn't let go of the feeling that a piece was still missing. There was a link I was overlooking, and that was what would make the whole thing make sense. Sleep came late, and my dreams were again filled with Allison sitting in my chair telling me to be careful.

Chapter Eight

Wednesday morning I arrived early as I had a lot of work ahead of me. A regular client had booked the entire day for her whole family, which meant I had seven appointments lined up back-to-back. I knew there wouldn't be much of a break in between, so I wanted to make sure I was stocked up with enough tapes, water, and incense. The phone rang almost immediately after I set my purse in my desk drawer, and I checked my watch wondering who could be calling at eight a.m. "Abigail Cooper," I said.

"Oh, Abby, thank God I caught you. This is Elaine Steinberg—I left you a voice mail late last night. Did you happen to get it?"

"No, I just got in."

"Oh, no. I'm so sorry, Abby, but my mom is in the hospital," she said, sounding worried.

"Oh my goodness! What happened?"

"We had a big family dinner last night, and we were all talking about coming to see you today. I think Mom just had a little too much excitement because she started having chest pains. I remembered that you'd told me in my last reading to watch for heart trouble, so we rushed her right over to Beaumont Hospital."

"Is she all right?" I asked, not really knowing what else to say.

"No, not really," she said and began to cry. "Abby, I'm so sorry, but we're going to have to cancel all of our appointments for today."

"Of course, Elaine, of course," I said, rushing to ease her mind. "Listen, is there something about a tube the doctors are thinking of inserting near her heart?"

"Oh! Yes, they are. She's in surgery right now and they're putting in a shunt to drain some of the fluid around her heart. That's what's causing her the trouble—she's got some excess fluid around her heart and it can't beat properly."

"The feeling I'm getting is that it may be a little touchy for the next couple of days with your mom, but I feel that she's going to pull through. This tube is really going to help her, but there may be an infection that could set in."

"The doctor warned us about that. He said it happens sometimes with older patients. Do you think she might die, Abby?" she asked me, her voice breaking into a sob.

"Elaine, I'm not a medical expert, but I strongly believe in the power of prayer. I believe it can work miracles. I want your entire family to pray for your mother to recover quickly, and every time you visit her, you tell her I said she's not finished yet, that there's a lot more life for her to live, okay?"

"Okay, thank you, Abby. I'll go get my brothers and sisters together right now, and I'll tell them what you said."

I hung up with Elaine and penciled a large *X* in the

middle of my appointment book. The loss of seven appointments was going to hurt my pocketbook something fierce. I sighed and thought about calling people to see if someone wanted to move an appointment up, but faced with an unexpected day off I was leaning hard on the side of playing hooky, no matter how much it cost me.

The question was what I should do with myself. I could go to the mall, or the movies or maybe the bookstore. I thrummed my fingers on my desk as I thought about each of those activities; nothing sounded interesting, and all required money, the thing I'd already realized was in short supply. Absently I picked up a pen and began tapping it on my desk blotter as I tried to decide what to do. Suddenly my intuitive phone began ringing loudly. I answered it and got an image of Perry Mason in my mind's eye. My pen stopped tapping as I followed the train of thought, and as a faint memory connected itself to the image of Perry, I knew I had the answer about what to do with my day.

I tossed the pen to the side and began rummaging through the clutter on my desk looking for a particular piece of scratch paper with a name and phone number scribbled on it. Locating the small paper square, I picked up the phone and dialed. After two rings I was rewarded with a "Hello?"

"Connie?" I asked.

"Yes?"

"Hi, it's Abigail Cooper. So sorry to bother you so early." My face reddened slightly as I realized it was only eight thirty.

"No problem, I was just on my way to work. What's up?"

"I have a question for you. You mentioned something about a lawyer for Allison making the arrangements for her funeral, and I was wondering if you knew his name and possibly his phone number?"

Connie laughed at me. "You still playing private investigator?"

"Yeah, I guess. Abigail Cooper, *Psychic Eye*, at your service," I deadpanned.

She politely giggled at my pun. "Hold on a sec and I'll get you the name," she said and I could hear paper rustling. After a moment she was back on the phone. "Okay, got it. The attorney handling Allison's estate is a guy named Parker Gish. He's in Birmingham on Merrill Street, but the phone number is smudged out—the paper must have gotten wet or something."

"No problem. I'll look him up in the phone book. Oh, by the way," I said, remembering something that had been bothering me. "Connie, do you know why Allison padlocked her sister's bedroom door shut?"

"You've been to the house?"

"Uh, yeah . . . I wanted to see if my intuition could pick up anything for the police investigation. I thought if I went to the house maybe I could hone in on the energy there," I explained, suddenly feeling like I'd been caught doing something I shouldn't have.

There was a slight pause before she spoke again. "I think it's a good thing the police have you on their side, Abby. Now then, back to your question. Allison padlocked Alyssa's door closed when she put the house up for sale. She was afraid that some real estate agent wouldn't respect her wish that no one go into that room. She said that she could still feel Alyssa's spirit in there, and she didn't want anyone to ruin it by walking around and invading that room. I hope you don't get the wrong impression of her, Abby. Allison really was a good person, but Alyssa's death did something to her. It made her do things a rational person might not, you know?"

"I understand—everyone handles grief in their own way. Thanks again for your help. I'll see you Saturday?"

"I'll be there. Good luck."

After hanging up the phone, I reached into the big bottom drawer of my desk and pulled out the phone book. I turned to the business section and located Mr. Gish right away. I called the number wondering if anyone would answer since it wasn't even nine yet.

A crisp female voice answered the line with "Parker Gish Law Offices, this is Jeannette speaking. How may I help you?"

"Uh, hi, Jeannette. My name is Abigail Cooper. I was wondering if I could schedule an appointment with Mr. Gish."

"Are you planning on setting up a trust? Or did you need some estate planning?"

"Estate planning." *Liar, liar, pants on fire . . .*

"I have an appointment for next Tuesday. How will that work for you?"

I hadn't even entertained the thought that Mr. Gish might not be immediately available. "Unfortunately, I'm headed out of town tomorrow morning"—*Liar, liar, pants on fire*—"uh, to Europe, and I'll be gone for the next few months. I really was hoping I could meet Mr. Gish and get the paperwork started. I had to fire my other attorney, you see, and I'm willing to pay extra if he can possibly squeeze me in."

"Hold on a moment," she said and clicked off the line. A few seconds later she was back with a curt question. "Ms. Cooper, whom did you say referred you?"

"Allison Pierce."

"Hold, please," and she put me on hold again. In a few moments, she was back on the line. "Mr. Gish can fit you in at one o'clock this afternoon if that's acceptable."

"Perfect," I said.

"His hourly rate is two hundred and fifty dollars, and he will expect a five-thousand-dollar retainer up front. Please bring your checkbook with you."

My eyes bugged out in spite of myself, as much for the hourly rate as for the rudeness at being told to bring my checkbook. I didn't like Jeannette much, and I wondered what Mr. Gish was like if this was the voice representing him. "No problem," I said breezily.

"We'll see you at one, Ms. Cooper," and she hung up before I'd said my good-byes.

I replaced the receiver and thought about what to do between now and my appointment with Mr. Gish. I really didn't feel like sticking around the office—the temptation to play hooky was just too strong. So now what?

I decided that since I was already devoting part of the day to running down leads on Allison's murderer, it made sense to devote the whole day to the endeavor. I pulled the phone book back toward me and began sifting through the local index. I found the number for the Oakland County Jail and called the operator there. I explained that I wanted to arrange a visit with one of the prisoners and asked about the process. I was told visiting hours were ten to noon and one to three and that all I had to do was come down, submit my name and whom I wished to visit, and if the prisoner was agreeable, we would meet in the visitation room.

A thought occurred to me, and I asked the operator if I could bring the inmate anything, like books or perishable items. She suggested I visit the jail's Web site to check the approved list of items listed there. I thanked the woman, hung up and turned on the computer. In a few minutes I had jotted down several grocery items and made some other notations about acceptable gifts and hurried out the door. I stopped at the grocery store first and purchased peanut butter, jelly, bread, cookies, potato chips, candy bars and pop. I had no idea what Marco liked to eat, but I figured if I was in jail I'd be craving comfort food.

Next I went to the magazine section and picked up every periodical I could find on cars, motorcycles, and hot rods. I avoided the porn section, but got a copy of *MAXIM* just to show I'm a good sport.

When I'd finished my shopping I headed over to the jail, a twenty-minute drive from Royal Oak. When I came to the colossal set of buildings that represent Oakland County's judicial process, I followed the signs that wound through long stretches of side streets, finally locating the jail. I parked my car in one of the monster lots and walked over to the front entrance.

After climbing several stairs, my grocery bags in tow, I entered through a revolving door and onto the Formica floor of a dismal gray interior. There were people lined up one by one in front of a security team and a metal detector. Everyone got the same careful treatment: Empty your pockets, take off your shoes and put all personal items on the conveyor belt; step through the metal detector, hold your arms out and spread your legs while a guard ran a hand-held detector along your body; open your mouth for the guard, then walk forward to put yourself back together. I groaned inwardly—there were half a dozen people in front of me, and this was taking forever.

After what seemed like an eternity, it was my turn and I went through the process without incident. I was directed to another line that was thankfully moving much faster.

Ten minutes later I stood facing a woman behind a

bulletproof plastic barrier who asked for my ID and which prisoner I was there to see.

"Marco Ammarretti," I answered.

She typed something into the computer, waited a few seconds, then gave me a clip-on badge with the word "VISITOR" in large capital letters. I was instructed to wear this at all times while inside the jail, and told that my ID would be returned to me when I turned in the badge. I was to enter through door C, and wait until my name was called. If I had brought any gift items, I was to give them to the guard after my name was called, and he would bring them to the inmate.

I nodded and walked quickly through door C into a rather large waiting room, with plastic chairs and blue industrial carpet. I sat down, wishing I had brought something other than Marco's magazines to read. About twenty minutes later my name was called, and I was led through another door, down a long corridor, and into a large room cut in half by a giant divider. A long set of chairs set close to small countertops was arranged symmetrically along the divider. I was told to wait at one of the countertops, and I was relieved of my grocery bags.

I sat down and stared through a thick pane of Plexiglas that had a small grated window set roughly at mouth level. I waited another ten minutes until every seat was filled, then a door on the other side of the wall opened and prisoners walked in, single file. We were told we had half an hour, and I felt the pressure of making the most of my time.

I spotted Marco right away, and my heart went out to him. He ambled over, the leg shackles making his movements slow and calculated. He took a seat and the smallest hint of a smile reached his eyes.

"Hi, Abigail," he said shyly.

"Hey there," I said, leaning in so he could hear me. "Thanks for the food and magazines. That was really nice of you."

"You're welcome—it was the least I could do. How are you holding up?" I asked, concerned for him in more ways than one.

"Okay, I guess. Just bored for the most part. I've got a decent lawyer, and my bond hearing is next week, so maybe I'll be able to get out of here before the trial."

I nodded encouragingly, suddenly at a loss for words. Marco helped by asking, "So, what did you want?"

"As you know, I'm trying to help the police with their investigation, and I've been to the crime scene." Marco flinched. For him it would always be Alyssa's place, so I moved on quickly. "Anyway, I have a few questions about what I picked up there and I was hoping you could help me out."

"Shoot," he said.

"First of all, do you know what happened to Alyssa's belongings? All of her personal things were missing."

Marco looked sheepishly at the ground, avoiding eye contact. He sighed heavily before answering. "Allison was really angry at Alyssa. I guess we all were. It just took us all by surprise, and Allison really wanted to blame someone, so she picked me. She found out a few days after the funeral that I was named as Alyssa's beneficiary and went nuts. Alyssa left everything to me, except a few small items. I had no idea, but Allison was bent on making a big deal out of it. So she hired a moving company, packed up all of Alyssa's things and had them sent over to my house. I was still really out of it at that point, so I called a couple of storage places, found one close by and had the stuff sent there. I haven't been able to go over there yet to look through it all—I don't know if I ever will."

"Did you know that Alyssa had named you her beneficiary?"

"I had no idea until her lawyer called me. It wouldn't have mattered to me one way or the other, though. I make a decent living, own my home, my car is paid for, and I've been socking away money in my 401(k) since I was twenty-one. It wasn't her money that I was interested in. I knew she and her sister had some, but I never knew how much. I haven't even claimed the dough yet, Abby," he said. His eyes pleaded with me to believe him. My lie detector hadn't gone off once since we'd sat down, so I was inclined to trust what he was saying. I nodded encouragingly and he continued. "Alyssa was my whole world. I didn't care if she was flat broke. I loved her—." His voice broke off, and he turned his head to one side, raising both cuffed hands to swipe a tear.

I gave him a moment to collect himself, then asked, "Can you tell me anything about Alyssa's behavior right before she passed away? Did anything seem out of sorts? Was there anything that might have warned you guys that she was leaning toward taking her life?"

Marco shut his eyes tightly and struggled with something, I wasn't sure what. In a barely audible voice he said, "Maybe, yeah . . ." That surprised me. I was so convinced that Alyssa hadn't killed herself that I wanted him to say there'd been no sign, nothing out of the ordinary, confirming my belief that she hadn't done it.

"Like what?" I asked gently.

"About two weeks before she did it, she was different, not quite heself. It was little things, like we'd go out and she'd just cling to me, you know? We usually held hands, but she started holding my entire arm with both hands, and she didn't let me out of her sight. Like this one night we went to a movie, and afterward I had to go to the restroom and she begged me to hold it until we got home. She wouldn't let me out of her sight. And then she stopped wanting to go out. We had all this stuff planned leading up to the wedding, and she didn't want to do any of it. She just wanted to stay home. I also noticed that she wasn't sleeping much. I tried to talk to her about it, but she kept telling me nothing was wrong. I figured the whole thing was just pre-wedding jitters, but apparently it was a lot more."

"What happened the day she died?" I asked as I pondered the change in Alyssa's behavior.

Marco took a deep breath and said, "I was at work and I called her at lunchtime. She said she wasn't feeling well and was going to take a nap. I called her a couple hours later, but she didn't answer. Something didn't feel right, so I left work early and headed over to her house—that's when I found her." He reached up to wipe another tear away.

I figured I should ease up about Alyssa if I wanted Marco to keep talking to me. He was kindly indulging me, but pretty soon I would push too hard on this topic and he might bolt. "So tell me about Allison," I said. You had dinner with her the night she died—what brought that on?"

He shook his head a little, "I'm not really sure. A couple of days before she was killed she called me out of the blue and apologized for acting the way she did at Alyssa's funeral. She also said she was sorry about the movers showing up on my doorstep and asked me if I still had any of Alyssa's belongings. I told her that they were at the storage company, gave her the pass code to the front gate and told her that I'd already given her name to the manager. I figured one day she'd regret sending away all of Alyssa's stuff, so I'd made sure she would have access whenever she was ready. She thanked me, and then I didn't hear from her again until the night before she died.

"I was surprised when she called and even more so when she asked if I was free for dinner the following evening. I was suspicious since it was such an about-face, you know? But I met her for dinner anyway and all she could talk about was you—that's how I knew who you were when you came to see me at the dealership. She said she had proof that Alyssa didn't kill herself and she wanted me to hear it, but the whole thing was freaking me out. I told her I couldn't handle what she was saying, and then I left. I know that was really rude of me, but she looked so much like Alyssa, and seeing her there, talking this crazy talk, I just couldn't handle it, so I left."

Again, my lie detector remained silent. He was telling the truth, "So what did you do between the time you left the restaurant and the time you got home?" I needed to know this one last piece of the puzzle.

"I was really upset when I left the restaurant. I missed Alyssa so much right then, so I went around to all of our favorite places. I drove to our favorite restaurant, then to the movie theater, and the park— a long trip down memory lane. I wanted to connect with her. So that's where I was, and by the time I got home it was midnight, and I bumped into my neighbor. I guess he saw how upset I was, and so now I'm in here."

We looked at each other through the Plexiglas for a long moment. We both knew he didn't belong here, and I hesitated before speaking again, unsure I could deliver on the promise I was about to make. Finally I worked up the nerve and said, "Marco, I believe you.

And somehow, some way, I'm going to get you out of here."

At that moment a buzzer sounded and several guards stepped forward from behind the inmates, indicating that visiting time was over. As Marco stood up, I thought of something and asked quickly, "Marco, what's the name of the storage place?"

"Millpond Storage," he answered. "Over on Franklin by Northwestern Highway."

But before I could ask anything else, he'd been shuffled away.

At twelve forty-five I was winding down Old Woodward Avenue in downtown Birmingham. Birmingham is a town I'm uncomfortably familiar with. I grew up here with my parents and went to school here.

The small city borders Royal Oak, but the energy and texture here is woven of completely different thread. Snooty is the only acceptable attitude in Birmingham, an enclave of wealth that hugs its larger, less opulent neighbor to the south with all the warmth of an evil stepmother.

In Birmingham, the women are maintained, the men are greedily lustful, and the children are named after high-end automobiles. You are just as likely to run into a Bentley, Mercedes, Porsche, and Lexus walking on the sidewalk as you are cruising the downtown streets.

I had no love for the town as most of my memories were uncomfortable ones of being ostracized for my gifts and being looked askance at for my fashion tastes. I had never fit in here and never wanted to.

So now I was driving the main strip through downtown, with an ever-increasing sneer on my face as people glanced sideways at my frugal and outdated choice of transportation. I passed small shops carrying fine china, soft linens, couture fashions, and gourmet foods that I couldn't afford.

I turned left onto Merrill and miraculously found a parking space with a little time left on the meter. I got out, poked another buck fifty into the meter, which netted me all of one hour, and hurried to the address I'd scribbled on my bit of paper. I walked into a two-story office building and up a marble staircase, passing expensive oil paintings with gilded frames.

Pushing through the wooden door of suite number two, I entered a richly decorated lobby, with cranberry wallpaper, plush leather love seats, glossy end tables and expensive magazines. I walked forward to the receptionist who sat behind a half wall, eyeing me expectantly. "Miss Cooper?" she asked.

"Jeannette?" I answered.

"Mr. Gish will see you in just a moment. Please take a seat."

Even though her words were polite, I could feel the ice falling from her like so much arctic wind. I sat down obediently and waited. Within five minutes I was told to come through the doorway, and Jeannette led me down a short hallway to a magnificent office, where a giant bear of a man stepped around his desk to greet me with outstretched hand.

Parker Gish was at least six five, with tanned olive skin, dark brown eyes and salt-and-pepper hair. He wore a custom-made suit of fine black silk and a tie that looked like it had been woven out of gold. His legs were long, his shoes were shined and his mouth held itself in a permanent grin. I liked him immediately.

"Miss Cooper, it's nice to meet you," he said.

"Thank you for seeing me, Mr. Gish," I said as my hand was swallowed by his.

"Please, call me Parker," he said and gestured toward a leather chair.

As I sat down, I took in his office. The wall behind Parker was one gigantic window of tinted glass, lending a voyeuristic aspect to the comings and goings of the downtown area. Parker's desk was a massive block of carved wood, with small leaves and berries expertly trimming the sides and corners. Expensive oil paintings hung in stylish groupings along one of the deep navy blue walls. To the right of the paintings was an enormous bookcase that housed row upon row of legal reference texts.

I could feel the richness of the carpet tickling my toes over the edge of my sandals, and I seriously considered hiring Parker for something just so I could visit this office.

Parker took his seat and pulled out a legal pad, preparing for our meeting. I felt a wave of guilt as I realized I'd have to come clean with this man, and in a flash of uncertainty I wondered what his reaction would be. "So, Miss Cooper, you knew Allison Pierce?"

"Please, call me Abby. And actually, I did know Allison but not well. In fact, that's really why I'm here today."

"Yes?" he said expectantly.

"You see . . . uh . . . the truth of the matter is that I really don't need your assistance with an estate," I said, my nervousness making me stammer out my words.

"I see," he said, holding that mocking grin for my benefit.

"Allison Pierce was also a client of mine. I'm a psychic intuitive."

I waited for him to laugh or throw me out of his office, but to my surprise he simply said, "Yes. Allison mentioned you."

"I'm sorry? She mentioned me?"

"Yes. I got a call from her about a week before she died, a week or so after her visit to you and she was very excited about what you'd told her. She was a real fan of yours," he said kindly.

That sentence cut me like a knife. Allison had spoken nicely about me to a lot of people, and I had been awful to her. My guilt was back, flogging my ego with self-recrimination. "Yes, I've heard that from a few other people," I said and looked down at my hands.

Obviously confused by my sudden mood change, Parker offered, "My wife reads her horoscope every day. It's been part of her morning ritual for years now, and she swears by it."

I smiled at that. This man had no idea what I was about but his ignorance on the topic was somehow innocent and sweet, not offensive. "Anyway, as I was saying, the police have asked me to offer them any assistance I can in apprehending Allison's killer, and I was wondering if I could ask you a few questions about Allison."

"This is about the cassette tape, isn't it?"

"How did you know about that?"

"I talked to the police a week ago. They filled me in on the details and pumped me for information. I'm not sure what else I can tell you. Besides, I thought they already arrested a suspect. Marco Ammarretti, I believe, has been charged with her death. Correct?"

Parker Gish was a shrewd poker player. His manner was warm, even fuzzy, but behind that beguiling facade turned the gears of a very keen mind. I had no doubt he was worth every penny of his two hundred fifty an hour. "Yes, Marco's been arrested," I said, "but I'm coming at this from a different angle."

"You don't think he did it."

"No, I don't."

Parker looked at me intently for a minute, no doubt assessing my mental acumen. I was pretty sure he didn't believe in psychic phenomena but was perhaps that rare individual who suspends judgment until he's investigated it fully for himself. Finally his grin widened and he said, "To be honest Abby, I don't believe he did it either."

This surprised me and I asked, "Really? Why?"

"I met Marco at Alyssa's funeral. That man was devastated. I know Allison blamed him for Alyssa's passing, but then something odd happened," he said.

"What?" I asked.

"Allison was originally trying to contest her sister's will. She didn't want Marco to have anything, and she called me to find out how to go about doing that. I advised her against it, but she was insistent. I was stuck in the middle, as both girls were my clients, and I represented them in two different ways. The bulk of their money was held in the trust set up by their parents, and as executor of the trust I oversaw this for both of them. However, they had each drawn up separate last will and testaments, and these I administered individually.

"If Allison wanted to contest Alyssa's will she was going to have to find a different attorney to do it because my interests were intermixed. About a week before she was killed, Allison called me and said that she no longer wished to fight Alyssa's will, that she was happy Marco would be taken care of. Then she started talking about you, and how, at first, she thought you were talking about Marco but then she realized you were talking about someone else. I'll admit that I didn't have a clue what she was talking about, and I was worried that she might have bigger psychological issues than just getting over the loss of her sister. I remember making a suggestion that she try and get some counseling to help her get through her grief, but she didn't want to hear it and honestly that was the extent of our conversation."

"And you told this to the police?" I asked, annoyed that Dutch hadn't filled me in on this little tidbit.

"Yes, of course."

I took a deep breath and mentally counted to ten. "Are you all right?" Parker asked.

"Fine," I said, recovering. "Sorry, just got distracted for a moment. Now can you tell me a little bit about Alyssa and Allison's background? Like how long you had represented them, and anything about their past that comes to mind, as long as it doesn't interfere with your attorney client privilege here of course," I added.

Parker waved his hand like he was shooing a fly. "Privilege is waived once the client has died, and since I don't represent Mr. Ammarretti, I can talk freely about the girls' estate. Let's see," he said rubbing his chin and thinking back, "The girls came to me about six years ago. They had just come up from Ohio, and they were living at a hotel at the time."

"A hotel?"

"Yes. I know it sounds strange, but they said they didn't want to rent; they wanted to find the right home and purchase it for cash. Their parents' trust had been set up by an attorney in Cleveland, and I took over the estate. Within a week or two they found the house they owned up until their deaths, and I worked with the real estate agent to purchase it for them. The girls were very private about all their financial transactions. They insisted on keeping the house in the name of their parents' trust, which had an odd name of its own."

"Oh?" I asked, curiously.

"Yes, the girls' parents had formed the trust fund years earlier and named it after the college where they met. The 'Cornell Trust' was the official name for the girls' financial holdings."

"Hmmm," I said, my mind spinning with this new revelation.

Parker nodded and continued, "The girls also asked me to administer the care of any property-related financial obligations, so I was the one who made sure that their property taxes, insurance and water bills got paid. I also set up auto pays for their utilities and made sure they had a weekly cash allowance."

Something struck me about that and I asked, "You mean you took care of all their bills?"

"Neither girl seemed very interested in keeping track of their accounts, so yes, for a fee I did it for them."

"So let me get this straight. The house wasn't technically in their names."

"Correct. It was in the name of the trust."

"And no bills were in their names," I said, getting excited.

"Correct—also in the name of the trust."

"Did they have any checking or savings accounts?"

"Each girl had a debit card that was attached to the liquid cash of the trust."

"Didn't that strike you as odd?" I asked.

"What?" asked Parker, not following me.

"These two sisters move up from Ohio, live in a hotel, buy a house that's not in their name, hide all their financial records behind the name of their parents' trust and avoid any public trace of themselves for six years."

Parker looked at me curiously. "You may be on to something, Abby. I remember Allison telling me once that she needed to go to Ohio for a quick visit. She said she needed to check on some property her parents owned and to renew her driver's license. I thought it was very odd indeed that Allison wanted to retain her Ohio driver's license, but she's my client, and I have a few others who are a little on the eccentric side."

"Very weird, but then Allison had a job, right? So she would have had some W-2's in her name."

Parker gave me an odd look, then said, "Actually, no."

"No?"

"She worked part-time at the Art Institute as an instructor, but she wouldn't let them pay her. She told them she didn't need the IRS headache every year. They never paid her a dime."

"So as far as you know, there were no public records that would place the girls in Michigan at all," I said, amazed that they had taken such measures to hide any trace of themselves.

"Just one," Parker said, looking at me with meaning. "Alyssa's application for her marriage license last May."

Cold chills rippled down my backbone, making me shudder. It made sense. The girls had been on the run. They had successfully hidden from someone for six years, and then Alyssa thought she was in the clear and applied for a marriage license.

Parker seemed to have the same thought, as his smile faded for the first time since meeting me. "You will be careful, Abby, won't you?" he asked unexpectedly.

"Yes, of course," I said quickly. "I think I've taken enough of your time, Parker. Thank you so much for all your assistance."

"You're welcome. Will we see you on Saturday?"

"Yes," I said, as I stood. "I'll be there—oh, and by the way," I went on as a thought and an image flashed in my head, "Maui or Kauai?"

"Pardon me?" he asked, startled.

"Hawaii. Are you going to Maui or Kauai in November?"

Parker looked at me with eyebrows lowered and a disbelieving smirk on his face. "Uh, both," he answered, sounding slightly unsure.

"It's a surprise for your wife, isn't it?"

"Have you been talking to my secretary?" he asked, trying to figure out how I'd gotten my info.

"Jeannette? I'd have better luck getting blood from a turnip." I said, then added quickly, "Your wife is going to love it. It's for something special, isn't it, some big anniversary?"

"The big three-oh," he said as he shook my hand, looking a little awed.

"When you look at time-shares, go for the one on Kauai with the white stucco and brown shutters. You can trust that one will be a good deal. Also you need to see a doctor about your knee. The arthritis is really starting to set in, and you shouldn't have to grin and bear it—that's what corrective surgery is for."

"My doctor has been pushing for arthroscopy, but I've been avoiding it," Parker admitted.

"Really? My feeling is that very soon you're not going to have a choice in the matter. You need to be careful of lifting something heavy. You'll be tempted soon to overexert yourself, but you need to say no. If you don't you'll be heading to the operating table sooner than you think.

"And, hey, congratulations to your daughter on making it into medical school. When does she start?"

Parker's jaw had dropped wide open, and he stared at me with wide, disbelieving eyes. "Next month."

"She'll do very well. And she's in love with one of her classmates—there's a wedding proposal for her in the very near future. You should start saving now because it's going to be a really big wedding." I smiled and patted him on the arm.

Parker laughed in spite of himself and walked me out to the lobby with his heavy hand resting fondly on my shoulder. "Abby, you're pretty unbelievable. Wait until I tell my wife. Say, do you have a card? She'd love to see you."

"Sure," I said, digging into my purse and retrieving a business card, "but send her to me after you go to Hawaii. I wouldn't want to spill the beans and spoil the surprise."

"Somehow I think she already suspects. Nothing gets by my wife. Prime reason I married her—she's the only one who can keep me in line."

"I wish you many more happy years together. And thank you again," I said, waving at him as I left the office.

As I drove home I thought about what I'd discovered that afternoon. I now knew that Allison hadn't provoked Marco into killing her. In fact now I believed even more strongly that he hadn't been responsible for either girl's death. It was clear to me that the sisters were on the run from something or someone in Ohio. They'd kept an exceptionally low profile, hiding away in Royal Oak under the umbrella of their parents' trust, but whoever they'd been hiding from had found them.

What I couldn't quite figure out was why, if both girls were in hiding, Alyssa had been killed first. Why not do both of them in at the same time? Why wait months, then brutally kill off the other sister without even trying to make it look like an accident? Why such a dramatic difference in the manner and scope of their deaths? What had these girls done to provoke such revenge, and who was it that had stalked them so stealthily for six long years?

For the rest of the day, these questions swirled in my head like a tidal pool sucking me down into a well of frustration and confusion, egging me to dig deeper and get to the truth.

Chapter Nine

Friday morning I finished with my eleven o'clock client early, so I went downstairs to get the mail before heading out to lunch. I hadn't been to the mailbox all week, a chore I usually found easy to forget, and as I turned my key in the little keyhole I knew immediately that I'd have to tip the mailman extra big come Christmas. The mail had indeed piled up, and the mailman had done his best to cram the letters, flyers, junk mail and a large manila envelope into the tiny compartment, causing everything to be squished and wrinkled. I pulled out the mess and then closed the metal door with a sigh. As I straightened out the squished envelopes as best I could, I vowed for the hundredth time to check my mailbox more regularly.

Killing two birds with one stone, I also stopped by to drop off the rent check for next month. While I was there I chatted for a while with Yvonne, the building manager. She told me she was interested in another reading—I'd read her a few months previously—and I told her I'd call her with the first available.

I walked back to my office, flipping through the

flyers, so when I finally glanced up I was startled to see a woman's head poking out of my suite and looking up and down the hallway.

I quickly realized it was Maggie, the massage therapist who had taken over Theresa's old office. I rarely saw her so hadn't recognized her at first. "Hi, Maggie! Long time no see. What are you doing here so early?"

"Oh! Hi, Abby. I thought you were around. I got here and found the door unlocked but you weren't here. I was setting up my room for a client who's flying to Munich tonight and simply *must* have a massage before he gets on the plane. As a favor I booked him at noon."

"You looking for him now?" I asked, referring to her rubbernecking the hallway.

"Well, it's weird. I was setting up my room when I thought I heard someone in the office. I figured it was you, so I came out to say hi, but no one was there. I was just looking to see who'd come in."

The hair on the back of my neck stood straight up on end and I felt a chill creep its way down my spine. Moving quickly past Maggie I walked into the suite, my senses on high alert. I had goose bumps on the full length of my arms, and I felt the distinct imprint of the intruder's energy. That same sense of malicious intent was present in the air, and on wobbly knees I followed it like an aroma through the lobby and into my inner office. I scanned my desk for signs of foul play but saw nothing missing. Maggie was watching my wide-eyed expression closely, alarm also marking her features.

"Abby?" she asked. "What is it?"

I glanced up at her, and it suddenly dawned on me that I hadn't told her anything about what was going on. What if whoever was stalking me had mistaken Maggie for me? I looked at her directly, doing a quick mental comparison. Maggie was tall, close to five eleven, with short wavy auburn hair and vivid sea-blue eyes. We didn't resemble each other physically, but then again I didn't know if Allison's killer even knew what I looked like. I breathed a sigh of relief that nothing had happened to her.

"Maggie, listen to me," I said, sitting down in the chair behind the desk. "You need to pull up a seat, because I have to tell you some things that are a little scary. We both need to be a lot more careful when we're in this office." She came over and sat down immediately. I had her full attention. I filled her in on everything that had happened since the night of Allison's murder, and as I told my story, I could see the fear creep into her eyes.

"So what do we do?" she asked, her voice soft.

"For starters, we have to be really careful about who we let into this office. If you can, work only with clients you know, not anyone new. The suite should always be locked, and we should both be careful when we go out to eat or to the restroom. I think you should always have Stu walk you to your car at night. I'll call the building manager and arrange it." Maggie was nodding at me with large, unblinking eyes.

"Why do you think someone's after you?"

"I'm not sure, but I think this guy may think I know more than I actually do. I'm guessing that he believes I can identify him or something."

"Can you?"

"I don't know. I've never tried that before and it's uncharted territory for me. My hope is that he will keep taking chances and that we'll eventually get to him."

"Before he gets to you, you mean," she said, finishing the thought that had been in my own head. I smiled bravely at her and shrugged my shoulders.

Maggie looked at her shoes for a moment, then asked the question we were both thinking. "Do you think he was in here just now?"

I looked at her, and I'm sure my eyes were just as large and afraid as hers. "Well, my intuition says if it wasn't him, it wasn't anyone I'd like to have back," I said.

"Oh," she said, wishing, I'm sure, that I'd said something different. "You know what? I think I'm going to cancel all my appointments for the next week or so. I'm due for a vacation, and it seems like this would be a good time to take it. What do you think?"

"I think that's a good idea, Maggie."

Later, after my last client had gone, I went into the office to make some phone calls and set up appointments. My first call was to Yvonne. I didn't necessarily want to alarm her, but I thought it would be a good idea to have Stu keep a close watch on this section of the building.

"Hey, Yvonne," I said when she answered.

"Hi, Abby. You ready to pencil me in?"

I had forgotten that she wanted to schedule an appointment but recovered quickly. "Absolutely. Let me just get my book over here," I said. However as I reached for it I noticed something peculiar. I always leave my appointment book open, turned to the current date and perched on the far left corner of the desk, so I can quickly check my schedule throughout the day. But now my book was closed and pushed over to the far right corner. I thought back through the day, wondering when I could have inadvertently done that. No memory came to mind and suddenly the goose bumps were back on duty.

"Abby? You still there?" Yvonne asked.

"Uh, yes . . . yes, I am, Yvonne," I said quickly. I

opened my appointment book and flipped to the back section, marking her in for the next available, three and a half months from now in November. Then I concocted a story about a client I'd had who struck me as a little unbalanced and was giving me some trouble. I asked if Stu could keep a close eye on this end of the building.

"Of course, Abby, I'll let him know tonight when he comes in at seven. Can you tell me what this client looks like?"

I thought for a moment and remembered standing inside Allison's house, and without pause said, "He's male, a little short, probably around five six or five seven with dark brown hair and brown eyes. He may be wearing clothes that are a little oversized too."

"I'll pass that along to Stu."

"Thanks, Yvonne." We disconnected and I turned back to my appointment book, wondering what someone could have wanted with it. I flipped through all of the remaining pages and found no notations or markings from anyone but me. It was all my handwriting. Shrugging, I turned back to the task at hand and returned all the voice mails that had collected since the day before, scheduling everyone I could get hold of. I then flipped the pages to Saturday, to see who I had coming in.

Since Allison's funeral was in the morning, I'd had to reschedule only a few clients. I set the appointment book carefully in the far left corner and turned my attention to the mail. Phone bill, electric bill, junk mail, junk mail, flyer, coupon booklet and a manila envelope addressed to me with no return address. I turned the envelope over but saw nothing unusual. Curious, I opened the flap and pulled out the contents—then sucked in a breath of shock and horror. Spilling out onto my desktop were several eight-by-ten glossies of yours truly, all taken from a few yards away.

There was one of me at the grocery store, one walking Eggy, another of me out with Dirk, yet another of me talking with Marco at the dealership. My hands shook as I pawed through each one, a feeling of vulnerability like I'd never known creeping down my backbone. Underneath the photos was a folded piece of paper with glued-on letters cut out from magazines and newspapers that read:

BACK OFF OR YOU'RE NEXT!!

That was all I needed. I pulled my appointment book close again and began dialing.

An hour later I'd rearranged my schedule and booked a flight to Boston. I was getting out of Dodge for a few days. I might be a yellow-belly, but at least I'd be a breathing yellow-belly. I called my sister and asked her if her offer for a visit was still open.

"Of course it is. What's happened, Abby?"

There was no way I wanted another visit from the Howler Monkey, so I simply said, "Nothing. I just had an opening in my schedule and thought I'd come visit you for a long weekend. I have Allison's funeral tomorrow, but I can catch a flight out right after that and stay until Tuesday afternoon."

"That sounds terrific! I'll take Monday off, and we can spend some quality time together."

We made arrangements for her to pick me up at the airport and then disconnected.

After we hung up I put in a call to Dutch. I figured he should know about the photos. I got his voice mail, so I left a message that I would try him again later. I felt weary now that my adrenaline high was wearing off.

I looked at my watch and noticed it was five thirty; not wanting to get caught here in the building alone, I grabbed my purse and beat a fast path out of there.

I drove home with an eye on the rearview mirror, again taking side streets. Once I reached my house, I rushed inside and bolted the door immediately. I checked all the windows and punched in the alarm code, carrying the cordless phone with me as I walked from room to room. I finished the night by tidying up the house, tending to Eggy and packing my suitcase. I had carried the photos home, intending to call Dutch again and hand them over to him, but then time got away from me and before I knew it the clock read midnight. Wearily I climbed into bed and fell asleep, a chair butted up against my bedroom door and the phone tucked under my pillow. Even with the alarm on I still felt vulnerable, but the chair and readily available phone at least allowed me to fall asleep.

Allison's funeral was all the more depressing because it was so sparsely attended. Other than Connie, Parker, his elegant wife, Doreen, and a few students from Allison's pottery class, there were only a handful of people. I took my place in the pew next to Connie and listened to a minister who'd barely known Allison speak about a woman in the sketchiest of phrases. His speech was evasive and lacked color, so he kept it short and general, leaving those few of us in attendance even more disheartened by her loss.

"She's with her Creator," he said. "We should celebrate her venture back to His loving embrace and rejoice that she has been returned Home."

I know the man tried his best, but his eulogy fell flat. It was like he was speaking about an infant who'd been alive only a few minutes, not long enough to dot the eulogy with the color of a lifetime of details. He referred to her love of pottery, plants and nature, and that was about all he could say. I wondered what else she'd done with her time on earth. Surely there must have been love, laughter, Monopoly, movies, boyfriends and . . . well, *life* filling up her thirty-two years. But then again, maybe there hadn't been.

Perhaps Allison had always been in the shadow of her younger, more vibrant sister. Maybe she'd always lived vicariously through Alyssa, and maybe, just maybe, when that was gone she had nothing but emptiness to fill up her days and nights.

There was a part of me that wondered if perhaps Allison discovered the truth about her sister's death, and in a self-destructive, suicidal move taunted the killer and invited her own sad ending. How ironic if the truth was the opposite of what everyone believed. What if Alyssa was the one who had been murdered, and Allison, heartbroken and lost, had thrown caution aside and for all intents and purposes committed suicide by setting herself up for certain death.

I shuddered in the church as these thoughts flitted through my head. Melancholy settled over me like dust, dulling the otherwise beautiful day.

The service carried over to the cemetery but I declined to go, saying good-bye to Connie, Parker and his wife. I walked quickly to my car, and once inside I watched Parker and the other pallbearers load Allison's casket into the waiting hearse. I couldn't help but scowl as I saw him heft a weight he had no business trying to carry, then watched as he stepped away limping, his knee clearly strained. Some people never listen.

*   *   *

A few hours later, with Eggy safely tucked away at the boarding kennel, I set the alarm and locked the front door, so I could wait for the airport shuttle out on the front walkway. I'd gotten a voice mail from Dave when I returned from the funeral. His shoulder was still bothering him, so he was going to take a few days to rest it but he'd be back on Tuesday morning. I thought about calling him and telling him I'd be in Boston, but he had a key and knew the alarm code, so I just left him a quick note tacked to the fridge that I was going away, and I'd see him Tuesday afternoon.

Dutch had also returned my call, but I didn't think I had time to call, explain the photos, and finish packing in time to make my flight, so I decided to fill him in the moment I got back from my sister's. If I had time before my flight, I'd call him from the airport.

As I stepped out onto the cement walkway I saw Mary Lou walking clumsily toward me, her arms loaded with two trays of flowers and several gardening tools. Leaving my suitcase, I rushed over to help her. "Got a full load there, I see," I said, taking the tools and one flat of flowers from her.

"Thanks. Yeah, we finished with this property in Birmingham and we had a lot left over. I thought they'd be perfect around your elm tree."

I had a huge elm tree in my backyard that offered luxurious shade in the summertime and, I imagined, brilliant color come fall. I pictured the flowers Mary Lou carried circling the elm and smiled at my neighbor. "I think they'll look fabulous. Thanks Mary Lou."

"Where you off to?" she asked, pointing to my luggage as she placed one of the flats on my front steps.

"Boston for a few days. Something's telling me to get out of Dodge."

"Oh?"

"Long story."

Just then the shuttle pulled up and I said, "Oops, that's me. Do you want me to help you get these into the backyard?"

"Naw, go on ahead. Just leave them on the step there and I'll get 'em in a minute. When are you coming back?"

"Tuesday. Can I square up with you then?" I asked, indicating the flowers I was setting down.

"Sure. I'll see you then," she said. *Liar, liar, pants on fire . . .*

I paused for a moment, wondering why my lie detector had gone off. Usually it didn't flash for the little stuff. Weird.

The shuttle driver beeped his horn, and I jumped into motion, grabbing my suitcase and waving goodbye to Mary Lou. As I took my seat, I looked back at my house and saw her heading for the backyard. My intuitive phone began to ring loudly, and I almost picked it up, but at that moment the man sitting next to me asked, "Where you headed?" So I set the phone aside, focusing instead on the good-looking guy in business attire. It would be the last time I ignored my intuitive phone for a very long time.

Chapter Ten

Cat lives in a suburb of Boston called Andover. It is an upscale community where modest million-dollar homes are built to appear smaller than they actually are. Most of the streets here wind through narrow hills, giving architects the opportunity to build houses that, from the street, appear to be modest-sized ranches but that, viewed from the side and back, fall gently away down low, sloping hills, accommodating great rooms, studies, gourmet kitchens and other hidden treasures in the backyard. The neighborhood is all about understatement.

Cat's house, of course, is the exception. There is nothing understated about it. Her house is enormous—tasteful, but *enormous* nonetheless. I smiled as we pulled into the large circular drive of "Chez Cat," as I had come to call it.

Chez Cat is a three-story colonial with a smaller wing on each side of the main house balancing the midsection, probably to keep it from toppling over. The house is complete with his and her twin offices, a weight room, a game room, a monstrous family room, and a gourmet kitchen. There are eight bathrooms scattered throughout the house. There are five bedrooms on the second floor and six on the third floor, making eleven total.

The master suite, one of the largest rooms in the house, features a sunken tub big enough for six and a seating area that rivals my living room. I'm sure my sister's walk-in closet is bigger than my bedroom.

In keeping with the gargantuan theme, the backyard is also immense, sporting swimming pool, tennis court, putting green and at least two acres of rolling gardens, artistic shrubbery and flower beds. To keep up appearances, Cat staffs a full-time nanny, housekeeper, gardener, and personal assistant. I figure being Catherine Cooper-Masters is probably exhausting, and she needs all the help she can get.

Many years ago, my sister came up with a brilliant marketing idea. It was one of those obvious things that everyone else in the industry had overlooked and Cat had managed to develop without all the restrictions of established competition. She began her marketing company with borrowed funds, heavy on the chutzpah, and turned a substantial profit within a short period of time. Within two years she had sold off most of her company to a larger conglomerate for more cash than I could count, but had retained the management rights. She was still holding court at a very large firm in downtown Boston.

Cat moved her family to Andover shortly after the construction of her dream home. I'm told that a small three-bedroom ranch once stood where the east wing of Cat's house now rests, but those rumors have yet to be substantiated.

As my brother-in-law removed my luggage from the back of the SUV, I stood in the driveway and looked up in awe. My sister came to my side and said, "I had it repainted since the last time you were here. Taupe is such a better color with this landscape, don't you think?"

I nodded and noticed for the first time that yes, indeed, Cat's house was now a more muted color. I stepped back and took in the structure and marveled again at the size of the place. It had to be nine thousand square feet if it was an inch, and it never ceased to amaze me that my sister owned this home.

Growing up, Cat and I had always lived in modest comfort. Our parents did well, and our homes were in upper-middle-class neighborhoods. I could only imagine the look that must have appeared on my parents' faces when they got their first peek at Chez Cat. They lived to climb the social ladder, and seeing my sister wrap herself in such opulence must have made them salivate with envy.

"You coming in, Abby?" she said, looking back at me as I continued to stare up at the house.

"Right behind you," I said, snapping out of my daydream. We walked in and were met by my four-year-old twin nephews, Matt and Mike. "Auntieeee! Auntieeee!" they shouted as they came crashing into my legs.

"Hey, little men! How are you?" I asked, stooping low to hug them. They're generally great kids—just as long as they're not on "seek and destroy" missions.

"M&M let Auntie go upstairs and get settled. You can visit with her later, all right?" my sister said, calling to my nephews by their conjoined nicknames.

M&M ignored her. Not an easy feat, mind you, but the twins had mastered it very quickly. They continued to hug me, shower me with questions, and use my body as a jungle gym. My sister withstood this blatant disregard for her authority for all of ten minutes before bringing in the heavy guns. "Sharon!" she called to the boys' nanny. "Can you please rescue my sister?"

A minute later I was relieved of my nephews and free to get settled upstairs. I walked heavily up the staircase, suddenly cognizant of how tired I felt. Traveling really takes it out of you.

My brother-in-law had already carried my luggage up for me, and when I entered the room I saw it sitting on a hope chest at the foot of the bed. Wearily I sat down and looked around the room, remembering its subtle decor.

The room itself was on the second floor toward the back of the house, and two of the windows overlooked the gardens below. It was relatively quiet, as it was one of the rooms closest to the west wing, which housed Cat's and Tommy's private offices. When I sat on the bed I also had a nice view of the pool. The walls were painted a very pale Peabody blue, with cream-colored bedspread, a French canopy and beechwood furniture. Everything was soft, elegant and finished. No construction to trip over, no ugly gray walls to stare at. I sighed and lay back on the bed for a minute as dusk descended on Boston, then closed my eyes and breathed deeply, feeling relaxed for the first time in ages.

Our mother had never been very interested in her children, and my father had traveled so much that we barely spent any time with him. Cat and I had been left to nurture and parent each other and as a result, had developed a bond much closer than most siblings. Even now we still took turns being the mother, except that Cat was far more serious about the role than I was. I attributed this to the fact that she was three years older and already had two kids of her own. She was naturally more inclined to offer advice, whether I needed it or not. Since I typically needed it, this tended to work out well.

I was lying there, letting the calm seep into my bones, when I heard footsteps approach from the hallway and enter the bedroom.

"Yes?" I said, not opening my eyes.

"Are you hungry?" Cat said.

"I could eat," I replied, opening one eye.

"Great because I had Marie whip you up a little dinner, and we can go over the weekend itinerary while you eat."

I stifled a groan. "I'll be right down." Cat retreated back down the hallway and I rubbed my tired eyes. Ugh, and I'd thought I was going to get a chance to relax.

My sister had the energy of a platoon of Green Berets. I had no idea where she got it from. I myself was typically content to sleep in and imitate moss on my days off. Cat also had the organizational skills of the Pentagon. She was an efficiency maven. She ran her entire day based on the second hand of her watch. In fact, her nickname was rumored to be Tick-tock. And I should know—I started the rumor.

Cat's wedding was a perfect example. Instead of having a wedding rehearsal *day*, she'd opted for a wedding rehearsal *week*. She came to every practice session loaded with index cards, measuring tape, a stopwatch, a whistle and, that essential necessity of every bride-to-be—a bullhorn. The rest of us brought our own individual bottles of Maalox.

Of course, on the day of the blessed event we were rewarded with rave reviews. Most attendees agreed that we, the bridal party, had performed our duties with the showmanship and professionalism of a Broadway cast.

Another great example was when Cat decided to take the twins to Disney World and invited me along. I received a seven-page itinerary for a three-day vacation via e-mail, then by registered post, plus two follow-up phone calls to ensure that I had indeed received the itinerary.

At Disney World, my sister actually timed the Dumbo ride. The five of us could be seen jogging single file through the park, grabbing fast passes and jousting for stroller space. It was the most exhausting vacation of my life.

Groaning again, I rolled over and got up. I looked at my luggage, still packed, and knew I had two choices. I could unpack it now, or leave it and just root around in the suitcase all weekend. The latter would drive my sister batty. I decided to wait until the itinerary unveiling before deciding which way to go.

I found Cat in the kitchen, making yellow highlighter streaks across several sheets of paper. Uh-oh.

"There you are! I was just making some quick notes for you here. I have it all planned out . . ."

Suddenly my intuitive phone began ringing. This happened a lot with Cat. I got all sorts of messages for her, mostly because she never stood still long enough for her own intuition to catch up to her. "Hold that thought, Cat. I'm getting something," I said and turned my head slightly—a habit I'd formed early in my development. When I was concentrating on getting a message, I liked to turn my head to the right and slightly down.

Seeing me cock my head, Cat bolted from her chair and sprinted up the stairs. She returned not even a minute later, holding a weathered notebook with ABBY'S PREDICTIONS neatly labeled across the front. "I'm ready!" she said breathlessly as she took her seat and held her pen poised over the paper.

"What's this big dinner party you're hosting? It's to celebrate something special? A birthday or something?"

"Yes!" Cat said, nodding her head vigorously. "Helen's seventy-fifth birthday is next month, and I've rented the Wharf Room at the Boston Harbor Hotel. It's going to be a huge party!"

Helen was my sister's mother-in-law. Cat and she had always been close. I'd met Helen several times and considered her an angel who'd fallen from heaven. She was very special and I could see why my sister wanted to go all out to make her birthday one to remember.

"I'm getting the feeling that there's a woman with blond hair who's going to spoil this for you. You're really hoping to keep it a surprise, and this woman is going to ruin it." There was a pause as my sister and I looked at each other and as one said, "The Evil One."

The Evil One was Dora, my brother-in-law's sister. Dora had taken an instant dislike to Cat, and the two were archenemies. At Cat and Tommy's wedding, Dora had sobbed hysterically when the two were saying their vows, and burbling, "He just *can't* marry her!" disrupting the ceremony. Cat had never forgiven her, and the two have been playing in a game of "Who Can Outdo Whom?" ever since.

"I knew it!" my sister said, thumping the table. "I haven't even sent her an invitation yet because I wanted to wait until the last minute."

"My thought is that she's going to try and put one over on you, Cat. I get the feeling she's already gotten wind of this and that she's also planning a surprise party of her own. She's trying to beat you to the punch by having hers the night before, or even on the same day. That way she can say she had no idea you were planning this and she comes out smelling like a rose."

My sister mumbled under her breath, and scribbled something I assumed was inappropriate in her notebook. I smiled and continued, "Now, here's my advice. She's going to plan this event at some sort of hall that's close to a harbor and has a view of a lighthouse."

Cat sucked in a breath. "The Cape Codder! I know that place! Oh, you're right, Abby. She goes there all the time!"

"Now all you have to do is beat her to the punch. Call up the hall and pretend to be Dora, cancel the reservation, and pay them some cash for their time. I'm telling you it's going to work, and Dora's going to end up with egg on her face."

I could already see the wheels turning in Cat's head. "I'm also going to move the date of the party," she said. "I'll have it a week early instead of on Helen's birthday, and I may even misprint Dora's invitation on purpose. Wouldn't it be hysterical if she missed the party altogether?"

"Hysterical," I agreed, shoveling some mashed potatoes into my mouth. I'd extracted a warm plate of roasted chicken, mashed potatoes and green beans from the oven and was happily munching. After a few more bites, I said, "She's also planning on sending Helen on a cruise. Did you know that?"

"No! Where?" my sister asked.

"Someplace south, maybe the tropics. She went cheap, though, and the trip is going to be a total dud. How about you outdo her by sending Helen and Paul someplace extravagant?"

"Europe!" Cat said excitedly, as she jotted down notes.

I checked my radar. "That works. Send them for a couple of weeks, and go all out." I had no problem telling my sister how to spend her money. She had plenty to spare.

"The *Queen Mary* cruise ship!" Cat exclaimed. I smiled at how excited she was. Helen would love the gift and the party, and the Evil One would get her just desserts. Sometimes I love being psychic.

"Wow!" Cat said when she'd stopped scribbling.

"Glad I could help," I said, taking another bite of mashed potatoes and fingering through the agenda spread out on the tabletop.

"Abby, this is great. How can I repay you?" Cat asked, turning the pages again in her notebook.

I looked at her, and then at the weekend agenda, which included a trip to the zoo, the mall, the aquarium, two museums and Faneuil Hall. I smiled as I gathered up all the pages and began to tear them into little pieces.

"Wha . . . ?! What are you *doing*?!" Cat shrieked. "That took me a full half hour to put together!"

"I'm sure it did, but I don't want to do any of it. The way you can repay me is to spend a few days relaxing by the pool with me."

"Abby, I can relax when I'm dead. Come on, don't be silly . . ."

"No, Cat, we're going to sit still, relax and enjoy the weather, the pool, the backyard and each other. We are going to plant ourselves out there poolside and lounge like lizards. And if you say no, then you can forget about ever getting another reading from me."

"You wouldn't!"

"Try me," I said, smugly eating another forkful of chicken.

"Not even the mall? But there's a *sale* at Neiman Marcus this week!" she insisted.

"Okay, the mall—but you will leave your watch behind."

"Now you're just being mean," she said, scowling.

Two days later I was sitting outside on a lounge chair with Cat, who was doing her best to relax with me by the pool. Puddled at her feet were two reference texts, a marketing plan, notes for an upcoming meeting, two cell phones, a Dictaphone, a Palm Pilot and a laptop computer. I had decided to take my small victories where I could. At least I'd been able to spend the last couple of days relaxing instead of running around.

I was contemplating flipping over to sun my back when the peace and tranquility of the day were suddenly interrupted by the sound of heavy equipment coming from somewhere at the front of the house. I looked at Cat, who was in the midst of yet another phone call, and took in that she didn't seem alarmed. Two minutes later a very large bulldozer and digger came tumbling across the edge of the property. I expected Cat to jump up and go chasing after them, but instead she waved to one of the men on the truck.

"What's all that about?" I asked when she'd finished her call.

"We're starting the construction of a guesthouse down there at the edge of the property," Cat said, pointing down the hill.

I squinted into the sun and saw where she meant. "Why so far away?"

"Claire and Sam are coming to visit this Christmas, and I want to make sure they're comfortable."

Claire and Sam were our parents. We hadn't called them "Mom and Dad" since we were teenagers as they preferred to be called by their first names. I no-

ticed a small tic form at the corner of Cat's eye, and
my heart went out to her.

Our parents were currently living in South Carolina
and hadn't asked to visit my sister since their last trip
here three years earlier. Apparently, nine thousand
square feet just wasn't enough room for my sister
and mother.

I had no such problems, as my relationship with my
parents had deteriorated to a Christmas card and an
occasional cable-knit sweater, which neither fit nor
flatted. My mother was very good at purchasing items
exactly two sizes too small, the subtle message being
"lose some weight, fatty." Claire and Sam had never
once in the ten years since they moved south asked
to visit me. I wasn't losing sleep over it.

Cat was a different story. She struggled through
hair-pulling conversations with our mother for the
sake of her children. She wanted her sons to know
their grandparents, which, in my mind, was a farce,
because my mother had never wanted to know her
own children, much less her children's children. I
stroked Cat's arm and smiled reassuringly. "Are you
sure you couldn't move them just a bit farther away?"

"I tried, but my neighbor wouldn't sell his property," she said, pointing to the neighbor behind her
house an acre and a half away.

I chuckled. "Aren't you a little worried, though,
about ruining your good relationships with all of your
neighbors who have to put up with all the construction?"

"Oh, *please*, Abby, I have money," she said matter-
of-factly. "They'll be back."

Just then M&M came running out of the house
wearing matching swim trunks plus yellow inflatable
floaties on their upper arms. Despite the awkwardness

of the floaties, Matt was precariously carrying an armload of small cars and trucks. "Here, Auntie, these are yours," he said and deposited several on my lounge chair.

I looked at the assortment and noticed that he'd given me a police car, an ambulance and a fire truck. "Thank you, Matty! I love them. But I thought you were into diggers and bulldozers."

"Yes!" he said, pointing excitedly to the far end of the property. Turning back to me, he added, "But those are yours!" He then ran to the far end of the pool, where Sharon was already helping Mike into the water. I watched my little nephew trot happily away and then I looked down at the assortment he'd given me and felt a small chill creep up my spine. A feeling of foreshadowing fluttered around the pile of trucks in my lap, and I shuddered even in the heat of the sun. Thankfully, my sister was on another call and hadn't noticed the exchange, or my reaction. I sat through the rest of the afternoon slightly removed, my thoughts troubled and my mind uneasy.

The next morning I was on the ten a.m. shuttle from Boston to Detroit, and as I stared out the window after leaving Logan Airport I thought again about the disturbing dream I'd had the night before. I dreamed that I was dead and that my body had melted into the ground so that I was one with the grass. All the people I knew were looking for me but couldn't find me. Everyone but my neighbor Mary Lou, who said she knew exactly where I was. She led a group of people that included Dave, Connie, Marco, Parker, Dutch and Milo to where I lay. Dutch walked right over me, and I could feel the rubber of his sole as it mashed down on my chest. He looked right and left and said he couldn't see me; everyone else nodded in agreement. I shouted up to him with my grassy lips, but he couldn't hear me, so Mary Lou began to plant marigolds in a flower outline of where I lay. When she was finished she stood up and said, "See? I told you she was here!" Then I woke up, startled and chilled by something I couldn't quite place.

As I sat on the plane I anxiously bobbed my knee up and down, staring out the window and pondering what to do to pass the time. I looked at the magazine I'd purchased for the flight and thought about reading it, but I was too wound up. The gentleman next to me was diligently making notes on a legal pad, and an idea occurred to me. When I asked if I could trouble him for a clean sheet of paper, he kindly paused in his scribbling and tore off several sheets, handing them to me with a smile. I thanked him and pulled a pen from my purse, then closed my eyes and concentrated for a moment.

When I opened them, I drew a circle in the middle of the blank page and labeled it "Allison's killer." I began drawing lines stemming from the circle and labeling these with whatever free associative thought I had. I had lines for "man," then branches off that line for "dark hair," "short," "big clothes," "Ohio," "Robin Hood," "Merry Men," "baseball," and "bat." I drew another branch off the circle and wrote out "Alyssa," "revenge," and "sins of the past."

This technique, which I'd learned years before, is called "mind-mapping" and it allows random streams of thought and information to be dumped out onto a sheet of paper in whatever order they tumble. It is a bit like emptying out the clutter held captive by both the right and the left sides of the brain, allowing for intuition to creep in as well. Later, after the clutter has been emptied, the thoughts can be organized into a more linear order.

When I'd finished with my map I stared down at the lines and labels on my web of information. I was looking for patterns or clues. Something new had appeared under the "man" branch—I'd drawn a line that said, "sports car." Interesting. I looked at other branches but couldn't find any discernible patterns.

Leaning back in my chair, I thought long and hard for a few minutes. I felt like I wasn't approaching this from the right angle, but what was the right angle?

A flash of insight occurred to me, so I took out another blank piece of paper and repeated the exercise, this time with "Alyssa's killer" written in the center. At this point, I was absolutely convinced that Alyssa did not commit suicide, so I thought it best to call a spade a spade. From the first circle I drew several branches in rapid succession: "wedding," "Marco," "open window," "heart-husband," "jealousy," "revenge," and "sins of the past." A sub-branch formed from here, and the same information from Allison's map appeared, including "baseball," and "sports car," "Robin Hood," "Merry Men," but without the word "bat." I continued to write for another few minutes and was sitting back to survey my handiwork when the flight attendant announced that we would be landing soon and asked us to please put all cell phones, computers and electrical equipment away. As I heard the term "cell phone," something flashed through my head, and I nearly ignored the stewardess's instructions and reached into my purse for my cell phone. I needed to call Dutch. I didn't know why, and I didn't know for what, but I had to call him.

I put my mind-map away, intent on studying it later, and tried to calm down. The thought, *Call Dutch, call Dutch, call Dutch* repeated itself over and over in my head, and the closer we got to landing the more I felt I needed to contact him immediately.

Finally the plane touched down and the moment I

deplaned, I whipped out my cell phone and pressed the ON switch. The phone bleeped on for a moment, flashed "low battery" on the display and promptly clicked off. Then I remembered I'd forgotten to charge it before I left Cat's. "Shit!" I said and snapped the phone closed, causing an elderly couple standing nearby to shuffle away from me. I looked around for a pay phone, but all I saw was a sea of faces, all happily talking on their cell phones and not a pay phone in sight. "Son-of-a . . ." I mumbled, as I hurried through the terminal.

I had gotten my luggage and was about to board onto the shuttle when the driver stepped in front of me and said, "Sorry, ma'am, we're all full."

"What?" I looked at him, my anxiety rising by the moment. I didn't know why I was so anxious, but I needed to get home and call Dutch as soon as I could. "Well, when will the next one come?"

"Ten minutes or so," he said. *Liar, liar, pants on fire . . .*

Twenty minutes later the next shuttle arrived and I quickly shoved my luggage on it and took my seat. I gave the driver my address and let my knee bounce out my impatience. I was hoping to be one of the first stops along the shuttle's route, and silently cursed when the other passengers verbally gave their addresses to the driver and I knew I'd be closer to the tail end of the drop off sequence. Finally we entered my neighborhood and I took in a deep breath, thankful that I was almost home. As we rounded the corner and turned down my street, several passengers gave a gasp of surprise. The end of my street was lined with police cars, fire trucks and an ambulance. I felt my stomach drop to the floor.

"That's not your house, is it, ma'am?" the driver asked, pointing ahead and glancing sideways at me.

"Oh my God! Stop the bus! Stop the bus!" I shouted, jumping out of my seat and scrambling over several passengers. The driver halted abruptly and I pitched forward, nearly stumbling out of the bus in my anxiety to get to my house. I ran through the line of spectators and stopped on the sidewalk in front of my home. I saw my front door open, and a policeman walk out, then trip over something and stumble, nearly losing his footing. After catching himself, he turned and looked back, then picked up the thing he had tripped over. It was a small gardening shovel. I followed his line of sight with open mouth and saw the array of other tools and dried-up flowers on my front step.

My mind had slowed to some foggy speed, and I couldn't really make sense of what I was seeing. The officer picked up the tools and carried them around my house to the backyard. I followed him.

When I came through the back gate I saw official-looking people all over my backyard. Most of them were wearing rubber gloves and carrying paper bags. They were combing my yard and parting bushes lining my back fence, poking at the ground with pencils, and depositing stray items into their bags. In the center of my yard a cluster of men stood in a semicircle, staring at the ground with grim looks on their faces.

Dutch and Milo were there, and Dutch looked particularly upset. I noticed he was wearing plastic gloves and holding a manila envelope. What the heck was going on?

I followed their gaze and saw something poking beyond the semicircle of men about 8-10 yards away that I couldn't quite recognize. The object in the grass was thin and clawlike, gray blue in color and surrounded by flats of dried, wilted flowers. At that moment I became aware of a buzzing noise, and as a slight breeze blew I noticed a horrible, suffocating scent that caused my stomach to bunch and roil. A gagging cough escaped from my throat, and the officer I'd been following turned and saw me standing there.

"You can't be here, lady. This is a crime scene," he said, angry at my trespass.

"No, you don't understand," I choked out, my voice barely above a whisper.

"Come on, you need to leave right now," he said as he grabbed my arm and began pulling me away.

"But—but—" I stammered to no avail—he wasn't listening to me. Then I saw my handyman, Dave, sitting on a chair near the back porch. Even from a distance of ten yards I could tell he was very upset. He looked pale as a ghost, and I could make out a wetness on his cheeks that gleamed in the afternoon sun. He seemed to stare listlessly at the ground in front of him as a flurry of activity scurried around him. My breath caught at the sight of him so distraught, and for a moment I forgot the officer pushing me back and called out to him, "Dave!"

In an instant Dave sat up rigid in his chair, looking around as if he'd been awakened from a sound sleep. I called to him again and this time he turned to look at me but it was a full ten seconds before he seemed to recognize me.

"Abby?! Oh my God, Abby?!" he cried, jumping out of the chair and running to me. The officer had stopped tugging on my arm and was looking from Dave to me. Dave reached me then and picked me up, crushing me to him. "Abby, I can't believe it! You're alive . . . you're *alive*!"

I couldn't say much because Dave was squeezing me so tight, but I did manage to look over his shoulder at the rest of the people in my yard. Everyone had grown silent, and both Dutch and Milo were staring at me as if they couldn't believe their eyes. They looked from me to the ground, then back again. I followed their gaze, and had a better view now that several people had moved slightly to one side. That was when I saw it.

I walked forward now unchecked, Dave following me as I edged closer to the group of men encircling a body that lay stretched out facedown on the grass, its skin gray–blue slightly bloated and horrid. I stopped just five feet from the figure and took in the claw-like object in the grass that I could now see so clearly was an arm, reaching its dead fingers forward to grip at small blades of grass.

The figure was a woman. She wore blue shorts and a pink T-shirt, her long hair wound up in a tight bun at the back of her head and a length of cruel rope knotted tightly around her neck making one visible cheek bulge outward to distort her features.

I took in the scene for all of twenty seconds, my breath coming in short ragged bursts as I felt my knees grow weak and my stomach border on the verge of emptying itself. Quickly I turned away stumbling back across the grass, away from the horror in my backyard. I made it just ten steps and my knees gave out. Dave caught me just before I collapsed and with care he lowered me the rest of the way to the ground. He then stepped back with sad eyes to look at me, aware that I now understood what everyone else there knew. Someone had been murdered in my backyard. The difference was that I knew the woman's name, where she lived and why she'd been killed. My neighbor and friend Mary Lou had been murdered because, from behind, she resembled me.

I felt clammy and light-headed, unable to focus. Dave was next to me and I remember him helping me up, but the details of what happened after that are a complete blur.

The next thing I knew I was sitting in a big caramel leather chair with an afghan over my shoulders, a bowl of fruit on my lap, and Dutch, who was sitting across from me, encouraging me to eat.

"Where am I?" I asked dully.

"You're at my house. Now eat," he said kindly.

As I looked down at the bowl of fruit, the realization that May Lou was dead came rushing back at me. "It's my fault," I said as tears spilled unchecked down my cheeks.

"Abby . . ."

"It should have been me, not her," I blubbered, reality finding cruel purchase in my guilty mind.

Dutch moved off his seat, and crouched in front of me. Holding my chin up, he looked directly into my eyes. "It's no one's fault but the son of a bitch that killed her," he said. "You had nothing to do with it. She was just in the wrong place at the wrong time. It's *not* your fault."

I looked into his eyes, feeling helpless and lost. I wanted to crawl under the afghan around my shoulders and shut out the world. Like how I used to watch scary movies when I was a kid, peeking through the tiny holes in a blanket, feeling safe from the horror underneath my fabric tent.

Dutch let go of my chin and reached behind him for a tissue, which he used to dab my eyes. He pulled the afghan closer, and I suddenly realized I was shivering. "Abby," he said gently, "you're in shock, and if you don't eat some of that fruit it's only going to get worse. If that happens I'll have to take you to the hospital and I really don't want to. Now, please eat. For me."

I looked dully at the bowl, and because I had nothing left in me to resist, I obediently began spooning the fruit mixture into my mouth, eating without tasting.

Dutch sat back again and watched me carefully, taking the bowl from me when I was done. Soon the shivering subsided and I did feel better, but I was also very tired, and my eyelids drooped heavily.

"Come on," Dutch said, and patted the sofa next to him. I shuffled over to him, holding the afghan close about me and taking a seat on the couch next to him. He wrapped an arm around me rubbing my shoulder, grabbed a small pillow next to him and placed it in his lap, then gently lowered my head to the pillow and stroked my cheek. I pulled my feet up into fetal position and closed my eyes as I listened to him say, "It's okay Abby. You're going to be all right."

I was sound asleep in seconds.

Chapter Eleven

When I awoke the room was dim, the last strands of dusk poking through the buttery sheers Dutch had hanging at the large window. I sat up, hearing voices, and turning my head, I saw that Dutch and Milo were in the kitchen, keeping their voices low.

I blinked several times. I'd slept with my contacts in, and my eyes felt like sandpaper. Finally, I got enough moisture circulating and stood up to take in my surroundings. Dutch's house was a total surprise.

I wasn't sure what I'd imagined his taste was like. I probably would have guessed he'd have lots of black leather, matching black lacquer, ratty tabletops with sports magazines, and a stack of remotes for every kind of electronic gizmo there was. Instead, as I looked around, I was astonished to discover the man had taste, and good taste at that.

His furnishings were leather, but a warm camel brown color, not black. Two end tables held a pair of auburn-colored Tiffany-style lamps. On the far wall was a large, flat-screen TV, but I could find no remote for it. I wandered into the dining room and discovered a long oak table with a cranberry runner and six high-back chairs. A buffet ran the length of one wall, and an antique cranberry beaded chandelier dangled delicately from the ceiling. The walls were painted a soft mocha, the trim a buttery cream, and everywhere soft accents of cranberry gave just enough color. The stairs to the second floor were on the far left, just behind the front entrance. I resisted the urge to explore there, but went around them and found a hidden study with a large wooden desk. The room was neatly arranged and set against a backdrop of shelf upon shelf of books, organized by Dewey Decimal. A desktop computer and a smaller laptop sat connected to each other by a power cord, and a used coffee cup still held its leftover contents. The large leather swivel chair behind the desk begged to be sat in, and I gave in, wanting to see the world through Dutch's eyes.

As I sat in the chair I noticed two reference texts on his desk, both marked in several places. Curious, I pulled one to me, scanning the title, and was surprised to find it was *The Life of Edgar Cayce, the Greatest Psychic of Our Time.* I had figured Dutch had a fairly closed mind about me, but the fact that he was doing a little research indicated he thought there was something to learn. The second text was called *Psychic Sleuths: Police Psychics and the Famous Crimes They've Solved.* "Go figure," I said to myself, as I pushed the books back in place.

" 'Go figure' what?" Dutch asked from the doorway.

I jumped in the chair, my hand coming quickly to my heart as I felt it begin to pound in my ears. "You should know better than to sneak up on people," I said tartly when I regained my composure.

"And you should know better than to snoop around in people's private business," he shot back.

My cheeks colored. "Sorry. You're right. I apologize. I didn't mean to snoop, I was just curious."

"It's fine. I was only playing with you," he said, his eyes kind again. "Are you hungry?"

"Not really, but I guess I should eat, huh?"

"You like pasta?"

"Love it," I said, relieved that he wasn't angry at me.

"Then follow me to the kitchen and you can sample my specialty, spaghetti alla carbonara."

"Sounds complicated," I said, getting up.

"You don't have to cook it, babe, you just get to enjoy."

We moved into the kitchen and I brought the afghan with me, only now noticing how soft and delicate it was. I looked at it appraisingly and remarked, "This afghan is gorgeous. The yarn feels like angora."

"My mother made it. She's a crochet queen, and every year I get something new from her. So far that's my favorite."

For a moment I envied him. His mother took the time to crochet something unique, just for him. My mother took a minute and a half to order something two sizes too small from a catalog. Then again, at least I got *something* for Christmas. I should just count my blessings.

I smiled at Milo, who was already seated. "How you feeling?" he asked.

"Better. I just—I don't know. It's just so hard to comprehend, you know? I can't believe she's dead."

"Sit," Dutch ordered as he brought over a heaping bowlful of pasta, filling the kitchen with a mouthwatering aroma. Dutch scooped a huge amount of pasta onto my plate, then handed the bowl to Milo, who took an even larger portion. Dutch shoveled what remained onto his plate.

The food was delicious. I ate quietly as Dutch and Milo talked about sports and cases they were working on, noticeably avoiding the one involving me. Finally we were finished and Dutch, a conscientious host, picked up our plates and deposited them in the sink, coming back with two fresh beers for Milo and himself. The two of them continued to make idle small talk, until I got sick of it. "So are we going to talk about it? Or just dance around it all night?" I said.

"We wanted to give you some time, Abby," Dutch explained.

"I don't need time, I need this psycho caught. I need to stop looking over my shoulder and get back to my life." For some reason this confession brought tears to my eyes, and I swiped at them, annoyed.

"All right, then, what can you tell us about Mary Lou?"

"What do you know so far?" I asked.

Milo said, "You told us she was your neighbor, and I found where she lived. According to the woman who lives in the other half of the duplex, she saw Mary Lou walking to your house with a bunch of flowers on Saturday afternoon."

I nodded. "Yeah, I saw her just before I got on the shuttle to the airport."

"Airport? Where were you anyway?" Dutch asked.

"I went to visit my sister in Boston for a couple of days. I left Saturday afternoon."

"You could have called, you know," Dutch said, giving me a look that said I should have known better.

"I did call, but I got your voice mail and I didn't feel like leaving a long drawn out message."

"Okay, so back to Mary Lou. You say you saw her right before you got on the shuttle?"

"Yes. She was going to plant some flowers around the elm tree in my backyard," I said, looking at my lap.

"She must have been killed very soon after she entered the backyard. You're saying you were home just before she was attacked?"

"Yeah, I was," I shuddered. "I went to Allison Pierce's funeral in the morning, then came back home to grab my luggage and wait for the shuttle."

"Where's your dog?" Milo asked.

"He's at the kennel. I was supposed to pick him up today. I'll have to call them first thing in the morning."

"Do you remember hearing or seeing anything out of the ordinary before you left?"

I sighed, trying to think back. "The only thing that comes to mind is that I was really anxious to get out of there. But to answer your question, no, I didn't see or hear anything unusual."

"Do you know of anyone who would want to hurt Mary Lou?" Dutch asked.

"No," I said automatically. But then something occurred to me, and I figured I had to come clean. "Wait—I forgot about her boyfriend. I saw a bruise on her upper arm about a week ago, and I suspected it wasn't the first time he got physical with her. I don't think he was the one who did it, though."

"Do you know his name?" Milo asked.

"Chad . . . uh . . . Levine, I think—that's it, Chad Levine."

Milo was writing the name down in a notebook he'd taken from his pocket when Dutch said, "So tell me about the photos, Abby." There was a hard line to his mouth, and for some reason I felt like he was angry with me.

I stared blankly at him for a moment, wondering what he was talking about. Then it dawned on me that

I'd left the manila envelope on my kitchen table. "Oh! I totally forgot. I got those on Friday, and that's why I went to Boston. I figured I'd show this psycho that I was listening to his instructions. If he wanted me to back off, then that's what I'd do. The whole thing really scared the crap out of me. Like I said before, I tried to call you and tell you about them, but I couldn't catch up to you before I left," I said, trying to explain the reason for my delay.

"You got them on Friday?"

"Yeah, Friday. It was the day before Allison's funeral. Why? Is the timing important?"

"Abby, the envelope is postmarked almost two weeks ago," Dutch said.

"Two weeks ago? You're kidding!"

"No, not kidding. We thought you'd had the photos for a week."

"No!" And then I remembered that I hadn't been checking my mailbox regularly. "Oh man, I can't believe this. They were in my mailbox, but I'm really bad about remembering to pick up the mail. I hadn't been to my mailbox in a week, so they probably were there and I just didn't get to them until Friday."

"Can you think of anything you did last week that might have set this guy off?"

I sucked in a breath and tears again welled at the corners of my eyes. I had. I'd gone to see Marco at the jail, and then I'd gone to see Allison's attorney. I'd stuck my nose right into the thick of things, and the whole time I'd been unaware that my actions were leading down a very dangerous road.

I told Milo and Dutch all of it. About going to see Marco, what I'd learned from him and what I'd learned from Parker Gish. The two seemed a little surprised when I told them that the only public record the girls had between them was a recent marriage license for Alyssa. I saw Milo make a note, and Dutch shifted in his chair.

"So you believe they were hiding from someone who eventually caught up to them?" Dutch asked.

"It's pretty obvious, isn't it? I mean, Marco could hardly have attacked Mary Lou from his jail cell, now could he?"

Dutch looked at his napkin, silent for a long moment before answering. "Abby, we need you to slow down a little. At this point, we don't know who attacked your friend. It could have been her boyfriend, or it could have been someone else," he said as he and Milo exchanged a glance.

"What?" I demanded. These two were starting to test my patience. Their insistence on ignoring the obvious was annoying me to no end.

"Did you know your handyman did some work for the Pierce sisters?"

I sat back in my chair, stunned. "What? What are you talking about?"

"Dave McKenzie recently brought a small-claims suit against Alyssa and Allison Pierce for money they owed him on a minor construction job he did for them."

I shook my head, trying to figure out where this was going. "So? I mean, yes, it's a pretty big coincidence, but I'm sure Dave didn't even know the girls were dead, so what's your point?"

"Let's see—the girls owed him money, they weren't paying and now they're dead. On top of that, he was the one who called the police this morning to report a dead body in your backyard. He had access to your house and knew your routine. Did you owe him money, Abby?"

The look I gave him was murderous, "You are an *idiot*!" I nearly shouted. "Dave McKenzie is an honest, hardworking, decent man! He's about as likely a killer as *you* are!"

Dutch regarded me with a cool expression, unphased by my outburst. "I agree with you, Abby. I don't think Dave killed anyone. Still, there are more angles to this thing than you realize, and we can't assume this mystery man from Ohio is the murderer, especially when we have no hard evidence."

I sat back, still fuming at the attack on my handyman. Then my intuitive phone suddenly gave a loud ring and I quickly answered it. After a moment I said, "Fine, then what we should do, gentlemen, is to sift through the past. Alyssa's belongings are in a storage shed on Franklin, and I really feel we'll discover something important there."

Milo looked at me curiously, then at Dutch, who nodded and said almost under his breath, "Edgar Cayce." Milo nodded and wrote something else in his notebook.

"Make fun of me all you want—" I began, my voice rising, but Dutch interrupted.

"Abby, I'm not making fun of you. Really, I've been telling Milo about this Edgar Cayce guy. From what I read, he was pretty incredible. So as much as I'd like to ignore this whole sixth-sense thing, the more I hang around you, the more I'm finding myself trusting your input. We'll go to the storage place first thing in the morning."

I nodded, then remembered something. "No, I can't. I've got readings starting at nine."

Milo and Dutch again exchanged glances and Milo then abruptly excused himself, leaving the room. "What now?" I said, exasperated.

"We don't think it's a good idea for you to be seeing clients right now, Abby," Dutch explained.

"What are you talking about?" I asked, slow on the uptake.

"If your theory is right, the guy who sent you the photos is the same guy who killed your neighbor, thinking it was you, and he's still out there. Conducting business at your office would make you a sitting duck, and Milo and I aren't open to that idea."

I looked at him with eyebrows lowered. "So what do you propose I do, Detective?" I had a suspicion he had done something behind my back, and I didn't think I was going to like it.

"I had Milo go over to your office and speak to your landlord. She agreed to rearrange your appointments and in fact she's already put in calls to everyone you were supposed to see tomorrow and she's rescheduled them for later dates. I know you can't just shut down your business, so we'll have to figure out something for the rest of the week. Maybe we can move you to another office, or you could have your clients come here and you could work out of my study for a while. I just don't like the thought of you being alone in that big building, and Milo and I can't babysit you."

I wanted to be mad, but I was actually relieved. I didn't want to go back to my office either. "Okay," I said agreeably, and was rewarded with a dazzling smile.

Dutch and I retreated to the living room where Milo was already immersed in a baseball game. I took one look at the score, and my intuition gave me a flash. "The A's are going to win over the Tigers, eight to six," I announced.

Milo looked sharply at me, "You sure?"

"That's what I'm getting," I said, taking a seat in one of the large leather chairs. Just then I saw a huge gray cat with bright orange eyes slink into the room, taking the three of us in with casual regard.

"So you can use your powers to predict sports events?" Milo asked, looking like a kid at Christmas.

"Sometimes. I'm much better at horses than I am with baseball . . ."

"Now you've done it," Dutch said, rolling his eyes.

"Horses? As in, if I took you to the track you could tell me which horse was going to win?"

"Usually. I just focus on what color the silks of the winning jockey will be and shazam . . . you have a winner."

"What are you doing Saturday?" Milo asked, his eyes wide as saucers.

"No," Dutch said, shooting his partner a warning glance.

"What's the big deal?" Milo said to him defensively.

"No," Dutch repeated, and took me in as well with the definitive word.

I looked at Milo, winking conspiratorially, and mouthed, "Call me" while Dutch's back was turned.

Milo smiled at me, then looked at Dutch. "Sure, man, whatever you say."

An hour later the game was over, the A's winning over the Tigers eight to six. Milo and Dutch both stood as the final score was settled in the last inning and looked at me with a mixture of respect and puzzlement. Milo patted Dutch on the back as he moved to the front door and said, "Okay, you take Abby over to the storage place in the morning. I'll track down Mary Lou's boyfriend and see what he can tell me about his whereabouts on Saturday."

"It's a plan. I'll hook up with you around noon," Dutch said.

Milo opened the door and stopped in midthought,

then turned back to me and asked, "Hey, Abby, can your spidey sense get the lotto numbers?"

I smiled at how eagerly he looked at me, swearing his pupils had been replaced by dollar signs. Unable to resist taunting him a little, I raised my hand to my forehead, closed my eyes and feigned concentration. "Ummm, okay, I'm getting the numbers twenty-nine, fifty-two, thirty-two, forty-five and five."

Milo mouthed the numbers in order as he pulled out his small notebook and jotted them down and waved a final good-bye before heading out the door. Dutch turned to me and shot me a small look of reproach. "That was mean," he said.

I snickered and answered, "Couldn't help it."

"Come on, Edgar, I'll show you to your room," Dutch said, grabbing my luggage from the landing and proceeding upstairs.

I followed a pace or two behind, suddenly full of mild trepidation. What was happening between him and me?

Since the night he'd come over to make amends about Nathaniel Davies, Dutch and I had circled each other carefully, keeping things businesslike and leaving out the flirt. We were both on equal footing then, secure in our own skills and abilities, but now the lines seemed muddled. I was in his house, he was taking care of me, and I was asking him to trust my gut, something he was definitely uncomfortable with. So where did that leave us personally? What waited for me at the top of the stairs?

Dutch reached the landing and paused so subtly before turning that I almost didn't catch his moment of indecision. Had I not been looking straight at his back I would have missed it completely. I followed him to the top and looked in the direction he'd almost taken:

master bedroom. I smiled, a dichotic mixture of relief and disappointment.

Dutch opened the door to a bedroom just down the hall. I was surprised to see that the room was painted a pale lavender with white trim. Lace doilies and antique porcelain knickknacks dotted every flat surface.

I cocked one eyebrow at him, as if to question his sexual orientation and he quickly explained, "This is the bedroom my parents stay in when they come to visit. My mom did the decorating."

"Ah," I said, nodding, "Knew it had to be something like that."

Dutch shot me a grin then and quickly deposited my luggage on the bed. "Bathroom's just down the hall. There are clean towels in the linen closet to the right of the bathroom and hangers in the closet if you need to hang up any of your clothes."

I moved to my suitcase and started to unzip it. "How long do you think I'll be playing houseguest?" I asked.

Dutch looked at me for a long moment, his eyes smoldering, the air between us suddenly erupting with electricity. I was completely caught off guard by it and stood there dumbfounded as I felt the magnetic heat rolling off him like lava. "I don't know, Abby," he said, his voice thick and rich. "Why don't we just play it by ear?" And then he was gone, out of the room and back down the hallway.

I sat down heavily, amazed at the instant transformation. This man played with my head, and I wasn't sure I liked it. I wanted him to make up his damn mind already.

I pulled my suitcase to the floor and dug through the contents, found my contact lens case, glasses, nightshirt and toothbrush, and headed for the bathroom. I hurried through my nightly ablutions, anxious to get to bed. Opening the door of the bathroom, I walked right into bare chest, and jumped like I'd been bitten, letting out a small yelp of surprise.

Dutch chuckled softly and caught my wrist. "Hey there, it's only me, Abby. I didn't mean to scare you."

My wrist was on fire, his grip strong and warm. I couldn't help noticing how good he looked half naked, and I'd bet dollars to doughnuts he looked even better when the other half was bare. "No, it's fine," I said too quickly, trying to brush past him.

He caught me by the waist, and brought me back against him, hugging me tightly. "I'm glad you're here where I can keep an eye on you. Get a good night's sleep, because we have an early start in the morning, okay?" he said.

My voice would betray me. I could feel it in my throat, wanting to burble and crackle with energy. I didn't trust it to answer, so I simply nodded, my body tensing with anticipation at what he would do next. Dutch gave me a small peck on the cheek, then stepped into the bathroom and shut the door. I put my hand over my heart, feeling it thud against my chest. What this man did to me was just *shameful.*

I walked back into my room and saw that Virgil the cat sat like a king in the center of the bedspread, his orange eyes glowing a silent challenge at me. "Go ahead," he seemed to say. "Just *try* and get me to leave."

I smiled and moved to sit by him, offering my hand for him to sniff and rub his whiskers against. Within minutes we were thick as thieves and I curled myself around him as I got into bed, weary with exhaustion. Sleep came quickly.

Chapter Twelve

Sometime in the middle of the night I was woken up by the sound of a phone ringing. It took me a minute or two to get my bearings; I couldn't initially remember where I was. When I figured it out I sat up and listened. On the clock radio by my bed, the digital display read two a.m. I could hear Dutch in the next room, his voice low and hushed, and wondered who he could be talking to at two in the morning.

At first I thought it was probably Milo, or the police station, but as the the call continued I knew it was something else. At one point I heard Dutch saying, "No, no, no!" his voice rising ever so slightly before he caught himself and spoke again in more hushed tones. Finally I heard the barest "Good-bye," then nothing more.

I was surprisingly upset by that call. It rankled that not only did someone feel comfortable calling Dutch at two a.m., but that Dutch had spent a good amount of time on the phone with them. The whole thing suggested intimacy, and I suddenly realized that I knew very little about the man sleeping next door to me.

I felt the spiny tendrils of that green-eyed monster circle in my belly, even as I tried to coax it away through reason and logic. After all, it could have been anyone calling—his mother, for instance. But try as I might, I still felt the bile of jealousy tickle my throat and knew I needed a reality check. I had to keep things platonic, for my own protection. It was a long time before I fell back to sleep.

The next morning I woke up to the smell of coffee. I blinked and rubbed my tired eyes, squinting as I looked at the clock on the night table and groaning when I realized it wasn't even seven a.m. Waffling between rolling over and trying to go back to sleep or getting up and finding the coffee, I pulled the covers over my head and cocooned in the warmth and darkness for a while. But after a few minutes I figured I was pretty firmly entrenched in my state of wakefulness, and sleep was no longer a possibility. Groaning some more, I pushed myself up and sat on the edge of the bed. I shuffled over to my suitcase and extracted my trusty flannel robe, then, bleary-eyed, I made my way down the stairs. I found the coffee, brewed and waiting in the kitchen, but no sign of Dutch. I walked into the living room and looked around, sensing that he was in the house but not really sure where. I walked through the living room and found him typing away on his computer. "Morning," I said from the doorway.

"Hey there," he said, his smile warm and inviting.

"What'cha workin' on?" I asked, nodding at the computer.

"I have a small consulting business on the side," he answered. "I'm just catching up on my e-mails."

"What kind of consulting business?" I asked. Maybe this would explain the late-night phone call.

"I'm a security consultant. I was a security specialist in the navy and put myself through college by consulting for the rich and infamous." He smiled at his little pun.

"What college did you go to?" I probed, taking a seat in a leather recliner to the left of Dutch's desk.

"I did my undergrad at State and my graduate work at U of M."

"You have a master's?" I asked. Somehow I just hadn't expected that.

"Yeah, in criminal psychology. Just because we're cops, Abby, doesn't mean we're not smart," he answered, picking up on my snooty surprise.

"Touché," I said, bowing my head. After a moment I asked, "So what's with the FBI?"

"What?" he barked, looking sharply at me.

"The FBI. There's a connection between you and the FBI. Am I right?" I was focusing on my intuitive phone, and I continued. "Something about an interview. Oh! Are you applying to the FBI?"

"I cannot believe you know that! I haven't even told Milo," Dutch said, looking at me like he'd just caught me sifting through his personal mail.

"Do you want to know if you'll get in?" I asked, teasing him.

"No!" he said automatically, then waited a beat and added, "Unless you know it's a lock. Then you can tell me." There was the smallest hint of a smile playing at the corner of his mouth, and I knew he was laughing at himself for giving in.

"Nothing in life is really a lock, Dutch, but I can tell you that there are a series of three intense interviews ahead for you, as well as a series of tests, both physical and mental, like a psychological profile or something. I feel like you're going to do really well, but you have major competition. There are only two slots open, and I think eight guys to select from. You'll need to study hard beforehand, but yes, I do feel like you'll get in. Just don't go in there expecting it. You still have to do your homework."

A wave of relief flashed over Dutch's features before he caught himself and reset his face. I noticed too that he'd been holding himself tightly, and his shoulders had noticeably loosened when he got my answer. He clicked off his e-mail, came around his desk and ruffled my hair. I watched him as he moved to the doorway, then turned and said, "Come on, Edgar, let's go eat."

Dutch made breakfast of eggs, bacon and hash browns, and the moment he took out the carton of eggs I slapped my forehead and called the dog kennel. Luckily they opened at seven and said it was no problem to keep Eggy for a few extra days. After breakfast we both got cleaned up and headed to Dutch's car for the ride over to the storage facility.

On the way Dutch made small talk by mentioning what he'd learned in the book about Edgar Cayce. He was talking about one of Cayce's more famous accounts about avoiding an elevator ride because when the doors opened he'd looked in and the passengers' auras had disappeared. He'd known something terrible was about to happen and hadn't gotten on board. A moment later the cable to the elevator had snapped and the passengers had all tumbled to the ground floor.

"I remember hearing about that story," I said. "I never read much about Mr. Cayce, but I know he was a remarkable talent."

Dutch lost himself for a moment in contemplation, then almost shyly asked me, "Can you see auras?"

I smiled in surprise at the question and answered, "When I focus I can."

Another beat, then, "Can you see mine?"

I hid my smile and said, "Probably. Would you like me to try?"

"If you want to," he answered noncommittally.

I turned in my seat to face him, just as he stopped at a stoplight. He looked at me, smiling, as if saying "cheese" for the camera. It was damn hard not to laugh, but I managed. I let my eyes go unfocused and looked at the space just above Dutch's head, and in seconds saw the white envelope that is the core of everyone's aura. I expanded outward and waited and then in a flash I had the brilliant Technicolor snapshot of his aura. "Oooooh," I said when I had it clearly in my vision.

"What do you see?" he asked, a hint of excitement and anticipation in his voice.

"Well, it's very pretty," I said, smirking at him. He scowled at me in a "get on with it," way, so I continued. "Around the top of your head there's this brilliant peacock blue, then it fades out over here," I said, pointing to his left. "It becomes lighter, like a soft turquoise. Now, coming down your trunk, it gets softer again, with traces of green and yellow, but there's a bit of brown somewhere near your feet. I can't really tell because you're sitting down, but my guess is that one of your legs or feet is a problem area that needs attention."

"Brown means trouble?"

"Sometimes. So does gray."

"I have a bad Achilles tendon that I strained the other day when I was out for a run. Could that be it?"

"Most likely," I said.

"So what do the other colors mean?"

"I'm not an expert on aura colors, but my feeling is that blue is typically the color of a thinker and an analyst. It would suggest that you are very analytical in your thought process and that you like things organized and functional. You're not so hot with spatial relationships, like geometry is tougher for you."

"That's true," he said.

"You're about order and structure—one plus one equals two. It explains why this psychic stuff is a difficult concept for you to understand analytically. The interesting part is this softer turquoise, because my feeling is that this is a recent change or shift in your aura, and this would suggest a softening of the hard-lined analyst in you. It's saying that you're opening your mind up and allowing for different possibilities. It suggests that you're evolving." I smiled and patted him on the shoulder.

My reward was a skeptical eyebrow. "Your aura can change color?"

"Absolutely. For example, if you become ill with the flu, your aura can get patchy or gray, and when you're in love it can take on a red or pink hue. If you're working on something creative, it can take on a yellow or orange cast. It can change many times over the course of your liftime, taking on a different shape, color or even density."

"Hmmm," Dutch said, lost in thought. I took another peek and noticed even more turquoise. I smiled in spite of myself.

A minute or two later he asked, "What color is your aura?"

I looked at him, again surprised by the question. He was genuinely interested, and I found myself liking him more and more. I thought back to the time when I first learned to see auras and was practicing by staring in the mirror. I recalled with a smile the moment I'd first seen the Technicolor dazzle of my own auric field. It was the first time I'd ever really thought I was beautiful. "At the crown of my head it's a gold color, and around my shoulders it becomes bright indigo. Sometimes it's a little more purple, sometimes it's a little more blue, but except for the top of my head it's all indigo shoulders to floor."

"What do your colors mean?"

"Both gold and indigo are indicative of psychic ability. The gold represents a strong tendency for claircognizant ability."

"What's that?" he asked.

"*Claircognisense* is Latin for 'clear-thinking.' It means that I can know something without really knowing why I know it. The indigo represents my other abilities, like clairsentience—clear feeling—and clairvoyance—clear seeing."

"So what you're saying is that you get your information from a bunch of different inputs?"

"Exactly."

"Cool," Dutch said, nodding his head.

Just then we reached the storage facility and Dutch pulled into a parking space in front of the office. We got out and walked inside. Behind the counter was a very short woman with beautiful soft brown eyes, long braided hair, and a figure as round as she was tall. For a moment she reminded me of the character in *Willy Wonka and the Chocolate Factory* who ate all the blueberry gum and blew up big as a balloon. "Good afternoon," she said warmly.

"Good afternoon," Dutch answered and flashed his badge, "I'm Detective Rivers from the Royal Oak Police Department and we're here on an investigation."

The woman's smile never wavered, and she didn't look very surprised. Dutch continued, "We'd like to get into the storage unit for Marco Ammarretti."

"Do you have a warrant?"

I looked on as Dutch almost imperceptibly blanched, then flashed an even bigger smile. "No, ma'am, not yet, and I'd hate to have to tie up a judge's time on this. The belongings in the storage unit previously were the property of an Alyssa Pierce, and we just want to look through her things for a few minutes. We think it may help solve the murder of her sister, Allison Pierce. You may have read about it in the paper . . ."

"Yes, I heard about that. But the storage unit is rented by Marco Ammarretti, and if I understand it, you are investigating him for that murder, isn't that correct?"

Dutch's face went the faintest tint of pink and I could read his frustration. "Yes, ma'am. However, we're actually trying to *clear* Mr. Ammarretti, and that's why we need to get into the storage unit . . ."

"Then by all means come back when you have a warrant, Detective Rivers."

I couldn't believe it—Dutch Rivers, bested by a blueberry. Dutch continued to force his smile at the woman, willing her to change her mind but she stood her ground, smiling back just as fiercely.

As I looked at the woman my intuitive phone began ringing, and I thought I might as well try; we weren't getting anywhere using Dutch's good-cop approach. "Are you the owner here?" I asked.

The woman turned her attention to me. "Yes, I'm Peg. I'm the owner."

"Hi, Peg. I hope you don't mind, but my name is Abby Cooper and I'm a psychic intuitive. I'm helping Detective Rivers with this investigation, and I have a message for you. May I share it?" This was a gamble, I knew, but most people, whether they believed in psychics or not, would want to hear the message.

There was the smallest change in the smile Peg held cemented onto her face, and I could see the wheels turning in her head. I waited patiently while she mulled that one over. "I suppose so . . ." She sounded unsure and I knew she thought this was a trick, but at least she hadn't kicked us out yet.

"Terrific. This occasionally happens to me when I'm around someone who's struggling with an issue. I'm so glad you're open to hearing the message. Okay," I said, rubbing my hands together for effect. "I feel there's this matter of insurance going on, and there's a lot of stress about someone owing you money but they're not paying up. It feels like there are these two separate events here, like there was a storm or natural disaster and something got damaged and the insurance company isn't paying up. Does this make sense to you?"

Peg looked taken aback, her hand on her chest. Her smile had disappeared and her mouth was slightly agape. It took a moment for her to realize I was waiting for her to answer me, but finally she said, "Yes, it does. We were adding some storage sheds onto the back of the property but a big windstorm came through about three months ago and knocked them down. The insurance company has been fighting us about a settlement."

"Uh-huh," I said, nodding. "There's also something about a fire too, but that feels like it wasn't here—oh my God!" I said, getting a rather intense flash. "Did your house burn down?"

Peg's eye's welled up and tears slid down her cheeks. "Yes, last year. No one was hurt, thank God, but our house did burn down and we lost most of our belongings."

"Now you guys are trying to rebuild, right? But the insurance company is giving you the runaround, like they don't believe that a fire and a windstorm could hit you all in one year, or that they don't think that what you're estimating as the value of your stuff is the correct value."

"You're right on both counts! They've come very close to accusing us of arson!" Peg was getting worked up and bouncing on her feet.

"I feel like you've already taken this to an attorney, but he's dragging his heels, right?"

"Yes!"

"And you may be considering taking it to someone else, like a female attorney, right?"

"This is unbelievable! I just told my husband last week that we needed to call a friend of mine whose sister does this sort of litigation."

"You should definitely make that call. It feels like the guy you've got right now is a minnow when what you need is a shark—and trust me, this woman is a shark. She isn't lazy like this other lawyer and you really need to call her. Follow your own gut on this. It's right on the money."

Peg blinked several times and wiped her watery eyes with her sleeve. She looked again at me and cautiously asked, "Can you tell me if this will turn out okay? I mean, will the insurance company give us what they owe us?"

I looked at Dutch a little conspiratorially, then looked at my watch and answered, "Peg, I'd love to answer that, but if we're going to get downtown and get a judge to issue the search warrant we have to leave immediately, right, Detective?" I asked, turning to Dutch.

"Time's a'wasting," Dutch answered, tapping his watch and looking stern.

"See?" I said to her, "I'm sure you understand." I smiled just as brightly as Peg had earlier and turned to walk toward the door.

"Wait!" she said quickly, coming around the corner with a ring of keys. "I'm sure if you're working to clear Mr. Ammarretti, he won't mind. Just don't tell him I let you in, okay?" She scooted around us and set a fast pace in the direction of the storage sheds. We had to trot to keep up.

Peg had the shed unlocked in a flash. She turned to me and said, "So, Abby, you were saying?"

I looked at her and patted her fleshy arm reassuringly. "Peg, I feel like this is going to go before some sort of authority figure, a judge or an arbitrator or something, and when that happens the truth will be revealed and you'll get your money. One thing you should look into is whether the insurance company has done this sort of thing to other clients as well. I'm getting the sense that they have an unspoken policy not to pay up, or to settle for less than they should. It seems like there's a real pattern here, and that's why you need to change attorneys. I think this other woman may have handled previous cases with this insurance company and either knows what they're all about or she'll connect some dots that your other lawyer hasn't. It could take a little time but there will be a resolution for you."

Peg looked at me, tears again dribbling from her eyes, and then threw herself at me in a tremendous hug. "Ooohmph!" I said, as I tried to suck in air.

"Thank you, Abby! Thank you!" To my great relief she let go and stepped back, waving a pudgy hand at the storage shed. "Take as long as you need, Detective," and with that she waddled back to her office.

I smiled triumphantly at Dutch, who was looking at me and shaking his head. "Awfully smug, aren't you?"

"Awfully," I replied as I turned to the shed. Dutch stood back and waited. I'd been the one who wanted

to come here; this was my call. I stood at the entrance
to the storage unit and closed my eyes, waiting for a
connection. Finally, a soft whisper came to me and I
moved into the unit, which was cluttered with furniture, boxes and bags of belongings. I felt a tug on my
right and moved a bicycle and two picture frames out
of the way. I looked at a set of boxes in front of me
and noticed that the one on top was the only box that
wasn't taped shut. I stepped forward and lifted the
box; it was heavy. I carried it awkwardly out into the
daylight, unfolded the flaps and looked inside. The
box held mostly paperback romance novels, and I
could see nothing out of the ordinary, other than the
contents had obviously been shifted around. I looked
at the side of the box; it was labeled BOOKSHELF. What
was here? I began to pull out the books and lay them
on the concrete, Dutch watching me patiently. As I
sifted through I discovered what Allison had been
looking for when she'd come here a few weeks earlier.
I pulled out a worn leather-bound book with the
words JOURNAL in flaking gold print embossed on the
cover. I opened it and saw that one of the entries was
from nine years ago. I looked back at the box and
pulled out more books but I found only one more
journal, this one eight years old. I put the romance
novels back in the box, noticing that they filled only
half of it. Something else had been in here. I was sure
of it—probably the journals from the past seven years.
My intuition, however, was screaming that I had all I
needed. I opened the first journal and flipped pages,
but nothing out of the ordinary popped out at me and
there was no incriminating note tucked safely away
in it.

"Should we keep looking?" Dutch asked.

"No, this is all we need," I said, standing. Dutch

took the journals from me and quickly scanned a few pages. "Abby," he said, confused, "these are from nine years ago. How are they going to help?"

"I'm not sure yet, but I'll keep you posted," I said as I returned the box to its place in the storage unit.

Dutch looked at me with skepticism but held his tongue, and we locked the unit and moseyed back to his car.

On the drive back to Dutch's house his cell phone chirped, and with one practiced quick movement he flipped open his phone and barked, "Rivers."

The conversation was abrupt, Dutch saying only, "Right. Meet you back at my place in twenty." He closed the phone and slid it back onto his belt.

"Who was that?" I asked.

"Milo. He's got something he wants to share with us. He's meeting us back at the house."

I almost asked him then, since we were already on the topic anyway, if Milo had called the night before, but I held my tongue. Dutch must have caught my indecision because he asked, "What?"

"Oh, nothing," I said. "I guess I'm just tired. I didn't sleep very well—you know, strange house, late night phone call . . ."

"Yeah, sorry about that. Hey, you want to stop and grab some lunch on the way back?"

So now it's a game of dodgeball we're playing huh? Okay, so maybe he's a private guy, and his late-night correspondence was none of my business. It was probably nothing anyway, an old college roommate looking him up, a navy buddy home on leave—something innocent and meaningless, right? Left side heavy feeling. Crap.

Milo was waiting for us by the time we got to the house. As we pulled up, I noticed how much charm the place had. A two-story Tudor, the house was yellow with black shutters, and well-manicured shrubbery lined the front in crisp rectangles. The walkway looked new, and a fine pattern of brick led the way to the front door. I marveled at how well maintained his house was—and felt a new pang of embarrassment that he'd seen my home in such a state of disarray.

Dutch carried the chili dogs and fries we'd purchased, I carried the Cokes and Alyssa's journals and Milo held the door open. We went into the kitchen and spread out the food, then took our seats. "What'd you find out about our boy Chad?" Dutch asked.

"I actually tracked him down this morning. Turns out he was a hundred miles away helping a buddy of his move. He was gone from Friday afternoon and didn't get back until Monday night. He had no idea his girlfriend was even MIA, and so far two other people have corroborated his story."

"He's not our guy," Dutch said, taking a sip of Coke. I nibbled on a fry, watching the pair work things through.

"And Abby's handyman's in the clear, too. He was at the doctor's office getting a cortisone injection Saturday morning that left him completely unable to use his arm for the next couple of days."

"Hard to strangle someone with only one hand," Dutch said.

I bit back my "told you so" and let the two continue to talk uninterrupted.

"Since I was two for two I decided to look into Allison's phone records," Milo said. "We found lots of calls to Ohio in the weeks before her death. I haven't run all of them down yet, but there's an interesting one to Toledo she made the night before she died. She placed a call to a residence that lasted forty-five minutes, and then immediately after that she called Marco."

"Coincidence, Mr. Watson?" Dutch asked, holding one finger up comically.

"I think not," Milo replied in a very poor English accent.

"Who's the forty-five-minute call to?" I asked, feeling like we were finally headed in the right direction.

"The number is registered to a Karen Milford. I ran a quick background on her and other than the occasional traffic ticket, she's got no criminal record to speak of. Her husband's a different story, though. He's serving three years at the State Pen on a drug conviction. Now, there is one particular detail I thought you'd be mighty interested in," he said, looking directly at me.

"What?" I asked.

"The name of Karen's subdivision is 'Sherwood Forest' and she lives on 'Little John Lane.' "

Dutch's jaw dropped and he whispered, "Robin Hood and his band of merry men."

"Yup," Milo said. It was obvious that Dutch had brought him up to speed on the clues I'd picked up at Allison's house.

I smiled in spite of myself. Even though the topic was rather morbid, I finally felt like I was contributing.

"I called Karen at home but didn't get an answer, so I tried the place where she works. Her manager hasn't seen her in two weeks. In fact, the last time he saw her was the day before Allison was killed. She works as a telemarketer, and her manager said it's not unusual to have their employees just up and leave without notice. What is odd, however, is that she hasn't picked up her last paycheck yet."

Dutch looked quizzically at me and asked, "Abby, let me ask you this: Is your spidey sense sure Allison was killed by a man? Your other clues were that 'he' was short, wore oversized clothing, and had dark hair. What if Allison was killed by a butch-looking female?"

I had to think about that for a minute. The way I differentiated between the sexes was by sensing the intensity of the energy that made up the individual I was speaking about. "Male" energy felt more dominant than "female" energy. But there had been instances when I'd gotten them confused. A very dominant female might come across as a male, and vice versa. I looked at the detectives and said, "I'd be lying if I said I'd never mixed them up before. It's absolutely possible, but this energy felt really dominant, and so I assumed it was male."

Turning back to Milo, Dutch said, "Looks like we're taking a road trip."

"You read my mind," Milo said, crumpling the wrapper from his chili dog.

Dutch looked at me and said, "Abby, are you going to be okay here by yourself?"

My eyes widened. "Why can't I come with you?"

Dutch and Milo exchanged glances, "I know you want to contribute," Dutch said patiently, "and you've already been a big help to us. However this is still a police investigation, and I'd get my ass chewed if my captain knew I was dragging you across state lines."

I scowled and crossed my arms.

"Listen, we'll only be gone for a couple of hours," he continued. "We're just going down for a little look-see. I seriously doubt we're going to find a smoking gun. We'll fill you in when we get back. Okay?"

"Whatever," I said as I got up and dumped the trash from my lunch into the garbage. Dutch came over to me after a minute, and gave me his business card. "Listen," he said, "my cell phone number's on the front right here. If anything weird happens, or if you find something in those journals that's interesting, call me. You should be safe here, but just in case anything out of the ordinary happens and you can't reach me, call the number I wrote on the back and talk to Detective Anderson."

I sighed, still annoyed, and took the card, turning away from him and nearly stomping to the couch. I picked up Alyssa's journals and pretended to become immediately immersed. A minute or two later the pair filed past me. "We'll be back around seven," Dutch said, ruffling my hair again.

"Mmmph," I replied.

"I'll take you out to dinner when we get home, okay?"

"Mmmph." I said again.

"Bye, Abby," Milo tried.

"Mmmph," I said and waved good-bye without looking up.

The moment the door closed, I set the journal down, and stood up, peeking through the sheer window curtain as the two pulled away in Milo's car. "Jerk," I said. I paced the floor moodily and then plopped back onto the couch. I stared blankly at Dutch's living room wall, my brow furrowed and my attitude pissy. Deep down I knew Dutch and Milo were right. They couldn't very well traipse across state lines with Jane Citizen in tow, but it still stunk that we were so close to catching the killer and I was left behind.

Catching movement out of the corner of my eye I turned my attention from the wall to Dutch's silky cat, who had decided to grace me with his presence. Softening, I patted the couch next to me and in a moment Virgil joined me, deciding my lap was prime napping country. I stroked his soft fur and calmed down a little, lulled by his purring. In a little while, my eyes became droopy as the warmth of the room, the softness of the couch and the lullaby of Virgil's purr coaxed me into a nap. I pulled the afghan around me and curled myself around the cat, drifting off into a light sleep.

Not long after I had dozed off something woke me and I sat bolt upright, sending the cat hurtling off the sofa and running to the recesses of the house. My heart was thundering in my chest as I heard someone outside, fumbling with the door lock. I stood up and grabbed the afghan, holding it up as if I were naked and trying to shield myself. I looked to my right and left, wondering what to do. Should I hold still? Should I run out the back? I looked for a phone and remembered there was one upstairs in Dutch's room. I bolted up the stairs and had just reached the landing when I heard the lock on the front door give and the door open with a creak. Someone stepped into the foyer and I stared over the railing, trembling in fear. Something told me that neither Dutch nor Milo had entered the house. As I waited, a tall figure with platinum-blond hair moved into my view. The head turned, looking around the room, and finally called out, "Dutch? Sweetie? I'm home." I stood rooted to the spot as the woman's words tumbled over me like an icy rain. She must have felt my eyes because she looked up abruptly and jumped a little when she saw me staring at her. Recovering her composure she said, "Where is Dutch?"

Her voice was rich and smoky, laced with a thick European accent I couldn't quite place. I took in her features: She was tall with long legs and a shapely figure. Her eyes were large and brilliant blue, her lips full and rich. She had a heart-shaped face with high, elegant cheekbones and a small, pinched nose. Her hair was cut short to accentuate her face, and the effect was stunning. She reeked of sexuality, and I became immediately self-conscious. "Hello?" she said, waving her hand at me, pulling me out of my stupor.

"Who are you?" I demanded. I might be outgunned, but that didn't mean I wasn't going to put up a fight.

She crossed her arms at my tone, one finely arched eyebrow snaking upward slightly, as if to say, "Who are *you* to question *me?*" After a brief pause she answered silkily, "Why, I'm *Mrs.* Rivers, and I'd like to know where my *husband* is."

Game, set, match to Mrs. Rivers. Time for Elvis to leave the building.

"He's in Toledo. He'll be back by seven. I was just leaving." I turned and walked down the hallway into the spare bedroom, where I quickly tucked what few belongings I'd unpacked back into my suitcase. I hauled this down the stairs, letting the bump, bump, bump of the suitcase announce my descent. Mrs. Rivers sat perched on the couch I'd just been sleeping on, thumbing through a magazine and ignoring me. For some reason this pissed me off, so I made a lot of noise as I gathered my purse and Alyssa's journals, tucking them safely into my purse. I headed into the kitchen, not really sure where I was going, but I didn't want to do my thinking in the living room where Blondie was looking her perfect, perky self.

I scanned the countertop, not really sure what I was looking for, and spied Dutch's car keys. "Screw him," I mumbled and took the keys, grabbed my belongings and headed out the back door through the garage. Outside in the driveway, I noticed that the heavy clouds that had threatened rain all day were finally releasing their moisture. Great. The Universe thought it appropriate to piss on my parade.

I loaded the suitcase into Dutch's car, noticing his lovely wife had parked her rental next to his—how romantic. I got in, turned the key and was backing out just as the door to Dutch's house opened and Blondie looked out. She raised a hand as if to stop me, and I smiled as I pulled into the street, waved to her, then squealed away down the block.

I didn't drive very far before common sense caught up with me. Mrs. Rivers was probably at this very moment calling in her husband's stolen vehicle. I headed out to Woodward and took a right into Burger King, parking the car toward the back of the building. I had to dump the car.

I took out my cell phone and tried to turn it on, but nothing happened. "Shit!" I said aloud. I hadn't had a chance to recharge it since getting back from Boston. I looked around the Burger King but didn't see a pay phone. I looked right, then left. There was a gas station across the street with a sign that said PAY PHONE. Perfect.

I got out and, dodging traffic I ran across the four-lane avenue to the gas station. The attendant sitting behind bulletproof Plexiglas let me borrow his phone book, and I began scanning the pages. I found a cab company that could have a cab to my location within an hour, and not wanting to push my luck, I agreed. Then I flipped the pages of the phone book to the area hotel section, and found a place about two blocks from my office. Perfect.

I couldn't go home—that would be the first place Dutch would look for me, and I was positive he'd come looking. Also, it would probably put me in the position of sitting duck for the psychopath who wanted to kill me and I was convinced was still out there. I considered going back to Boston, but I had clients to read, and mortgage payments to make. I *had* to work.

My head began to pound, so I rubbed my temples and decided to quit thinking about all of it. I played dodgeball with traffic again and made it safely back to Burger King. I had some time to kill and I was in dire need of some comfort food, so I went in and ordered a Coke and fries. Then I sat in a booth and looked dully out the window as I ate.

As I stared out the window the rain clouds grew thicker and more menacing, and within a short period of time the drizzle turned into a torrent. Lighting and thunder flashed across the sky in dramatic brilliance creating an orchestra of light and sound. I sighed heavily. The tempest outside mirrored the one raging in my head. I didn't know whether I was angrier at myself or Dutch. The truth was that I was extremely attracted to the guy, and I still fostered the occasional fantasy about our on-again off-again romance turning its way back to ON. But all that was a moot point now. He'd lied to me. He was married. To a beautiful, exotic goddess. How the *hell* could I compete with that? I couldn't and I didn't even want to bother trying. I was angry for not picking up on it. My intuition should have mentioned this little fact, and it rattled my cage that I hadn't had a clue.

Finally my cab pulled up, windshield wipers flying. I ran out and pulled my stuff from Dutch's car. I threw his keys under the mat in the front seat, and shut the door. If the car ended up stolen, I figured it would only serve him right. I loaded everything into the cab, then quickly jumped into it myself but not before I was completely soaked. Realizing how soaked I was I quickly checked my purse to see if Allison's journals were still dry. They were. Luckily, on the floor of the cab was an empty plastic bag. I grabbed this and put the journals in the bag, then stuffed them with some difficulty back into my purse for safekeeping.

I had the cabbie drop me at the bus station. Once there I pulled my luggage through the double doors and over to a row of pay phones. I rummaged around in my purse, withdrew Dutch's card and, flipping it over, dialed the number on the back and waited. On the third ring, a man with a voice that sounded like gravel on an iron grate barked, "Anderson."

"Hi, this is Abigail Cooper, and I have a message for Detective Rivers."

"Go ahead," he said, no note of surprise in his gruff voice.

"Please tell him he can pick up his car at the Burger King on Twelve Mile. Thank you," I said and hung up the phone. I knew that the caller ID on Anderson's phone would indicate I'd called from the bus terminal, and I liked the idea of throwing Dutch off my trail. I was pretty certain he would think, for a while at least, that Greyhound had taken me to places unknown. Thankfully, the bus station was only three blocks from the hotel I'd chosen, although I knew I'd still get drenched.

I wheeled my luggage behind me and headed back outside. The rain hadn't let up, and I hurried as fast as I could to the hotel. By the time I got there I was nearly drowned.

The clerk looked at me slightly askance when I checked in, paying in cash and registering under my sister's name, but other than offering me a towel he made no comment about my state of disarray. As soon as I got to my room, I unzipped my suitcase and began pulling out my clothes. Everything that had been on top was soaked, but in the middle there was a pair of dry, albeit slightly worn, jeans and a cotton shirt.

I was freezing by that time, so I took a long hot shower and tried not to cry while I soaped myself down. It was a struggle.

However, while I was in the shower I came up with a game plan: Tomorrow morning I'd go to my office early, get my appointment book and my recording equipment. I had a small device I used when I did readings over the phone that recorded the reading. Thanks to my sister I'd added a considerable number of clients to my list from Boston so the device definitely came in handy.

Once I had the recorder, I could come back to the hotel and do the readings from the safety and privacy of my hotel room. I could order room service so I wouldn't even have to go out. All I had to do was make it to Monday when I didn't have any clients. Then I could fly back to Boston and do my readings from my sister's house. I figured four days stuck in a hotel room wasn't so bad.

Later, after I'd dried my hair and crawled into my nightshirt, I climbed up onto the bed and puffed up the pillows. I thought about turning on the TV, but I wasn't really into reruns. I looked around and spied my purse, with Alyssa's journals sticking out. I reached over and looked down at the worn leather-bound books. "Eenie, meenie, minie, mo," I said as I balanced each book in my hand, shifting them like a scale.

My attention kept going to the more recent of the two, the one Alyssa had written eight years previously. I put the first one down, opened the second and quickly became engrossed in the life of Alyssa Pierce at seventeen. I smiled as I remembered being that age myself, and how things were always bigger and more important in adolescence.

The journal itself was rather innocuous, filled with stories about parties she'd gone to, her boyfriend, volleyball tournaments and final exams. On one page she'd doodled little hearts inserting things like, "Frank and Alyssa forever" and "Mr. and Mrs. Milford" into the center.

I smiled, remembering a boy I'd been that gaga over when I was her age. That, however, made me think about how I'd been gaga over Dutch, and I sighed again. Shaking my head and refusing to give in to my moody thoughts, I went back to reading the journal. My intuition kept buzzing in my mind and I knew I was missing something here. I closed my eyes and focused, and the words "Mr. and Mrs." kept swimming around in my mind. My eyes popped open and I quickly reached for my purse and pulled out the mindmap of Alyssa's murder that I'd drawn on the plane. My eyes darted across the page until I found the branch I was looking for, "Heart Husband." My heart began to race as the dominoes fell into place and I put the picture together. Alyssa had probably been married before and her ex-husband must be the man who had stalked her. I looked back at the name encircled in the hearts—"Frank Milford,"—and I knew I'd heard that last name before.

I thought for a moment, tapping my finger anxiously on my lower lip. Then I had it—Karen Milford was the name of the woman Allison had called the night before her death. The same woman Dutch and Milo were currently on their way to Ohio to talk to. There had to be a connection; Karen was either a close relation or Frank's current wife. I thought hard again remembering that Milo had said that Karen's husband was in jail. That meant that she must be the sister— but wouldn't she have a different last name?

My brow furrowed, and I shook my head to clear it. I didn't know yet how Karen figured into this, but if I was right, and Alyssa was married to Frank Milford before, that could be why she and her sister had fled Ohio without leaving an obvious trail. Frank must have found her somehow, all these years later, and staged her suicide by leaving at the scene the Dear John letter she'd written him when she left him. It also explained the shredded wedding dress. Frank would have been furious that Alyssa was about to marry someone else, and after shooting her, he would have taken his rage out on her dress.

When Allison put it all together she must have contacted him, setting him off on his bloody rampage. I thought back to the reading I'd given Allison. I'd told her that there was a brother figure who was responsible for the loss of her sister and now I was sure Frank was the "brother from Ohio" that I'd picked up on. A brother and a brother-in-law are indistinguishable to my intuition. They have the same psychic connection for me. It all made perfect sense. Excited by my conclusions, I got up to pace the floor.

The question that remained was what should I do about it? I could call Dutch, but I didn't want to talk to him. I eyed the phone guardedly. I could call Detective Anderson again and leave a message with him. I paced the floor again, thinking. If I called Anderson now, he would know that I was calling from a nice quiet hotel room instead of a noisy Greyhound.

I paced some more and fought with my conscience. I wanted to get the information to Dutch, but I didn't want to give myself away. I looked at the clock radio and sighed. It was nearly nine-thirty. I sat back down on the bed and ran my fingers through my hair. I was very, very tired. All of the events of the past few weeks had taken their toll. With a sigh I concluded that eight hours wouldn't make much difference in tracking down Frank Milford anyway. If he was responsible for murdering Allison, Alyssa, and Mary Lou, then he was definitely holed up somewhere and taking great precautions to hide his whereabouts. No, it was better to get some rest tonight, then call Anderson first thing in the morning, making sure to block my number, and leave Dutch a message with all the information. He could track Frank down as best he could, and I could continue to operate incognito without having to talk to him.

Wearily I pulled back the covers of the hotel bed and crawled in. I was asleep within seconds.

Chapter Thirteen

The next morning I woke with a start. Something was out of place. I bolted upright and looked around at my fuzzy environment. For a long, dreadful minute I had no idea where I was. Then it all came back and I had another panicked thought and snapped my head around to look at the digital clock radio. I squinted and made out the time. Eight o'clock. I snapped my head around to the window. A.M. "*Shit!*" I swore and tore off the covers. How had that happened? I swore I set the alarm for seven! My first client was at nine and now I might not have time to make it to the office and back in time to call them and schedule a phone reading. I rushed into the bathroom and punched in my contacts, then combed my hair with one hand while I brushed my teeth with the other. I quickly pulled up my hair in a ponytail, and threw on jeans and a T-shirt, grabbed my purse, and ran out of the room.

I reached the sidewalk outside and noticed with dismay that it was still raining. "Can I catch one break here?!" I said to the sky, then ducked my head and took off. I ran the two blocks to my office flat out, and by the time I got to the double doors I was huffing and wheezing and drenched again. I pushed through the doors into the lobby and had to grab the molding along one wall as I stood bent over, fighting for air. I noticed that two women walking by gave me a wide berth and looked disapprovingly at my dripping, wheezing form. If I'd had the breath I would have told them what hobby they could pick up in their spare time.

When I was merely panting, I straightened up and checked my watch. 8:15. Son of a bitch. I took the stairs two at a time, my legs burning, and walked quickly down the hallway to my suite. I extracted my key, turned the bolt, dashed inside and closed the door. I grabbed the large package sitting just inside the door, and carried it into my inner office. As I walked through the doorway, my phone rang and reflexively, I picked it up.

"*puff*-Hello?-*pant, pant.*"

"Abby? What's wrong? Are you okay?" Dutch asked.

"You!-*puff-pant*-Are!-*puff-pant*-AnAsshole!-*pant-pant.*"

"Do you know how worried I've been about you?" Dutch roared.

I shook my head at the phone, giving it a particularly vulgar look as I slammed the receiver down. I plopped into my chair and while I caught my breath I pulled the package close and inspected the sticky note affixed.

Abby,
I rescheduled all of your appointments for Wednesday and tucked your appointment book into your top drawer. This arrived while I was

calling your clients. Call me if you need me to help with anything else.

I'm so sorry about your friend.

Yvonne   8/29

I smiled and made a mental note to call Yvonne and give her my personal thanks, then quickly tore open the package. It was from Theresa and contained a beautiful angel figurine by my favorite artist, Kim Lawrence, who had been designing such abstract art pieces for quite some time. This particular statue was called *In His Grace* and depicted a white, faceless angel complete with halo and wide wings. The statue's head was slightly bowed, and he wore an overcoat that flared outward. It was beautiful. I hurried to open the letter that accompanied the statue.

Abby,

Brett and I have settled into our new home in Santa Monica and I'm starting to get used to the routine here. I'm meeting with my new producer next week and we're going to go over story ideas for the show. Part of me still walks around pinching myself that this is all happening, but I'm trying to remember to be grateful.

I found this figurine in a little shop in downtown Santa Monica and immediately thought of you. He reminds me of Archangel Michael, and I know he's your favorite, so I thought what the hell—happy early birthday!

Anyway, I miss you like crazy! I swear I felt your energy last week when I was out at the beach. It was like you were standing right next to me. Call me soon!

Love to you and all you do,

Theresa

P.S. Oh! Almost forgot! Someone named Mary keeps coming through to me and is telling me to tell you that she and Lou are fine and busy planting flowers but she wants you to be careful; in fact, she was the one who made me buy the statue! She said it's for your protection and that I had to rush the delivery. Hope that makes sense!

I dropped the note onto my desk and shook my head. Theresa's talent still left me dumbfounded at times, and I felt tears of relief fill my eyes as I thought about Mary Lou traveling to a heaven where she could busy herself planting flowers and create a beautiful garden.

I swallowed hard, remembering that I had a client showing up in forty minutes and several calls still to make. I had already decided to read my first client at my office, then quickly bolt back to the hotel in time to call the second. My readings typically only last about forty-five minutes, so I'd have fifteen minutes or so to make it safely back and set up for some phone readings.

I settled the figurine at the center of my desk and was reaching for the phone when it rang unexpectedly. Startled, I jerked it up. Tentatively I put it to my ear and asked, "Hello?"

"Abby, please do not hang up on me," Dutch again, controlled and calm this time.

I sighed audibly in his ear and snapped, "I have *nothing* to say to you! You are a *liar*, you cheat on your *wife* and you pretend to be this upstanding police detective who obeys all the rules when you're really just a lying *jackass* who thinks he can *use* people!" Hmmm. Apparently I *did* have things to say to him.

Just then there was a soft knock on my door. I took a deep breath and blinked away the tears of frustration that had welled up in my eyes. "Who is it?" I called out, putting Dutch on mute.

"Abigail Cooper? Hi, it's me, Mike Pad. I have a nine o'clock appointment? I know I'm early, but I was just really excited to see you . . ."

"Abby, listen to me, I swear it's not what you think," Dutch said in my ear.

Liar, liar, pants on fire.

Mike and Dutch had spoken at the same time, and I shook my head to clear all the traffic. I popped the phone off mute and said, "Just a minute, I've got to check something," then put Dutch on hold. I pulled open my desk drawer, took out my little blue appointment book and flipped quickly to today's date. There was Mike's appointment. I called out, "Okay, I'm on my way," and quickly walked to the outer office door. I opened it to find a gorgeous, casually dressed man wearing a white bandana and oversized jeans, dazzling me with an electric smile.

I smiled back and said, "Hi, Mike, come on in. I'm finishing up a call, and I have one more quick one to make after that but then we'll get started. It's actually a good thing you got here early."

Mike nodded and passed in front of me while I held open the door, then locked it behind him. He looked at me quizzically as I turned back again. "You're soaking wet!" he said.

Rubbing my arms, which were peppering with goose bumps from the chill air in the hallway, I said, "Yeah, I got caught in the rain. Uh, just have a seat and I'll be right with you, I promise." I rushed back into my inner office, closing the door. I had to dispense with Dutch quickly, then call my ten a.m. and tell them about the change of plans. Walking back to my desk, I was slightly flustered by the very good-looking man in my lobby. I thought suddenly of how I must look, wet, and rumpled. I grabbed my purse from the floor, setting it on the desk, and then picked the receiver back up. I depressed the HOLD button again and said, "Dutch, I'm sorry, but my first appointment is here and I really don't have time to talk to you about this." I emptied my overstuffed purse on my desk, hunting for a comb.

"Abby, listen to me," Dutch said with forced patience. "I don't like the idea of you doing readings at your office. You're too vulnerable over there. It's fine if you don't want to stay with me—"

"You got *that* right," I said, pushing aside Alyssa's journal, some folded pieces of paper, my wallet and a lipstick.

"I know you're upset, but you don't have to run around taking chances and giving me a heart attack in the process."

For some reason my intuitive phone suddenly went haywire the moment Dutch said "heart attack." I homed in on the thought and followed it, my eye darting to Alyssa's journal. I recalled little hearts she'd drawn with "Mr. and Mrs. Frank Milford" in the middle. With a jolt I suddenly remembered my theory on Frank Milford from the night before. Interrupting Dutch, who was continuing to explain himself, I said abruptly, "I know who killed Allison and Mary Lou."

There was a pause, then Dutch surprised me by saying, "Frank Milford."

My breath caught for a moment, then I remembered that he and Milo had been to see Karen Milford. "Karen Milford told you, huh?"

"No, she can't tell us anything Abby. She's dead. Frank killed her, too."

I sat down with a thunk. "He killed his own sister?"

"No, Karen was his second wife not his sister. We believe that Allison called Karen to warn her about

Frank and that Frank overheard the conversation, then killed Karen to keep her quiet about Alyssa's murder."

"But I thought Karen's husband was in prison."

"No, Frank got out of prison six months ago. I guess the guys in Ohio are a little slow updating their records. We checked with Frank's P.O., and currently Frank's missing in action. We know he killed Karen by the bloody fingerprints he left all over his home. They're a dead ringer for the ones on record with the Toledo P.D. We found Karen's body in a shallow grave out behind the house. Even though she's been dead for two weeks, you can tell he beat the hell out of her, probably with the same bat he used to kill Allison.

"My guess is that he thought he could kill Karen, then head up to Michigan, take care of Allison and you, and make it home in time to clean up the house before skipping town for good . . ."

Dutch was still giving me the details when something fell to the floor in my lobby. I heard a loud *thunk*, and for some reason it unsettled me. My eye darted to the closed door separating me from my client in the lobby, and suddenly feeling uneasy, I pulled my appointment book closer. My intuition was going haywire and I didn't know why.

I glanced at the appointments written down for the day and couldn't see anything to be alarmed about, but something was definitely off. I picked up the book and looked closely at Mike's appointment. My eye kept darting to his last name. "Mike PAD, 9:00 a.m."

It was weird that I'd put his last name in all caps. Weirder still that I hadn't written down his phone number next to the name; I only did that with clients I knew personally. But I didn't know the man in my lobby. I was sure I'd never met him before in my life.

Dutch had stopped his description of the murder

scene at the Milfords' and was now trying to get my attention by saying, "Abby? Abby, you there?" but I wasn't listening to him. Instead I was listening hard to a little jingle that had started to play in my thoughts, *When you want some lunch and you're in a crunch, come on down to Pic-A-Deli . . .*

My eye refocused on Mike's last name. "PAD—Pic-A-Deli. I dropped the book on the desk as my breath caught in my throat.

Mike from the Pic-A-Deli was not in my lobby.

Frank Milford was.

I looked down at my arms. Goose bumps stretched from my wrists to my shoulders, and the damp hair on the back of my neck was standing straight up on end. I wanted to run screaming. I wanted to crawl under my desk and make it all go away.

"Abby? Hello, Earth to Abby. I can hear you breathing . . ." Dutch said.

Panicked now, I squealed into the phone, "Yes, Mr. Rivers!" my voice rising in harsh crescendo with fear. "Of course I can squeeze you in, especially if it's an *emergency!*"

There was a beat or two on the other end of the line as I heard Dutch's breath catch. I gripped the phone with white-knuckled fear and added, "I have an opening on September eleventh. Would *nine-one-one* be good for you?" I was trembling in fear now, willing him to understand.

"Abby, I'm calling the Royal Oak police on my cell. *Do not* get off this line!" Dutch said, his voice a hush of tension.

I could hear him punching three numbers into his cell and pictured him holding me up to one ear and his cell phone to the other.

"Hurry," I said, trying to whisper but it came out louder than I'd liked.

At that moment my inner office door slammed open and Frank Milford stood with menacing fury in the doorway. He'd clearly heard my plea for help. "Hang up the phone, Abigail," he said from the doorway. My eyes darted to the twelve-inch blade gripped tightly in his hand. My vision blurred as my terror rose. I couldn't move, couldn't breathe and couldn't scream.

I could hear Dutch on the other end shouting into his cell phone for the police to hurry, and I had a wild thought, that as long as I could physically hear Dutch I'd be okay.

"*Hang up the FUCKING PHONE!*" Frank shouted.

I jumped in terror, dropping the receiver. It clanked loudly on the desk and I could hear Dutch calling out from the earpiece, "Abby?! Abby?! Are you there?! Abby?! Talk to me!!!"

At that moment Frank rushed toward me, raising the knife. I darted around the desk, pinning my eyes on him. "P-p-please . . . !" I stuttered. It sounded pathetic, even to me. I could still hear Dutch, shouting now for me to answer him.

Frank's grimace turned into a sick smile as he reached over and gripped the phone, and holding it to his ear he said, "Abigail can't come to the phone right now, she's too busy playing a game of butcher shop," and with that he slammed the receiver into the cradle. My lifeline was gone.

Frank then turned to me with eyes that were wild and dilated. " 'P-p-please,' 'p-p-please'!" he said, laughing as he mimicked me.

I grew very cold inside. I had to think, figure a way out. But I couldn't get past the knife poised to arc down at me at any moment.

"Listen, you don't want to do this, Frank. It won't solve anything!" I said, my words tumbling out and mixing together. He moved toward me, around the desk. I moved the opposite way. "The police know who you are! They'll hunt you down anyway!"

Frank ignored me and moved closer. I scooted farther around the edge of the desk, away from him, and he laughed at my effort. "Round and round the merry-go-round!" he sang.

Oh my God, I thought. *This man is insane!* "Listen to me!" I shouted, willing him to see reason. "The police are on the way, they'll be here soon . . ." and with that Frank lunged across the desk, knocking objects onto the floor as he came at me. I reacted too late trying to twist away and run at the same time. He caught my shirt and brought the knife down. Instinctively, I thrust an arm up in the nick of time. The knife caught me mid-forearm and I howled in pain as searing white-hot heat erupted from my arm, moving through my shoulder and sending sickening waves of pain down my spine. I felt the knife hit bone, then it stuck there and my stomach roiled. Frank pulled up on the blade, taking my arm up with him, the knife still firmly stuck.

Small arcs of blood spurted from the wound, squirting me, the walls, and Frank. He struggled to pull the knife free, the blood making it slippery and difficult for him as I screamed in agony. Far off, I heard footsteps in the hallway, then urgent knocking at the door. My screams became panicked and I inserted cries of help in between the screams of pain. Frank shook the knife back and forth, trying to dislodge it from the bone in my arm, and I crumpled to the floor in agony.

Frank bent down, sweat dripping from his face. "*Fucking bitch*!" he screamed as he grabbed my arm without mercy in one hand and firmly gripped the blade with the other, giving a tremendous yank. With a sickening sound the knife came free and I felt darkness pooling in the corners of my vision. The room was swaying and I knew it was over. I wasn't going to make it.

I felt Frank come around me and pull my head up by my hair. I saw the knife swing up under my nose and without realizing what I was doing, I flailed out with both arms, desperate for something to stop him. My left hand connected with an object at my knees, and I grabbed it with both hands, panic making my right hand cooperate, and hurled it upward with all of my might. I felt contact, and heard the sound of glass breaking, a howl that wasn't my own, a crash and then several explosions like cannon fire. Then I heard nothing at all.

Chapter Fourteen

My mouth was dry. That's what woke me. I felt like I hadn't had anything to drink in days, and my mouth felt dry as dirt. I became aware of the hum of electricity, the soft noise of a television, and the smell of antiseptic. I opened my eyes but everything was foggy. I squinted, compressing my eyes to see a little better, and wondered where my glasses were.

The room seemed too bright, and it suddenly occurred to me I had no idea where I was. I blinked several times to jog my memory, but for the life of me I couldn't remember going to sleep in this place. Something felt odd. I looked down at my right arm, which was throbbing dully at my side. It was bound in a plaster cast and tubes had been inserted in my left arm. I saw they were connected to an IV. Oh! Hospital! Okay . . . why was I in the hospital?

Then like a wave to the beach, it all came back, and I winced. I heard voices in the hallway just outside of my room, and immediately recognized the insistent voice of my sister. Cat was talking in her most businesslike tone. ". . . Yes, I understand that, but I think

Abigail would be better served recovering at home, so again, Doctor, I would like a firm commitment as to when she can be released into my care?"

"Cat . . ." I croaked out. Tears welled in the corners of my eyes. I wanted to hug my sister. I wanted to be held and told that everything was going to be all right, because the magnitude of what had happened to me was just starting to hit home.

She must have heard me, because she came running into the room, followed by the fuzzy outline of a man in a long white coat. "Abby! Oh, honey, we were wondering when you were going to wake up." She came close to my bed and leaned in to wrap me in her arms, being careful of the tubes and my injured arm. I held on to her for dear life, and the tears turned into embarrassing sobs.

The white-coated man stood off to one side, allowing my sister and me to have our moment. Finally Cat released me and stepped back to survey me with a critical eye. "How are you feeling?" she asked, stroking my cheek.

"Thirsty," I said, my tongue sticking slightly to the roof of my mouth.

Cat nodded, walked briskly into the bathroom and returned a moment later carrying a plastic cup with attached straw. She looked at the doctor, who nodded, then she handed it to me. I drank deeply, savoring the delicious taste of cool water. When I'd had my fill I looked back at her and asked, "Do you know where my glasses are?"

Again Cat was in motion. She swept over to the other side of the bed and pulled my glasses out from a drawer in a small nightstand. Coming back across the room, she handed them to me and I put them on, bringing the room into focus. Cat leaned in again and swept a stray hair out of my face, then kissed my cheek. I could see that my usually reserved sister had tears of her own in her eyes, and as I took her in I noticed there were deep lines of worry on her forehead and circles under her eyes that indicated she'd gotten even less sleep than normal. "We were worried about you," she said, her voice softened with emotion.

The doctor stepped forward. He was a tall man of Indian descent, and he had kind eyes. "Abigail, how are you feeling?"

"Like a golf ball after it's been hit by Tiger Woods."

The doctor laughed politely. "I'll bet. You've had quite an ordeal, young lady. We performed surgery on your arm, and we don't think you've sustained any nerve damage, the knife seems to have damaged only the bone. We had to insert a pin because you sustained a small fracture. You lost a great deal of blood, and when you first came in here it was pretty dicey. However, we've given you several new pints, and if you're feeling up to it I think we can release you as early as tomorrow."

I heard everything the doctor was saying, but it was really difficult to take it all in. I nodded absently and suddenly was overcome with lethargy. I looked at Cat and she read my mind. "That would be wonderful, Doctor," she said. "Now I think Abby is very tired and needs a little more sleep." The doctor smiled and nodded, taking his cue and leaving the two of us alone.

I lay back on the pillows and let out a heavy sigh. "How did you know?"

"Your Detective Rivers called me. Your landlord at the office had me listed as the emergency contact, and I flew out as soon as I heard. I could strangle you, you know, for not telling me about all of this." I looked at my sister and realized for the first time how I'd hurt her by keeping her in the dark about everything that was going on.

"Cat," I said and grabbed her wrist with my good hand, "I knew you'd do something stupid like fly out here and kidnap me and squirrel me away. I guess I just had to see this thing through."

Cat flattened her lips into a thin line, and I saw several emotions flutter across her face. She had always been the mother figure to me, replacing a real mother who'd never really cared. It was so hard for her to let me fly on my own, and even harder when she knew I was taking chances. "Well, missy, if you *ever* keep me out of the loop again, I swear I will charter a private plane and do exactly that!"

"So, what you're saying is that it's a win, win either way, huh?"

"Exactly. Now, you need to lie back and rest. I can see that you're tired. You don't need to worry, I'm taking care of everything, so you just get some sleep, okay?"

Uh-oh. When Cat said she was taking care of "everything," she usually meant it, and I was worried about what that might mean. I closed my eyes, thinking that if I just rested them for a minute I could pick the argument back up, but instead I fell fast asleep.

When I woke up again the room had the half-light of dusk about it. I couldn't see again, so I looked around and saw that my sister had considerately removed my glasses and placed them on a sliding table next to the bed. As I reached over to put them on I noticed movement in the corner of the room. I sucked in a breath of alarm and hurriedly pushed the glasses onto my nose. Dutch came into focus, one hand outstretched in a *hold on there* gesture. "It's just me, Abby. You're safe. It's okay."

My breath had quickened and I put a hand on my chest to slow the rhythm down. Dutch came forward and kissed my forehead, then pulled a chair up to sit by my side. "How long have you been here?" I asked.

"Only for an hour or two. You're cute when you sleep, you know."

"I've been told," I lied. If this guy thought any part of my disheveled self was cute right now I wasn't about to spoil the myth. "Can you tell me what happened?"

Dutch's face grew stern. I saw a great deal of emotion flash in his eyes, but what those emotions were I could only guess. After a moment he asked, "What do you remember?"

"Well," I began, suddenly uncomfortable, "I remember Frank lunging at me across the desk, and I remember getting stabbed in the arm." I winced as I recalled what that had felt like. "He had me by the hair from behind and I saw the knife in front of me. I remember thinking I was a goner and then . . . I don't know. I think I hit him with something?" I said this last part as a question, because the details were just too foggy.

Dutch was nodding. "Yeah, you hit him all right. You rammed some sort of porcelain angel figurine right up his nose. In fact the coroner had to remove one of the wings from his eye socket."

My heart dropped low into my chest. "Coroner? You mean I killed him?"

"No, Abby, Royal Oak's finest did that. Luckily the station is just down the street from your office, and those guys got there just in time to pump a few into him. I'd like to think he felt the bite of that statue before he died, though. I thought I'd go insane when that bastard hung up the phone on me. I've never moved so fast in my life. I got there just as they were pulling you out from underneath him."

I was playing with the bedsheet, trying very hard

to compartmentalize the whole event. "He was crazy, Dutch. I mean, I saw it in his eyes."

"Yes, he was. When Milo and I got to Toledo we could tell right away something was wrong. The Milfords' house was locked up tight, but there was a pretty distinctive smell coming from the backyard. We called Toledo police and they broke the door down and led the investigation to the backyard. Karen Milford probably died the night of Allison's phone call. Like I told you before, we think Allison talked to Karen, told her what Frank had done and he caught her trying to flee. We found some of her clothes stuffed into a suitcase.

"We also know that Frank was obsessed with Alyssa. We got onto his hard drive and found that he diligently worked a public records search for her until one day he got lucky and found the application for a marriage license on Alyssa and Marco. We found some pictures of her in his glove box, pretty much like the ones he sent you. We also found all of her other journals, the ones Allison took out of the storage unit. We haven't gone through all of them, but Alyssa used to write a lot about her abusive husband and how she and Allison fled to Michigan.

"He must have been following her for a couple of weeks, and knew she was in the habit of taking an afternoon nap now and then. We think that's when Frank made his move. He shot her while she was sleeping, ripped up her dress and left the suicide note.

"Allison never bought the suicide theory, and your reading, Alyssa's journals, and the photos she found that Frank sent Alyssa confirmed it for her. She went in search of him and finally found him through Karen. We're pretty sure she called Karen to warn her that her husband was a killer and to run before it was too late.

"After killing Karen, Frank headed to Michigan, and waited to make his move. We think he probably waited in the bushes the night she met Marco, and when she got home he attacked her from behind. It's just too bad Allison didn't listen to your warning. If only she'd come forward with all of her evidence to us, maybe most of this could have been avoided."

Dutch and I sat silently for a minute, letting that sink in and thinking about how different things would have been. After a moment he continued, "Oh, and we found the rest of the 'suicide' note. It was actually a three-page Dear John letter to Frank, begging him to leave her alone and not come after her, dated about six years ago. Just sheer luck that those last cryptic sentences were alone on the third page, making it really look like a suicide note. We also found a latent print on that screen that you found behind the bush at the girls' house. You were right—it was Frank's."

I sighed deeply, lines of sorrow furrowing my forehead. "Is there anything tying him to Mary Lou's death?"

"Yeah. Footprints we found at the back of your property by the fence exactly match Frank's shoe. There were also some fibers we pulled off Mary Lou that didn't match her clothing, and we're hoping we can trace them back to Frank. We also found the cassette holder from your reading with Allison in Frank's hotel room, along with the newspaper article about Mary Lou. The scary thing, kiddo, is that Frank was actually staying in the same hotel you were."

"How's that for creepy?" I said. Then something dawned on me. "How did you know which hotel I was staying in?"

"We found two key cards at the scene. One was yours, the other was Frank's."

I shuddered as a flash of me in my hotel room with

Frank chasing me around the bed came into my head. I abruptly got the feeling that if I hadn't arrived at my office at exactly the moment I did to receive Dutch's phone call, Frank would have spotted me at the hotel and would have done me in before help could have arrived. I shivered as I thought about how close I'd come to buying the farm. Wanting to change the subject, I said, "So, tell me about Mrs. Rivers," my good hand back to twirling the bedsheet.

Dutch looked at me for a really long time, his midnight blues pinning me to the pillow. I couldn't read his expression; the man should play professional poker. Finally he answered me, sort of. "Her name is Fenia, and I swear to you, Abby, that she is a part of my past. You, however, I'd like to make a part of my future."

I waited, listening with my intuition for the sound I expected, and it wasn't there. For once my *Liar, liar* indicator was silent. Hmmmm. "I see" was the only witty comeback I could think of.

"No, you don't, but you will," he promised. Dutch smoothed his hand over my head and leaned in to kiss me softly on the mouth. Then he walked out of my room and into the night.

The next day I was released from the hospital, and Cat was prancing around me like an excited poodle, opening doors, helping with my luggage, fastening my seat belt. I wanted to sock her. "Will you just—" I said a little too loudly.

"What?" she asked, blinking innocently.

"Cat, I'm not broken. I can click the friggin' seat belt already."

"Of course you can, Abby," she answered patiently and waited as I fumbled with my left hand to do just that. My casted right arm wasn't of much use, and I had a hell of a time trying to get the buckle to snap into place. After a full five minutes, I finally gave up.

"Fine! I can't do it by myself! Whatever!" I flailed my good arm in the air. I was frustrated, and pissed, and Cat's soft laughter wasn't helping any.

"Abby, you are a stubborn mule, you know that?"

"Like I said, Cat. Whatever."

My sister gingerly leaned over and fastened my seat belt, clicking it into place like it was the easiest thing in the world. She then pulled away from the hospital curb and drove me in the rental car to my house. We parked in my driveway and I had the same damn trouble unfastening the seat belt that I'd had fastening it, and again Cat had to help me out. This was just getting stupid, if you asked me.

Free from the seat belt, I managed to open the car door and get out as Cat raced around the side of the car and withdrew my luggage. The door to my house opened just as we made it to the front walkway, and a chubby brown bundle of excited energy bounded to me and tried to climb up my leg. "Eggy!" I cried. God, it was great to see him. "Mommy missed you!"

Eggy refused to hold still long enough to be hugged, so I settled for letting him slobber my face until it was good and wet.

Then I heard a familiar voice above me say, "Well, it's about time you two got here! I've been waiting all morning."

"Hi, Dave!" I was so glad to see him I nearly cried.

"Hey there, Abby. Eggy's been underfoot all morning. I think he knew you were on your way home."

I stood up and moved with Cat into the front hallway and came up short. I must have entered the wrong house. This house was freshly painted and fully furnished. "What the . . . ?" I said aloud as I gazed at my unfamiliar surroundings.

"Well, what do you think?" Cat asked at my side, nearly dancing with mischievous excitement.

"But I thought we agreed, Cat, that you weren't going to overdo. Remember our pact from when I bought the house? No furniture?"

"Oh for God's sakes, Abby! You were in a coma!"

"I was unconscious . . ."

"To-mate-o, to-maht-o," she said, waving a hand in dismissal. "Besides, I came here the other day when you were in the hospital, and I can't believe you've been living like this, it was like 'haute garage sale' or something—really *appalling*. Anyway, I noticed that you had a catalog from the Pottery Barn, so I just ordered, ordered, ordered!"

"Cat, I've been in the hospital for four days. How the hell did you get this stuff here so fast?"

"Where there's a will . . ." Cat sang. Nothing pleased her more than doing the impossible. She *lived* to hear someone tell her "no." "So, do you like it?"

I looked around at the creamy suede couch and matching love seat, the deep wood end tables, the multicolored wool carpet, the ottoman, new lamps, new curtains, and wall hangings covering crisp clean soft yellow walls, and my eyes welled up. Cat had damn fine taste, and this place was gorgeous. "Very, *very* cool, Cat."

Cat swung an arm around my waist and squeezed. "Wait till you see the rest."

I shook my head. My sister was one of the most generous people I had ever met, and her gift was just leaving me speechless. We walked into the study, which had a new coat of pale blue paint and was now furnished with a new desk and a plush office chair, with a small settee in the opposite corner. Shelves had been installed on the walls, and I noticed that all of my books were neatly displayed. I took in everything, even the decorative candles that seemed to dot every surface.

"The settee folds out into a bed for when you have company," Cat explained. I smiled because I knew that Cat wouldn't be caught dead sleeping on a settee. Whenever she came to town she always stayed in the penthouse of some four-star hotel; she believed in the kind of pampering that only twenty-four-hour room service and chocolate mints on the pillows could provide.

We moved to the kitchen, where I found the walls coated in lemon yellow and the room newly furnished with a glass breakfast table, upholstered chairs and curtains to match the walls. The porch also sported a new table and chairs, and the backyard held two additional surprises. A hammock swayed softly in the morning breeze, and a koi pond had been started in exactly the place where Mary Lou had been killed. I grabbed Cat's hand at her thoughtfulness, and tears fell softly down my face. "That's amazing," I said, pointing to the pond.

"I remember once you told me about a reading you'd had with a mother who'd found her son dead in her backyard. He'd overdosed or something." I nodded as the memory of that reading came back. "Anyway, I remember you told her that her guides wanted her to put in a koi pond to help change the energy of that space, to take it from a place of sadness to a place of peace."

I was speechless, mostly because it was absolutely the perfect thing to do. Mary Lou would have loved a koi pond, and I vowed that when it was finished, I would plant all her favorite flowers around it.

We moved off the porch and Cat led me upstairs. Dave was in my bedroom standing on a ladder and screwing a canopy to the ceiling. I looked at the new wrought-iron bed and my mouth fell open. I'd always wanted one of those. "How did you know?" I asked my sister.

"Abby, you've only told me like four million times how someday you were going to have a wrought-iron canopy bed."

"Oh," I said, just nodding, now feeling *very* guilty about yelling at her in the car.

Dave got off his ladder and came around to pat me gently on the shoulder, "You okay, Abby?" he asked, concern wrinkling his forehead.

"Sure, Dave, I'm glorious," and meant it.

Later that night after Cat had gone back to her hotel suite, I managed to shower and wash my hair, a real trick considering my right arm was bound up in a plastic bag. I wasn't quite sure I'd gotten all the shampoo out, but at least I was clean. I padded downstairs in cotton shorts and a tank top, intent on an evening snack. I checked out the cupboards and smiled. Cat hadn't stopped at just furnishing the house; she'd gone grocery shopping too. Rooting around for something sweet I moved from the cupboards, to the fridge, and finally to the freezer. My sister, the health nut, had lavished me with fruits and vegetables, avoiding anything that would rot my teeth. A little deflated, I reached for an apricot just as someone knocked on my door.

Eggy went bounding into the living room and barked like a banshee, warning my visitor that he was on duty. Trying Dave's hand signal and marveling that it worked, I moved past a suddenly quiet Eggy and flipped on the porch light while peering through the peephole. The view was completely black. Rolling my eyes, I sang out, "Who's therrrrre?"

"The big bad wolf," replied a husky baritone.

Snickering, I opened the door and smiled, genuinely glad to see Dutch. "Hey, sailor, just get into port?"

"Yes ma'am, and I thought I'd bring by a little present," he said, holding up a brown paper bag that looked like it had possibilities. I smiled at him in the doorway, wondering what he had in the bag.

He surveyed me for a moment and said, "You look better. How ya feeling?"

"Better. What's in the goody bag?" I asked hopefully.

"Ice cream."

"What kind?" I'm particular.

"Vanilla."

"Oh," I said, disappointed. "Story of my life."

"What?"

"Nothing. It's just that I'm really in the mood for some chocolate."

"Got that too, sweet-hot," he said, doing Bogey and holding up a container of fudge topping.

"Well, are you going to make me a dish of that, or do I have to whistle?" I asked, doing Bacall.

"Go sit on the porch and I'll be right with you," he said, stepping past me into my living room and coming up short.

I was closing the door and as I turned back toward him, I had to laugh out loud at the expression on his face. "Holy cow! How?" he asked, sweeping his hand in a sideways motion to indicate the room.

"Cat," I said. No further explanation necessary.

"Ah," he said, nodding. "Yeah, that woman's got moxie. I remember when I first met her. I just wanted to get out of her way."

We both laughed. That was my sister. "Come on, I'll show you the rest." I took Dutch on a tour of the new furnishings, and he politely whistled at all the new decor. We moved out to the porch after he'd scooped us both some ice cream and liberally applied the fudge. We sat down at the new table, close to each other, just enjoying the company.

We talked about little things for a while. Dutch had been wrapping up the case on Frank Milford; the press had run wild with the story and Dutch asked if I'd seen the article in the paper yet with the headline POLICE PSYCHIC ATTACKED BY SERIAL KILLER!

I had.

The article had favored me with all sorts of abilities I'd never known I had, including levitation and bending spoons. The reporter had gone so far as to look up several clients, who had all testified to my accuracy and said they weren't surprised I was working with the police to solve crimes. Dutch had been quoted too, saying only that he had been able to glean important clues from my intuition that had in fact helped lead the police to Frank Milford.

Cat, who had rearranged all of my appointments for the next several weeks, had even gone so far as to recruit a fellow psychic, Kendal Adams, to handle the overflow while I recovered. Kendal was a good friend of mine, and I wondered what I'd owe him for agreeing to work double time over the next few weeks.

Meanwhile, the deluge of phone calls into my office generated from the article was keeping Cat busy. I'd only recently found out she'd flown in her own personal assistant to help with the flood of new business. According to Cat, I was now booked solid for the rest of my life.

"Soooo," I asked, stirring the last of my melted ice cream, "are we going to talk about Fenia?"

Dutch grimaced. "I knew that was coming. Yeah, okay, Abby, what do you want to know?"

I looked at him like he was stupid, but gave him

credit for perhaps just being simple. "Uh, how about you tell me how it is that you're still married?"

"Okay, I can see that I'd better start from the beginning," he sighed. I nodded encouragingly. "As you know, I was in the marines many moons ago, and I was stationed in Holland for a couple of years before coming back stateside. That's actually how I got my nickname. I speak fluent Dutch." He paused for a moment, gathering his thoughts, then he continued. "Anyway, I met Fenia, who was born in Holland, while I was stationed there, and we dated on and off for a while. A couple of years after I came back to the States and after I'd left the service I got a call from her saying that she really wanted to come for a visit. I wasn't seeing anyone at the time, so I told her she was welcome. She was only supposed to stay for a couple of weeks, and she ended up staying a year. I was never in love with her, and I know she was never in love with me, and just about the time I was hinting that she needed to go back home she told me she was pregnant."

There was a long pause and I waited, holding my breath and stirring rings in the bottom of my bowl.

Dutch continued, "Well, I was really caught off guard by the pregnancy thing, and I guess I panicked. I ended up popping the question to her and of course she jumped on it. We got married in Vegas about two weeks later. So then a few months go by, and I'm thinking, 'Wow, for a pregnant woman she really is hiding it well,' and then a few more months go by and it finally dawns on me that she's not pregnant and that this whole thing was just a way for her to stay in the country. We talked about it, and she finally came clean and begged me not to divorce her. Apparently there's some INS thing that states that an alien resident who gets married and claims citizenship that way can't divorce for three years without getting deported."

"So how long ago was all this?" I asked.

"Well, we got married eight years ago."

"You have *got* to be kidding me!"

"I know it looks bad, Abby, but she left the house pretty much after I agreed not to divorce her, and I really haven't seen that much of her since. I figured that when I was ready to commit to someone again I would file and that would be that."

"And when do you think that will be?" I demanded a little too harshly. I was angry, or jealous, or something.

"Yesterday."

"I'm sorry?" I asked, making eye contact with him for the first time.

"I filed yesterday. It should be final in about three months, and I've had a long talk with Fenia. She's not welcome in my home or my life ever again."

"I see," I said, a little too stunned to say anything else.

"No, you don't, but you will," Dutch answered, and reached over to squeeze my hand.

I squeezed his back, looking him full in those midnight blues, a silent truce growing between us, and the first strong threads of trust finally taking root.

After another hour of talking, we got up and moved into the kitchen to deposit our bowls in the kitchen sink. Thinking of something suddenly, I asked, "Hey, Dutch?"

"Yeah?"

"Where's Milo been? I haven't seen him since the day you guys left for Toledo."

"Oh, yeah. He's in Hawaii," Dutch answered, a mischievous smile playing across his lips.

"Hawaii?"

"Yeah, and he had a special message for you."

"For me?"

"Yeah, he said, 'Tell Abby thanks for the numbers.' "

"What numbers?" I asked.

"The lotto numbers. Milo won the Michigan lotto last Friday."

"No joke?!"

"No joke."

"Damn!"

"Damn toot'n, Abby," and with that he carefully pulled me close, stroked my cheek, then kissed me softly.

"Mmmmm," he said as our kiss deepened.

"You like?" I giggled, relishing his skilled lips.

"You taste like a hot fudge sundae," he mumbled against my lips. "It's yummy."

I laughed and answered, "And like I've told you before, Detective, you have *excellent* taste!"

VICTORIA LAURIE

The Psychic Eye Mysteries

Abby Cooper is a psychic intuitive.
And trying to help the police solve crimes
seems like a good enough idea—but it could
land her in more trouble than even she could
see coming.

Available wherever books are sold or at
penguin.com

OM0014